# It had to be you

## LUCY MERRITT

Heartline
Books

# LUCY MERRITT

LUCY MERRITT was born in a snowstorm and has never got over it.

She ran away from home when her ultra-green father decided that the family didn't need central heating any more. Since then she has had many jobs – from serving Sangria in a bar in Spain, to marketing fantasy hot-water bottles at Christmas.

When she fell in love with a hill farmer, she made him put a Scandinavian wood-burning stove into the marriage vows.

Lucy is adaptable, she writes in bed, solves problems in the bath and makes love in front of the fire. Everything else is negotiable.

RED HOT LOVER, Lucy's first novel for Heartline Books was a great hit with readers, and we're sure that IT HAD TO BE YOU! will gain this talented author even more fans.

Did you miss RED HOT LOVER, Lucy Merritt's first novel for Heartline Books? If you did, why not call the Heartline Hotline – 0845 6000 504 – and pay by credit/debit card, or send a cheque/postal order for £4.49 (including p&p), made payable to Heartline Books Limited, to us at HEARTLINE BOOKS Ltd., PO Box 400, Swindon SN2 6EJ and we'll send you the book by return.

# Heartline Books –
# Romance at its best

*prologue*

The newspaper cutting was on the floor when she got home. Some helpful person had pushed it under the door and Cleo recognised it at once. It was the third in two days. Her support group took their responsibilities seriously.

*Where is she now?* the headline yelled up at her.

'Where indeed?' said Cleo savagely.

She kicked the door to behind her and levered her pile of books down onto the table. Then she bent and picked up the smeared scrap of paper. She did not bother to read it. She knew it by heart now. Instead, she scrunched the little piece of paper up and lobbed it hard at the opposite wall.

At once, she felt the sweat break out on her temples. Not surprising. It was a hot, hot night in LA and she had just walked up four flights of stairs to her one-room apartment. Not ideal conditions for a pitching contest. Or taking out her frustrations on her mail.

'What do I have to be frustrated about?' said Cleo aloud. 'I've got all my own teeth and I'm making the rent. What more can a woman ask?'

*To be sitting by a cool lake, maybe.*

There was a fridge in the tiny kitchen corner. She wrenched it open and grabbed a bottle of ice-cold water. She drank deeply, then let some of the water dribble down between her breasts. It soaked the sticky T-shirt but it made her skin tingle. Cleo gave a little shivery sigh of relief. The sudden cold was blissful. She closed her eyes, abandoning herself to sensation.

*A cool lake with a waterfall and a breeze in the trees . . .*

The answering machine was blinking. She was nearly sure that she knew what the message was but she switched it on anyway.

Sure enough, there was her mother's voice. All phoney brightness.

'I know you won't be home yet, darling…'

*You bet she knew. She wouldn't call at a time when I could talk back.*

'But I wanted to tell you. I've decided to go back to the Braybourn.'

Cleo let out a long breath. So her mother had scraped together enough money for more cosmetic surgery. It could be worse.

*A lot worse.*

At the thought of how much worse it could have been, she shuddered. And shut off the thought immediately.

*Don't think about it. You got away. You told her, never again. She believed you. She agreed.*

Yes, Margaret had agreed. She had not really had much choice. Cleo had been incandescent with rage. Well, it was either rage or fall apart! Margaret had not known that, of course. Margaret had never seen her daughter angry like that.

Neither had her daughter. It had frightened her. She would have died rather than admit it, but it had scared her witless.

*I couldn't take that again. I don't know what I'd do if my mother let me down like that again.*

Cleo took hold of herself. So Margaret had tricked her into auditioning for a movie that was close to porn. She had sworn she didn't know. Maybe Cleo believed her…on a good day.

*But the important thing is you got away. You didn't do it. You realised what was going on and you walked out. It's in the past. Get over it.*

She shrugged and wandered over to the window. The glass was hot to the touch.

She unbolted the door to the fire escape and went out onto the ironwork landing. Outside, the night sky was a soup of reflected sodium light. Maybe a couple of the weak twinkles up there could be stars, she thought. More likely, though, they were high mounted beacons to guide in aircraft. There was not a lot of the natural world visible in the urban landscape all around her. And, even outside, there was still no air.

Cleo pressed the cold water bottle to her forehead. Other people were sitting on their fire escapes too. Families eating. A party of teenagers hanging out. Across the rooftops, a pair of lovers were entwined. They had lit candles. The flickering light showed two abandoned glasses and a bottle of wine that had been barely touched. Somewhere, someone was playing a haunting saxophone solo.

Cleo leaned on the iron rail and closed her eyes.

*A waterfall, a breeze, no mothers, no support group. A long, long way away from here. With a man who loves me.*

Her eyed flew open, startled. The waterfall was a customary fantasy these hot nights. Understandable in this airless urban desert. But a man who loved her? That was a new one.

*Real fairy tale, that one.*

Since her encounter with the euphemistically named 'Adult Film Company', she had been trying hard not to thing about men or love at all. That way she got to keep her dreams bearable. Of course, it had not done much for her social life.

Still, who could afford a social life anyway, with classes in law four nights a week?

Cleo pushed back her damp auburn curls and thought without enthusiasm of the pile of books on the table. Two were borrowed. She had to pass them on tomorrow. So she would either have to do the work out of them tonight or get up at first light tomorrow. She knew tonight was better, while the teacher's lecture was fresh in her mind.

But… But…

She sank onto the top step and leaned against one of the iron soldiers. The saxophone sound drifted up to her – smoky, languid, and voluptuous. Virtual sex, thought Cleo. For the first time in over six months she thought about sex and managed to smile.

Now, if she had wanted to be sitting by a cool lake with a

sex god, she could have understood it, she told herself ironically. It was this trash about *love*d that was worrying.

At twenty-three, Cleo knew a lot about sex. She knew that
it could be anything you wanted. But it was usually part of a
package deal and only the unwary or the very young forgot
to look at the small print. Even when very young, she had
never been that unwary.

These days she just steered clear, even before adult films
played their part. At best, sex was a complication. Just at the
moment, she was not looking for any complications.

So why was she sitting on a fire escape, looking up into the
polluted sky and dreaming of a man who loved her?

The saxophone started to play something else. It had lots
of runs and jumps, with a sweet tune running underneath all
the virtuoso stuff. In spite of herself, Cleo's eyes drifted shut
again.

*A waterfall, the spray on my skin, the air electric with it.
And a man. The man. Breathing in my scent as if he can't get
enough of me. As if he can't believe I'm here.*

In spite of herself, her lips curved at the thought. Her head
tilted against one of the iron rails, as if she was putting her
head on someone's shoulder. She gave a long sigh. She was
nearly asleep and she knew it. She was just too tired to shake
herself out of the reverie and go back and deal with life.

Too tired and too allured by this new drowsy fantasy. She
could almost feel him there at her shoulder. Strong as a rock.
Intensely, vibrantly alive.

*His hand along the curve of my neck. Looping my hair
back, so he can kiss me. But not kissing yet. Just holding.
Wanting me. Protecting me. Treasuring me.*

*Waiting for me…*

If only.

*chapter one*

Another hot, hot day in LA. Too hot to shop, too hot to work, too hot to *think*.

*But I've got to think*, Cleo told herself. She was desperately trying to hang on to common sense with both hands. *No man is going to come striding into my life to rescue me.*

In real life, there were no rescuers. No pristine waterfalls. No men who treasured you. Or protected you. Or waited for you to love them. In real life, there were problems. And no knight in shining armour was going to deal with them for you. You either found a solution or you drowned!

And just now, her problem was very simple. Her mother's largest creditor had stopped her as she had crossed the street outside her building and explained it with brutal clarity.

Between her gambling and her cosmetic surgery habit, Margaret Darren had finally come to the end of her options. She had not noticed it yet, of course.

The man in the sunglasses did not really care about that. His boss wanted his money. He did not expect Margaret to pay up. He was a realist. But her daughter was a different matter.

And now, her daughter sat at the plastic table in the diner where she worked and tried not to shake. Her long, curly red hair was clipped into a severe plait down her back. But the residual curls stuck damply to her neck. *Think. Think quickly.*

She had spread the newspaper out on the plastic table in front of her but the words danced in front of her eyes. Her hands were clammy on the tabletop.

There were not many ways a waitress and part-time law student could make the sort of money Margaret had lost, Chloe knew. Maybe – just maybe – the little newspaper article that people kept giving her was her way out. Not a knight in shining armour, but a little piece of luck, just when she needed it.

Luck? An invitation to jump into the shark-infested sea of Hollywood all over again, was *luck*? To do what? Drown? *More likely, be eaten alive*, she thought, morbidly.

But an idea was taking shape. If she had a halfway decent agent…if she kept control of the thing…the clearer it got, the more alarmed she felt.

*You'll never get away with it.*

But what sort of coward was she, if she didn't even try?

A coffee pot appeared at her elbow. 'You'll need to go wash before you can serve food,' said George.

Her employer topped up her cup. He peered over her shoulder at the column. She had smoothed it so often, it was beginning to smear.

'*Where is She Now? Brian Paul Seeks Lost Teenager,*' he read aloud. 'Don't we all?'

It was a joke. George was a conscientious husband and father, owner and manager of the downtown diner and all-round good citizen. He sent underdressed teenage girls home to their parents regularly!

Cleo smiled dutifully, but it was an effort.

George was not used to this perfunctory response to his witticisms from Cleo. 'Hey,' he said pained. 'I said, don't we all?'

She pulled herself together and stood up. The diner would be filling up all too soon. It was now or never.

But first, she had to do her duty. George needed a response to his jokes.

'How much not to tell Naomi?' she said rapidly.

Naomi was George's wife. She had seen George pink-eared with embarrassment at some of her students' revealing designs. She would not take his excursion into lechery seriously. But the threat delighted George.

'A rocky road for your silence?'

'You know all my weaknesses.' Honour satisfied, Cleo looked round the diner. 'Mikey in?'

George leaned forward to peer out of the window. Carefully. The glass was hot to the touch, in spite of the ferocious air conditioning.

'The limo's in the parking lot. He must be in the washroom.'

As he spoke, a man in a grey suit came out of the door to the cloakrooms. He saw Cleo and George looking at him and raised a hand.

Before she let herself think about it any longer, Cleo beckoned him over.

'Mikey, I need to borrow your mobile.'

He grinned. In spite of the formal suit, he was no older than Cleo's twenty-three. He had a pleasant face and freckles. They matched Cleo's. There was a time when that had been important.

'Sure. Diner's phone broken again, George?'

George looked surprised. 'Not the last time I looked. When did you try to use it, babe?'

Cleo shook her head. 'No, Mikey, I mean *really* borrow. Just a couple of days. I need to give out the number to someone else.'

Mikey looked alarmed. 'I need this phone. How do you think I get messages about jobs?'

'That's OK. You can hang onto it. Just take a message if they call.'

'If who call?' said Mikey suspiciously.

She held out a hand. It was a small, competent hand. A working hand. There were a couple of rough patches, a reaction to detergent, and a burn mark where hot fat had splashed on her last week The nails were cut short and practical. Mikey remembered when she had had a manicure three times a week and her peacock talons were as spectacular as any Hollywood fashion queen's.

She put her head to one side and opened her wide, wide

aquamarine eyes. They hadn't changed. Still an amazing colour. Still wickedly expressive. And just a bit world-wearier than they should be. Heartbreaking.

'I need to make a call,' said Cleo, wheedling. 'One itty-bitty call. Quick, I promise. Pretty please?'

Mikey sighed. He could never resist her when she wheedled. She always dug out a dimple from somewhere to go with it. It made her look young and hopeful, for once. Too often, she looked twice her twenty-three years and as if she had the Hollywood Hills on her shoulders.

'OK,' he said, resigned. 'But *real* quick. ' He surrendered the phone.

But he didn't go away. He slid along the bench opposite her and waited expectantly. George hardly hesitated a minute before succumbing to temptation and joining him. They both sat there, agog, and making no bones about it.

Cleo ignored them. She peered at the printed page, then keyed in the number carefully.

And when she spoke, their eyebrows flew up.

'Hello?' Suddenly you remembered that Cleo was an actress. This was Joan Crawford playing a tycoon. She took her voice down a couple of octaves, and aged it twenty years. Twenty years of effortless authority too. 'CPM Agency here. Brian Paul, please.'

'CPM?' mouthed George at Mikey.

'Agency?' mouthed Mikey.

They looked back at her, anticipation intensified. She turned her shoulder.

'Hi. I gather you're looking for Patti Darren – the British girl who used to be in 'Snow Mountain'. I'm her agent.'

Mickey's laughter died. He seized the newspaper. Cleo lifted her elbows and let him swing it round so she and George could read the column.

Still in that businesslike contralto, she said, 'She's been in Europe.' That was vague enough. 'If you're serious, I can get a message to her. Yes, I'll hold.'

Tinny Khatchaturian sounded in her ear. She held the handset away from her head, wincing.

Across the diner, the Nunez family waved to her. It wasn't difficult to interpret. Banana milkshakes all round. Cleo raised a thumb, indicating she had understood, scribbled the order on her pad, and pushed it across the table to George.

'Jeez,' he muttered. 'The kid'll throw up in the car.'

Cleo glared. 'What am I, a waitress or the gut police?'

He grinned, getting up. 'Love you British girls when you talk dirty.'

She made a rude sign. His grin widened and he went back behind the counter to start ladling ersatz flavouring into tall glasses.

As soon as he had gone, Mikey leaned across the table. 'What are you doing?' he hissed.

Cleo smiled. But she did not answer.

Khatchaturian broke off mid-climax. Thankfully.

The voice on the other end had clearly received instructions. 'Agent? You're Margaret Darren? We've been trying to get hold of you for days.'

'No,' said Cleo, telling herself that her heart was not jumping all over the place. 'I'm not Margaret Darren. Patti changed agents. Margaret's been out of the loop for ages.'

Mikey's head reared up.

'Oh, that would explain it,' said the telephone, relieved. 'We called and called but there was no answer. We've looked in the casting books but we couldn't find the kid listed anywhere.'

*You wouldn't*, thought Cleo. *Nobody has produced a directory of ex-child stars working in downmarket diners. Not yet, anyway. Maybe I will, one day. When I get my crusade on the road.*

Aloud she said, 'I represent her now. If you want to see her, I'll call her. See if she can make it over to LA.'

'Great.' The voice did not sound as if it was great. The voice sounded as if this was another complication it could do without at the end of a long hot day.

The voice, thought Cleo, probably did not want Patti Darren resurrected. After all, the star of a teen soap that had hit the big time and died more than ten years ago could well turn out to be more of a liability than she was worth. Cleo knew the feeling. She would even have sympathised, if the voice, however reluctantly, had not been holding out a life-line.

She said briskly, 'E-mail me the details.' And gave the e-mail address Mikey had helpfully taped to the bottom of his phone display screen.

The voice seemed to realise that this might actually be going to lead somewhere at last. Which, of course, was when the voice said, 'Who am I talking to?'

Cleo drummed the talk button up and down several times. She hoped that it sounded like electronic interference at the other end.

'Goodbye,' she said loudly over her own percussion.

She clipped the phone shut and handed it back to Mikey. Then she stood up and did a neat line-dancing sequence – forward hop, back hop, smack on the thigh, dip.

'This caravan's ready to roll. Yeah!'

At the counter, George was unimpressed. He pushed four banana milkshakes across the counter.

'Go help Ricky Nunez brighten his mother's life.'

Cleo gave him her wide, wicked smile. It wrinkled her nose. Most women, as George had often told her, looked cute when they wrinkled their noses. Cleo looked dangerous.

Maybe that was the aquamarine eyes. They were very level, those eyes. And cool. With just a hint of challenge. Made a man stand up straighter, thought George, father of three and not normally a poet.

Or maybe it was the freckles. Or the jut to the small, determined chin. Or the way she held that auburn head, high and proud as if she was ready to take on the world.

Anyway, definitely not cute.

'You want me to tell the paying customers to lay off the banana milkshakes?'

'Micaela Nunez is a nice woman and she only bought that truck last week. Ricky is a greedy little skunk,' said George, the father of three similar.

Cleo executed a neat box step. 'You got it.'

She whisked three of the foamy drinks onto a tray, left the fourth, and pulled a glass of water from the dispenser instead. Then she grabbed some breadsticks and went over to the table where the Nunez grandfather and three grandsons were discussing hot rods.

'You'll want water and starch with all that icky stuff,' she said briskly. 'Day like this, it'll cook inside you. You want to go home with a gullet blocked by toffee?'

Grandfather Nunez laughed. 'OK, Cleo. We'll take more water with it.'

She nodded. 'And Ricky had two milkshakes before you guys got here. Do you really think another is wise?'

Grandfather stopped laughing abruptly. He yelled. The other boys gloated. Ricky whined.

Cleo slapped the glass of water down in front of the glowering nine-year-old. He did not say thank you.

'You're welcome,' she told him, smiling into his furious face. 'No charge.'

And sped back to the counter.

'George, I need a favour.'

'If it's time out, no. You can see how I'm fixed…'

And she could. The cars were beginning to pull into the lot outside. School must be out. The kids would be coming in for cold drinks and fries and to hang out with their friends. This was the time the diner really hummed. And she was the only waitress until Marcy came on at six.

'No time out. I just need to use your printer.'

George shrugged. 'You got it.'

She went back to Mikey. 'Has the e-mail come through yet?'

He clicked the phone to see. Then shook his head. He looked up, sober. 'So Margaret's out of the loop? Does she know?'

'No. And no one's going to tell her. She's up at the Clinic having her eye bags fixed. If I'm lucky, I'll get this deal done and dusted before she finds out that it ever existed.'

Mikey looked at the paper in front of him. 'If you can read the press, so can she.'

'Yes, but she doesn't when she's in the Clinic. She says it stops her relaxing.'

He looked at her gravely. 'So when are you going to tell her?'

Cleo's pale face went rigid. 'Do you want a banana shake on the house? George has got one going begging.'

'She's a bloodsucker and an awful agent. No question. You need to get out from under her. No question about that either. But she's also your mother. You can pretend she doesn't exist.'

Cleo whisked a menu card from its stand and handed it to him. 'Today's special is *Fusilli alla Carbonara*.'

He looked down at the page of newsprint again. 'Forget the eye bags. She'll get her ass back down here damn fast if she gets a sniff of a job like this.'

'Cynic. The chicken caesar is good too.'

He leaned forward and looked up at her earnestly. 'Look, I know the trap you're in. Nobody better. But this is crazy. If you get the part and don't cut her in, Margaret will sue you for every cent.'

There was vivid resistance in her eyes. 'She can try.'

He gave an exasperated sigh. 'We've been through this before. What she did to your contract was criminal, no question. But it's not illegal. Or not until you go on your crusade. No lawyer will take your case and you're not qualified yet. What does that leave?'

Cleo was cool. 'Publicity.'

He said slowly, 'You think this producer guy will do it for you?'

'Mikey,' said Cleo, 'how long have you known me?'

'But you said…'

She laughed aloud. 'You're not only a cynic, you're a sexist cynic. When did I ever ask a man to fight my battles for me?'

'Never', said George, leaning over the counter. He had been listening unashamedly. 'Come on, Mikey, you know it. How many guys have come in to the diner and tried to hit on Cleo? And ended up with the scar tissue to prove it.'

She nodded. 'I'm not denying, I make mistakes by the truckload. But I sort them out all by myself.'

Mikey said, 'This isn't a mistake. It's illegal.'

'Dubious,' said Cleo briskly. 'Breach of a contract that Margaret should never have drawn up in the first place. Hell, I didn't even sign it. I was thirteen, for Heaven's sake. She signed it as my guardian. That's going to look great in the papers, isn't it? Mother signs daughter to her own deadbeat agency for life?'

Mikey said, 'But…'

'Don't look so worried.' She buffed her knuckles against his chin. 'That's what this producer is offering me. All those lovely chats to the Press, promoting the movie. I'll tell them exactly what Margaret has done. It will make a great story.'

He was not comforted. 'She'll stop you before it gets that far.'

'No, she won't. Not if I'm clever. And maybe I can do us all some good.'

Beyond the window, the first soft top with a crowd of kids in it screeched into the parking lot.

'School's out,' said George, going back into his kitchen. 'You listen to her, Mikey. She's a smart cookie.'

Cleo smoothed the crisp apron over her jeans.

'You'd better believe it, buster,' she said cheerfully. 'All I need is a following wind and a bit of luck.'

Mikey looked apprehensive.

'And a little help from my friends,' she finished blithely.

He cast his eyes to Heaven. 'I knew it. I'll get sued too.'

She chuckled. 'I'll tell them you weren't responsible. I hypnotised you.'

The kids piled out of their car, laughing, and wandered over to the diner that was their second home.

Eyeing them, Cleo said, 'Better make it the special if you want to eat in the next hour. Here come six burgers and fries.'

Mikey succumbed, as he always did. 'Whatever you say.'

'You'll like it. And don't forget the stuff from Brian Paul's office. George said you can use the printer in the office when it comes through.' She made for the counter.

'One day,' said Mikey with restraint, 'you'll meet a man who won't do every damned thing you want.'

Cleo blew him a kiss.

But later, after she had taken orders, and served and billed until she felt she had as many arms as the goddess Kali, and all the customers had gone home, she sank onto one of the bench seats. Now that she did not have to convince anyone else, all the bright confidence had gone. She knew exactly how scared she was.

Oh, not scared of the law. Not even scared of Brian Paul Productions, though she knew, none better, that the film industry took people up only for as long as they were useful then threw then away like last week's trash. But she could handle that. She had been there before, after all.

No, she was scared of something altogether bigger and darker. She was scared of all the things that she had set in motion and she couldn't guess at.

And, most of all, she was scared of her mother's reaction. Margaret was getting more and more frenetic. Living more and more in a fantasy world. If that fantasy suddenly exploded because Cleo took control of her own life... Cleo's stomach clenched sickly at the thought.

George came out of the kitchen, switching off the lights. 'Want a ride home?'

*Tell him. He's kind. He won't judge. And he might help.*

Only you didn't ask a father of three to lend you money it

was going to take you twenty years to pay back, no matter how fatherly he was.

She remembered suddenly something that her own father used to say before he left. 'Live dangerously and you live alone.'

*I'm living dangerously. And there isn't a single soul I can share it with.*

George stopped beside her, his kindly face concerned. 'Hey, kid. You OK?'

She stood up, smoothing her hands down her jeans. Margaret was her problem and hers alone. It was up to her to sort it out. She squared her shoulders.

'Just tired, George. Just tired.'

*And scared as hell. But it's not going to stop me.*

It was pitch dark. The lake was black ink, nearly still. No breeze.

Rafael Gonçalves Dourado stood in the cover of the pines and listened. He was all in black, unnaturally still. Like a spy, he thought with grim humour. Or a very, very high-class burglar. If anyone saw him, they would have every justification in gunning him down.

His smile twisted. That was not very funny. Not in the circumstances.

Still, he could not have looked more threatening if he tried. Every inch the villain. Bent on robbery. Violence as an optional extra.

Except – he was not trying to get into the gracious mansion up the little hill. He was trying to get away.

A little breeze ruffled the water suddenly and he shivered. It was not really cold but the adrenaline was getting to him.

*I'm a respectable medical researcher. How on earth did I turn into James Bond?*

But he knew the answer to that. It was the price of vanity. Vanity and stupidity and not looking hard enough at a deal that was too good to be true. The deal and the woman, both.

Though the woman had not been exactly *good*, he amended.

This time, the humour was more than grim. It was savage. How could he have been such a *fool*?

There was a flurry of movement in the distance. He tensed, slipping deeper into the shadows. Someone had come out on to the terrace beyond the smooth swathe of lawn. In the dark, Rafael saw a gleam of white. A nurse? An orderly?

Whoever it was came to the edge of the formal steps and looked out. By day, they would see the designer urns, the formal garden, and the wheelchair-friendly paths. But by night, there was undifferentiated darkness. So why were they standing there, scanning the shadows? What were they looking for?

Rafael felt his mouth dry. His hand went to the little waterproof pouch taped to the skin under his thin T-shirt. The evidence. Would Paul-Henri Toussaint kill to get that evidence back?

Had Paul-Henri killed already?

Rafael put a protective hand over the package. The cold that had nothing to do with the night touched him again.

He did not want to believe it. Of course, he didn't. Paul-Henri was his *friend*.

Correction – Paul-Henri had *said* he was his friend. But Paul-Henri had said a lot of things. Most notably, that Rafael was going to take charge of a state-of-the-art facility. That the Toussaint Centre's research into cancer was second-to-none. That he would get all the support he needed to pursue his own line of enquiry. That a Nobel Prize was a real possibility one day.

*Oh, vanity! What a trap you are!*

How long had it taken him to detect that the Toussaint Centre was all discreet luxury and public relations? That the research was quick and dirty? That almost none of their famous results would stand up to scrutiny? And that people who said so, did not survive? He shivered at that word 'survive'.

The watched must have opened the long windows onto the terrace. He could hear the cheerful buzz, the clatter of cutlery on good china, laughter. Patients and their physicians and guests ate together in the evenings. Oh, it was very civilised, the Clinique Toussaint.

Civilised and profitable – and totally false!

He looked up. Even in the black night, the mountains were unmistakable, great jagged peaks pointing at the sharp Swiss stars. He could feel the cold pour down off those peaks, now the summer sun had gone.

Just as he had felt the cold pour down his spine yesterday when he looked at that message from the young American researcher who had left and realised, at last, so stupidly, criminally late, exactly what was going on. And later in Paul-Henri's office. And, again, when Suzanne crossed her legs and laughed. So that now, though the cold was still pouring, unstoppable as a waterfall, he was numb.

*I nearly had it all.*

Yes, he had. The research facilities he wanted. All the time in the world to pursue his theory. The chance at last to prove that he was more than a playboy scientist with more money than sense.

Rafael gritted his teeth. He had not cared about the perks that Paul-Henri boasted of. The Swiss bank account. The lakeside villa. Subscription to the opera. A Mercedes that was so top-of-the-range, it was virtually unique. Not even the proximity of the mountains that he loved to climb. He had cared about the *work*.

And that, of course, was why he was standing here alone in the dark, preparing to dive into the lake. Because the work was all a fraud. The playboy scientist had fallen right into the trap.

*Deal with that later*, Rafael told himself grimly. *Now you've got something more important to do than massage your self-respect. You've made a complete cock up, so far. This time you've got to get it right.*

The trouble was that he had not believed the evidence of his own eyes. The first thing he had done was reveal his doubts about the research to his boss. Paul-Henri smiled and said he must be mistaken, and offered to upgrade the Mercedes to a Lamborghini. Rafael explained again and again, every way he knew how. Paul-Henri Toussaint did not take it in.

*No 'Receive' button*, thought Rafael with irony. *All broadcast, that was Paul-Henri.*

So then Rafael had gone to Suzanne. She would know how to deal with her father. She would help him make Paul-Henri see that what he was doing was *wrong*. Suzanne would understand. She was Rafael's friend, as well as his lover. She had even recruited him into the Clinique Toussaint in the first place. Suzanne had a 'Receive' button. Lots of them.

Suzanne listened, as Rafael had known she would. In silence, which surprised him. He would have expected protest, shock, and dismay. He got none of them.

When he finished, she sat back, smiling faintly. She had come to the door of her apartment straight from the shower. Her bathrobe gaped a little. Now she crossed her legs and it fell open to the thigh. She did not adjust it.

'Oh, come on, Rafe. You're whinging about a few graphs?'

'More than a few,' he said levelly. 'Every single one.'

She lowered her lashes. They were spectacular lashes, black and thick and curling, in almost shocking contrast to the vivid blue eyes. In anyone else, her eyes alone would have stopped traffic. But Suzanne would already have brought it to a standstill with her fabulous legs and sinfully voluptuous body.

Oh yes, he had nearly had it all, all right.

'You're not turning Puritan on me now, are you darling?' she said softly. 'I thought you Brazilians were supposed to be party animals.'

And he realised – she knew. She *knew*.

That was when he knew just what a trap he was in.

All last night, and then again this morning, he had e-mailed and telephoned everyone he could think of. The sponsoring university, the medical schools, the editors of respected journals who were supposed to have subjected the Toussaint research to peer review. None of them wanted to know. Paul-Henri was a terrible investigative researcher. But he was brilliant at PR. Everyone who mattered either owed him or was afraid of him.

And then, this evening, Rafael got the e-mail from Matt Gottlieb. In spite of his qualifications, he was now teaching science in an obscure Californian high school.

'If Paul-Henri tells you he'll see that you never work again, believe him,' he e-mailed. 'And watch your back. They said Erik died from drink and drugs after a party. But I roomed with him and he was a diabetic. Never touched alcohol. Still, the official line is he was a party animal. Take care.'

It chilled Rafael's blood. *Party animal! That's what Suzanne called me*.

'Thanks for the warning,' he'd e-mailed in reply.

He downloaded all the evidence of the forged results onto a diskette. Then he copied it three times. They would search for it. He would need plenty of copies, so that they could find one when he let them catch him up.

Hell, he was even beginning to *think* like James Bond.

So that was why he was standing in the shadows, dressed from head-to-toe in figure-hugging black, a plastic bag containing his papers, his car keys, and the precious diskettes taped to his chest under the dark shirt.

*This is crazy. What am I doing?*

But he knew the answer to that one. The only thing possible if he was to hang on to his soul.

Rafael looked up at the stars again. His *soul?* That sounded like one of the aunts in their crazy Amazon wilderness. His mouth twisted. What would the aunts say if they could see him now? Or his grandfather?

His jaw tightened. 'Dourados never run away,' his grandfather had asserted all through his childhood.

*Well, I'm running this time, old man. I'm running to keep my soul and to keep my sanity. I'm running from women who think a man will be so deafened by his blood that he will say black is white if they want him to. I'm running from women with focus and drive and ambition, and not a glimmer of principle anywhere in the whole sexy package.*

And then suddenly – out of nowhere – Rafael remembered something else that old Carlos Dourado had said to him once, when he went to say goodbye to him before going north to study.

'You watch out for these crazy women in the States, Rafael. They call themselves independent. Huh! No woman is independent. No woman wants to be independent when there is a man worth his salt around. And women will always want you, my handsome grandson.'

Rafael, eighteen, loose-limbed and broad-shouldered, with speaking dark eyes that had melted more than one girl's heart already, had seen nothing wrong with that.

'So you just take care now. If any woman tells you she's independent, you just give her a wide berth. She wants something. Or she's lying.'

*Or both.*

He thought of Suzanne, all perfect legs and absolute certainty that she was going to get what she wanted.

Learn from this, he thought grimly. From now on, Rafael Gonçalves Dourado dedicates his life to the pursuit of scientific truth alone.

And, with a return of that graveyard humour, he wondered if they would let him get away with it?

Well, there was only one way to find out. He slid into the water and struck out for truth.

*chapter two*

'You'll never get away with it,' said Mikey Lambert. His crumpled clown's face, which had been so charming when he was an eight-year-old soap star and made him unemployable at twenty-five, was awed as he looked at her in the mirror.

Cleo shrugged her thin shoulders. 'Why not?'

'You'll be found out.'

'Why should I? ' She looked at herself crucially. 'This black suit makes me look like every hotshot agent I've ever met. Besides, lying is my trade.'

Mikey sighed. Lying was his trade too, though it was a long time since it had earned him a living. 'It's different when there's a camera between you and the audience. Up close and personal, people are going to *see.*'

Cleo narrowed her remarkable eyes at him. Underwater eyes, someone had once called them, Mikey remembered. That was just before the man suggested she take her clothes off for an audition for a washing machine commercial and she had kneed him in the groin. He grinned, remembering. Cleo was not one to overlook invasion of her personal space.

She said now, 'They'll see what I want them to see.'

Mikey spread his hands, helpless. 'I know you're as smart as paint, Cleo. But this lie is just too big.'

She shook her head, mulish. 'No lie is too big.'

He knew that look. They had worked together for too long for him not to know what it meant. Cleo had always been the one who had got them into trouble on the set of 'Snow Mountain'.

'But no one will believe there's suddenly an agent they've never heard of before.'

Cleo had an answer for that, as she had had an answer for

every objection he had raised so far. 'That's because I'm a *British* agent.'

'Why would you, I mean Patti Darren, have a British agent?'

'I've got a British passport,' said Cleo with complete sangfroid. 'My father still lives in London. For all anyone in Hollywood knows, I went home with him ten years ago.'

Her voice was level but Mikey looked at her quickly. Ten years ago, she had been thirteen, coming to the end of her useful life acting a ten-year-old in 'Snow Mountain'. They had been axed on the same day, he and Cleo.

'Can you sound British?' he said, to distract his thoughts as much as hers.

She stuck her nose in the air. 'I *am* British. I've just lived here so long, you've forgotten.'

'So have you,' he challenged.

She pulled a face. 'I'm a pro, aren't I? I can sound like the Queen if I have to.' She pursed her lips and launched into a demonstration. 'How do you do? Have we met? My footman eats producers like you for breakfast.' Her cut-glass vowels were very good.

Mikey made a discovery. 'You really, really want to do this thing?'

The aquamarine eyes darkened. 'Time we started fighting back,' said Cleo quietly.

'Oh Cleo…'

'How many are there of us, Mikey? The cute kids who no one forgave for growing up?'

There was a pause. He looked away.

'I don't know,' he muttered eventually.

'No, we don't keep up with each other much, do we?' said Cleo bitterly. 'Even going to a stupid support group is a sign of failure.'

He looked away. She had never persuaded him to join.

But Cleo was not recruiting at the moment. She was looking inward, angry.

'From time-to-time, we see that another ex-child star has tipped over into crime or madness and we thank God it wasn't us. And then we go back to pretending that we're doing just fine. But how can we? How much schooling did you get in those five years on 'Snow Mountain'? And what happened to all the money you earned?'

'About one semester's worth of school,' agreed Mikey. 'And my parents split the money between them when they divorced, I guess.'

'Mine is still going on my mother's fantasy life. Clothes, make-up, plastic surgery. And gambling, of course.'

They stared at each other, ashamed of their parents. Ashamed of their own helplessness.

Cleo leaned forward and put her hand on his. Her hand was hot, urgent.

'Help me, Mikey. We can do it.'

He was never proof against that eager look. 'What do you want me to do?'

'Set dressing,' she said coolly. 'Help me look like a visiting agent. George's Naomi is gong to get a couple of her students from college to do the costumes. I'll do the business. If I look sharp, I can sign the contract before Margaret gets back and tries to highjack it.'

'It's crazy. You'll have to be two people.'

Her chin lifted. Cleo at her most determined. In his experience, a determined Cleo shifted volcanoes.

'I'll be twenty people if it gets me out of this trap.'

He shook his head. 'But I thought you didn't want to act again.'

'I don't,' she said. Her intensity beat at him like a forest fire. 'But I want to finish my law course and qualify.'

Even to Mikey, her oldest friend, she was not going to talk about the man in sunglasses. Or Margaret's debts. Mikey would think he ought to do something. Help out. Maybe even play the knight-errant.

*Not fair*, thought Cleo. She always tried to be fair. Somebody had to. No man could be expected to play the knight-errant in the twenty-first century. That was not the way the world worked any more.

Besides, if she were going to confide in Mikey, she would have done so last year after her run in with the pornographers. She knew that. She also knew that Mikey would not have understood. He had heard her blistering tongue. At least once, he had seen her raise welts in the ego of a sleaze ball director on a set for a commercial. He would never have believed that anyone could outface her.

But that pornographer had. When she let herself think about it – which, mostly, she didn't – Cleo could still recall the ugly taste in her mouth. The way she shook with loathing as he looked her over, the way that loathing was edged with fear. And a terrible sense of betrayal, as well, of course.

It was not that she did not trust Mikey. It was just that she did not think he could help. Nobody could. And nobody helping sometimes made Cleo feel like the loneliest person in the world.

*Still, at least if I don't rely on anyone but myself, no one can let me down.*

She said aloud, 'This job will pay for the rest of my tuition.' And then fiercely, as if it was torn out of her, 'Then I can go out and be an advocate for every other poor seven-year-old with a cute profile and star struck parents. One way or another, I'm going to make that damned law work, even if it kills me.'


He got off the island all right. He even left the Mercedes in a massive car park in Marseilles where it would take weeks to find it. He was beginning to think that James Bond had been a thundering incompetent. Being on the run was a piece of cake.

And then it all went wrong. The one thing he had not calcu-lated. The one thing he had been certain was always there.

He rang the aunts to tell them that he would be joining them unexpectedly. They would be delighted, he thought. They were always saying how much they missed him. How a man's hand was much needed at the remote Amazon estate. Well, now they would get what they wanted. Ruprechago was just the place to duck out of sight.

Only the aunts did not speak the lines he had written for them. Not at all.

'Oh no dear. You can't come now. We're renting the place out for a few weeks.'

That was Aunt Violetta. She was his great aunt and probably certifiable except for her world-class work on Amazon spiders. She had clearly lost even more touch with reality and regressed to her student days in rented Parisian apartments, thought Rafael.

'I don't think so,' he said patiently. 'Let me talk to Luisa.'

Luisa was his father's much older sister. Rafael often thought that she should have been an ambassador, instead of a rich girl with nothing to do except marry one unsuitable man after another. She went to Paris for her clothes and New York for her entertainment, and she would know that people did not rent decaying Amazon mansions as a holiday let.

But Luisa had a shock for him.

'A Hollywood film company has taken it for six weeks,' she said.

'Hollywood? – Which Hollywood film company?'

She gave him a name he did not recognise, saying, 'We are all going to Europe while they are here.'

Rafael went blank. 'But Violetta never even goes to Manaus.'

'She has a standing invitation to visit the Keeper of Arachnids in London, Berlin and Stuttgart,' said Luisa coldly.

'But – why?'

'We need repairs. You have not been back so you don't know how bad it is.'

This was an old complaint. 'I've never refused to pay for any repairs.'

'It is not,' said Luisa loftily, 'a matter of payment. It is a matter of having a man to make sure they do the work properly.'

Rafael groaned. Some years ago, Luisa had looked at feminism and decided it had nothing to offer her. The men of the Dourado family had been on the hook ever since. 'You have Alberto. It's his job to manage the place.'

'It is not the same,' said Luisa unanswerably. 'And you have not been back for three years. So, when the film company approached me, I thought it an ideal opportunity.'

Rafael banged his head against the hotel room wall. But he did not say anything. He knew there was no point.

'They will repair the airstrip and restore the main salon to the original. A very nice man has already visited and taken measurements,' said Luisa triumphant.

Rafael started to fight back at last. 'How do you know this film company will pay up?'

Luisa lost patience. 'We had the bank check them out, of course. But if you're so worried about us, all of a sudden, go see them.'

He was the main trustee of the Ruprechago Estate. And Luisa was right, he had not been back for three years. He had a duty. He knew nothing about Hollywood film companies and he had far more pressing problems, but the aunts were family. And weird. And ripe for exploitation by a quick talker with a clever line.

He said wearily, 'OK. I'll go see the producer.'

At least Paul-Henri Toussaint's agents – that is, if they were really after him and it was not all paranoia – would not think of looking for him in Hollywood.

Mikey drove her to the hotel on 'The Day'. As London agent, Cleo Kelly, she wore the dark suit, designer heels, and a cool magenta wig. She was pleased with her look. It made her appear fearsomely efficient.

And Mikey, driving the executive saloon, made it look as

if he had just picked her up from the airport. He carried a discreet overnight case up to the reception desk for her.

'Thank you. Ms Darren is arriving at twelve-thirty,' Cleo told him loudly.

No one seemed very interested. That didn't matter. They were getting into their parts, she and Mikey. The audience came later.

He nodded. 'The stretched limousine is already there.'

That was a lie. The stretched limo was parked three blocks away. They had just left it.

The receptionist gave her the cardkey to her room. She wrote a note, scribbled *Patti Darren* on the envelope and left it with the clerk. Then she nodded farewell to Mikey, let the busboy take her small case upstairs, tipped him, and closed the door behind him.

As soon as he had gone, she whipped off the wig and black suit. She tied a headscarf over the auburn hair. It was still in its rollers. Then she scrambled into loose trousers and a tabard. It made her look like one of the hotel's lowliest cleaning staff if you didn't look too closely.

She had already located the service stairs. She half-ran down them, out past the industrial size trash bins. Then she was home free, walking rapidly to the side street where Mikey was waiting.

He gunned the engine as soon as he saw her. Cleo dived into the back seat.

'I really have got a pick up at the airport,' said Mikey, pulling out into the main boulevard. 'They paged me five minutes ago.'

'No sweat.'

Cleo pulled the tabard over her head. Suddenly it was clear that the trousers were fashionably loose and soft, and that the blouse was silk. All very expensive. She pulled the rollers out of her hair, fluffing it up as she had practised.

While he returned the borrowed car, she climbed into the back of the opaque-windowed limousine and finished the job of turning herself into Patti Darren, returning star. Fortunately, she had always been good at rapid make-up. Then it was just a matter of a comb through her hair, a lot of hair spray, gold hoops in her ears. By the time Mikey returned, she had shrugged on a soft ivory jacket with the designer label that no one who knew what was what would need to see, and was slipping her feet into ivory-and-gold shoes. They were the only things in the whole ensemble that she had bought rather than hired or borrowed. There was a reason for that...

'They're the only thing that will give me away,' she told him dryly. 'I've been practising. But I could still just fall off those heels.'

Mikey grinned. 'Not you. Go get 'em, tiger.'

He closed the door and drove her sedately to the most nerve-racking performance of her life.

It was a good entrance. *No, hell, be honest, Cleo*. It was a *great* entrance.

Only it wasn't Cleo, sashaying through the lobby. It was Patti Darren, all grown-up and gorgeous with it. And everybody looked. Against the soft cream of her trouser suit, her skin was smoothly honey-gold. She was all cloudy auburn hair, swinging hoop earrings, and long lazy stride.

And every celebrity-sated hack in the place *looked*.

She did not allow herself to notice that, of course. Or anything else either.

The lobby was more like Versailles than a hotel, even a Hollywood hotel. Two of the walls were a mosaic of mirrors. They reflected infinity of hothouse lilies, chandeliers, and designer dresses. Cleo disdained to notice mirrors, flowers, or ornate lighting arrangements. As if her thrift shop outfit had come from the starriest designer around, she strolled over to the reception desk. She looked – she worked very hard at looking – as indifferent as the moon.

For a moment, the hum stilled. A story! She could almost *hear* it in their silence. A story – and they were hungry for it.

*Cracked it!*

She could have whirled or danced or punched the air in triumph.

Instead she said, 'My suite?'

The desk clerk was well trained. 'The Lollobrigida Suite, Miss Darren.'

She checked Cleo in and gave her a wafer to unlock the door and a pile of mail. Cleo's surprise was excellent, taking into account that she had posted most of it herself in the last couple of days. Preparation pays, she thought.

'Thank you,' she said.

Very gracious. No one would recognise pugnacious Cleo Kelly from George's diner. Or the magenta-haired super agent theoretically already upstairs. 'No calls. It's a long flight from London.'

The desk clerk made a note. Then paused. 'Your agent, Miss Darren? Ms Kelly has already checked in.'

Cleo did a glamorous red head shrug. *Thank heavens I can still remember how*, she thought. *It has been such a long time. But all those years of watching the stars pout, they stand you in good stead.*

'OK,' she said. 'You can put Cleo through. Nobody else.'

Having thus established that there were two of them, she gave a wide, theatrical yawn and sauntered off to the elevator.

She pushed the mane of spectacular auburn hair back. Against her skull, she could feel her fingers under its scented softness. They were trembling. An armful of bangles clattered. You would not have known it from her world-weary smile though.

She pretended not to hear but the whispers were everywhere.

'Who is she?'

'Great hair!'

'Don't I know her?'

And, inevitably, 'What is she in?'

Thankfully, someone knew. Someone still remembered.

'She was the clever kid in "Snow Mountain".'

'The teen soap? But that was years ago.'

*Gee thanks.* She kept walking.

'Not that long. What did it do? Two seasons?'

'Yeah, well, it built in obsolescence. The cast were all growing up too fast. It was pulled at the top of the ratings.'

*Ah, the voice of reason.* She could have kissed whoever it was who had said that. She didn't, of course.

The bellhop had taken her to the elevator. She stood beside her luggage while he pressed the button.

The hum of the lobby was starting to rise again. She could still pick out the conversation nearest to her, even though she had her back to the speakers. She had got used, over the years, to paying attention to what people said, even when it looked as though she was concentrating on something entirely different. Survival technique.

'So which one was she?'

'The youngest in the class. Red hair and bad dress sense.'

'Oh yeah.' The slow note of recognition. 'The genius. She was a real dog. But boy, was she funny.'

'She's not a dog now.'

'Guess not.'

The elevator came before she could hear what they thought of her now.

Her skin prickled with distaste. She had forgotten what it was like to be a commodity. Now she remembered.

On the penthouse floor, the bellhop used her card to let them in, pulling in the brass-columned luggage trolley after him. It was taller than him and piled to capacity with cream leather cases. Rented for the next three days and packed with anything she could find in her room. But no one was going to guess that.

The suite was like a full apartment, with a discreetly lit entrance hall and some elegant *fin de siècle* prints on the wall. Cleo had not seen luxury like this in ten years, but she gave no sign of it. She yawned again and waved him to take the cases into the bedroom. The bellhop deposited them and wheeled his tall trolley back, massaging his arm instinctively. Those suitcases were *heavy*.

She bit back a smile. 'Thank you.'

The tip was carefully judged. Generous enough to look as if money was no object. Not so generous that it suggested she was trying to impress. Hotel staff had an acute nose for desperation. She knew that. She'd worked as a chambermaid in her time and she knew all the signs the bellhop would be looking for.

She'd debated over the tip almost more than anything else. Though you would never have known it from the careless way she slipped it into his hand.

He did not even look at the notes. But he would. As soon as he got out of the door he would count them. He would read the signs she had so carefully set up for him, and would pass on the message to his co-workers. Who, in turn, would tell their contacts. And the buzz would start to go round the town. Patti Darren was *back*.

But, meanwhile, she had a role to play.

She whipped into the bathroom and flung off her thrift shop Armani. A quick shower and the trembling stopped. She was doing fine, Cleo told herself. Just fine. So far.

Her agent gear was as different as the thrift shop could provide. Dark and well-cut but tailored. The clever magenta wig was sleek, as different as possible from Darren's abundant auburn tresses. Most important of all were the tinted glasses. Anyone who looked properly would be suspicious of two women with aquamarine eyes. In all probability, no one would look. But Cleo wasn't chancing it anyway. She surveyed herself in the mirror.

Older, she thought. Lots older than pretty Patti Darren. Hell, she even looked smaller somehow.

'Small but deadly,' she said. And went off to talk to the production company.

They were disappointed that she had not brought her client.

'She's resting. Rough flight,' said Cleo briskly. 'You saw the tapes though?'

Yes, they had seen the videotapes she had sent them, both old work and the audition piece they had asked for. Yes, they were very interested. But they still wanted to see her in the flesh.

'Sure. That's why I got her over here.' Cleo was cool. 'But let's put our cards on the table. Your second lead got herself pregnant. So, you've got a hole to fill. And you start shooting on Monday. Right?'

The director jumped. The producer was made of sterner stuff. 'So? This town's full of actresses. I could go down to the coffee shop and hire four right now.'

Cleo sighed elaborately. 'Experienced? Union member? Name recognition with the under twenty-five's?'

The director leaned towards the producer. 'Amanda is supposed to be British. Darren's got the right accent, right manner,' he muttered under his breath.

Cleo looked at him with contempt. She wanted to yell at him, 'That's acting, you jerk.'

But she didn't. She just smiled. The guy was making her case for her, after all.

'I'm sure you'll just love working together,' she said. She pulled a contract out of her brief case and pushed it across the desk at them. 'She's signed. See what you think.'

The producer frowned heavily. This was not the way it happened in Hollywood and any decent agent would know it. On the other hand, the woman had delivered so far and, he saw with some astonishment, she was not being greedy. The only thing that was unusual was the provision of an imme-diate payment for the Darren girl's trip to Hollywood. And they would have picked that up eventually anyway.

'No,' he said. 'But we can negotiate.'

The tinted spectacles glinted. 'Sure. And I'll have a bank draft for the audition expenses today.'

The director stirred uneasily. The producer shrugged. It

was not enough to make a fuss about and the Darren girl did look like a lifeline. 'You're a hard woman, Ms Kelly.' He picked up the phone and told his secretary to make out the cheque.

Cleo hoped that she did not sag in her seat with relief. Without that cheque, there was no way she was going to be able to pay all the bills she would run up for this charade. Payment for filming was notoriously late.

She said, 'Thank you. You'll want her measurements.' She handed over a single sheet with everything from bra cup to glove size listed on it. 'And I'll tell her to be here, when?'

The director said, 'Three. We want to do a read through.'

'Fine. Give me a script. Which scenes are you doing?'

She was a fast study. In a couple of hours, she could be word perfect on a couple, at least.

The director had marked them. He handed them over.

The producer said smoothly, 'If we agree – *if* – we would like you both to join us this evening. The writer is picking up an award and we have taken a table.'

The writer was a hugely eminent Latin American novelist. Cleo was prepared for this. Brian Paul's PA had hinted heavily that it would be advisable to bring a dress. Naomi's craziest student had produced a creation that made Cleo's eyes cross, but it would be a headline getter and that was the important thing.

'We'll be happy to,' she lied, mentally crossing her fingers. And she started to make good her debt to Mikey. It was not much but it would be a start. 'Of course, you'll provide a suitable escort for my client? She's been out of Hollywood a long time. She won't want to go to the awards ceremony alone.'

'Escort?' said the producer blankly.

Cleo stood up. 'Think Rent a Hunk,' she advised. 'Or you could try the kid who used to be on "Snow Mountain" with her. Mikey Someone.'

She sounded totally indifferent. It was so clever, she could have hugged herself.

She raced back to the suite, turned herself into Patti Darren, and then went back to the producer and director who did not recognise her – and gave the audition of her life.

Then she went back to the hotel and waited for the film company's call. She even pulled on the magenta wig again, to get herself back into the character of Cleo Kelly, the agent with knives in her smile.

They took their time. She had almost given up when the call came. She was running a foaming bath and had wrapped herself in one of the hotel's warm and fluffy towels. But her wig was still firmly in place.

They did not call the hotel suite, of course. That was the client's. They rang the mobile phone that Mikey had surrendered to her for the day. She flicked it open and saw which number was calling.

'Yes!' she said, swirling off the tap and dancing out into the main suite.

She composed herself determinedly. She even sat at the elegant desk under the window, to put herself more in the mood.

She picked up the telephone and lowered her voice to a terrifying contralto register. 'Cleo Kelly.'

'You were right, Ms Kelly. You were *right*. Patti Darren is the one for us.'

'Fine,' said Cleo, clipped and British and completely deadpan. Under the chair, her bare feet were doing a tap dance. 'And the contract?'

'Well now, just a few modifications…'

They wrangled for several minutes.

'You know your business,' said the producer at last, reluctantly admiring.

*I should. I've worked through enough disasters that Margaret put together.*

But all she said aloud was, 'I have a very demanding client.'

'Well, she's lucky to have you. And we'll be seeing you

both later.'

She had prepared for that one. 'I'm not sure how soon I can get away. If you get someone to pick Patti up from the hotel, I'll see you at the ceremony.'

He accepted that without interest and ended the call. Cleo rocked back in the chair and closed her eyes.

*I've done it. I've done it!*

And Margaret had not appeared in a puff of red smoke to stop her. Margaret was still out at the Braybourn Clinic, unaware that her daughter, client, and sole investment had just got out from under her. Cleo should have felt triumphant but, quite suddenly, she found her eyes filling up behind her closed eyelids.

If only Margaret had been a different sort of mother. If only she had not put her daughter into acting. Or not tried to keep her there well past her sell-by-date.

'Sing out Louise!' said Cleo, trying to see the funny side.

She opened her eyes and stood up. This was not the way to greet her best breakthrough ever. She should be singing and dancing. Or at least swigging something celebratory.

She went to the well-stocked fridge in the bar area. Sure enough, there were several bottles. Napa Valley sparkling rosé. Sonoma County Chardonnay. Real champagne…

Now was not the time for stinting, she thought. Besides, Mikey would be picking her up later. Champagne it was. He would share it.

But when the door bell rang only ten minutes later and she opened it, champagne flute in hand, the escort who stood there was not Mikey Lambert with a rented tux and a conspirator's smile.

Cleo took one look at the boxed orchid in his hand and realised that she had made a big mistake. Subtlety was obviously a mistake with Brian Paul. She gulped and clutched the glass of champagne to her breast. And realised three things simultaneously. The glass was icy enough to make her jump where it touched her bare skin. She was still only wearing a bath towel. And the man's eyes had gone straight to her breasts and stayed there.

Second mistake! Two in twenty seconds! And up to then the plan had been brilliant and her execution flawless!

'Oh hell!' she said, unwarily. She was so dismayed that, for once, she failed to think well on her feet. 'Rent a Hunk!'

And then blushed to the roots of her magenta wig.

Because his eyes lifted to her face, in astonishment. And he was *gorgeous*.

*chapter three*

Rafael had had a bad ten days.

No editor of the medical journals he contacted wanted a paper on the Toussaint's research methods.

'Wouldn't touch it with a barge pole,' said one frankly. 'Allegations like this are just scandal. Malicious too. Probably actionable.'

Another one, of even higher prestige, put it even more simply. 'I've known Paul-Henri for years. Frankly, Mr Dourado, who are you?'

That made Rafael wince. But it was a salutary reminder of how he had got into this trap in the first place. He put pride to one side and called his old professor at medical school.

'Not entirely surprised,' came the e-mailed reply. 'Let me have a look at your evidence.'

Rafael sent him one of the precious diskettes. Unnervingly, his hotel room had been turned over twice. Once in Paris. Once in New York. On both occasions, his overnight case was searched thoroughly. But then, the diskettes weren't there. He carried them with him at all times.

Still, it was worrying that he was so easy to track down. Rafael decided that James Bond had not been such an idiot after all and threw away his air ticket to LA. He zigzagged across the continent, using small carriers and airports.

He got another e-mail from Matt Gottlieb in California.

'Talked to Eric's sister. He thought he was being followed. She says, he told her the week before he died that girls kept coming on to him, out of nowhere. So watch new people. Mistrust coincidence.'

Rafael took that seriously.

He took it even more seriously when he logged on the next

morning and found that his professor has sent him an e-mail at midnight.

'Had an approach about you. Take care. Avoid e-mail. Don't use your credit card. They're too easy to trace. Keep out of sight. I will be in touch.'

*How?* thought Rafael.

But Professor Schenke was no James Bond fantasist and Rafael trusted him. So he stocked up on ready money and got himself a seat on the bus to LA.

By the time he arrived in Hollywood, he was grubby, tired and edgy. He had never realised how much his wealth made life easier. He had thought he did not let his inheritance make any difference. He had always worked and worked hard. Never been a playboy like his father and his Uncle Tomas. But he had never had to travel coach or sleep in airport lounges before.

People were polite to a well-dressed stranger, positively warm when they knew he was a millionaire academic. He found they simply did not see a foreigner with an overnight case and a day's growth of beard.

To crown it all, when he finally made it into Anitra Productions, responsible for the '*Cloud Orchid*' project in Hollywood, they talked to him quite kindly but as if he was a backwoodsman. And then they offered him a job for the night.

'A job?' said Rafael, too startled to draw himself to his full height and blast the man.

'You've got nowhere to stay, right?' said Brian Paul, the producer, with an experienced eye on the overnight case. 'We can fix that. My secretary will get you a room. You go freshen up and take a look at that contract your aunt signed. You'll find it's OK. But I appreciate you want to make sure we aren't ripping off the old lady.' He beamed benevolently. Well, he tried. 'And then you do this part.'

None of this made sense. Rafael's temples were thumping with the tiredness, tension, and the ice-age air conditioning in the office. 'Part?' he said, blankly.

The benevolent grin widened until it nearly cracked.

'You want to act, right? That's why you're here really. Don't have to kid me. Well, now's your chance. We've got an agent demanding an escort for a lady we're taking to dinner. We'll get a tux and a limo over to your hotel and you go collect her. Bring her to the Award Ceremony, take her back. Make sure she has a good time. Know what I mean?'

And Rafael, out on his feet after two near sleepless nights, did not take in the full implications. Or any implications, indeed. He just nodded wearily. He knew there was something odd here but he shelved it until after he had slept and showered and looked at their legal contract with Luisa. He just needed to *sleep*. The details of an escort job he didn't want could wait.

But now, face-to-face with a purple-haired Maenad whose nipples, vividly outlined under damp towelling, looked as if they were ready to fire bullets, he snapped to attention. And realised that he should have focused on this before.

Rent a Hunk? *Rent a Hunk?*

That was when, too late, he did draw himself to his full height.

'Don't get carried away,' he said coldly. 'I'm just here to take you to dinner.'

To be honest, it was not just the crack about Rent a Hunk that took him aback. It was the woman herself. He was not prepared for either that slipping towel or the naughty look in her eye. And he was frankly outraged by the dismay which replaced it.

He did not know much about starlets but he read the papers. He had been braced for a teen queen in a micro skirt. Probably she would giggle. He was faced by a woman – no doubt about that, he thought, trying not to look at the sagging knot between her breasts – wrapped insecurely in towelling and looking as if she was ready to kill.

Not just ready to kill. In a flat panic, he thought. For all her purple hair and aggressive state of undress, she looked flustered. More than flustered. Her face was distinctly pink.

His eyebrows twitched together. Did film starlets who demanded a hunk for the evening blush? What was going on here?

He said in a gentler tone, 'That was the deal. I put on a tuxedo and accompany you to the Diamond Awards, where you and I are dining with the producer of "Cloud Orchid".' And he offered her the boxed flower.

She looked horrified.

Rafael was annoyed. He had been mildly proud of himself for remembering the courtesy. OK, it had been at the last moment. And something of a delaying tactic before he launched into what promised to be a mind-numbingly dull evening. But after the limousine dropped him off and went to wait, he wandered around the art deco lobby, trying to find out if the hotel could produce an orchid for the woman.

The florist had been helpfulness itself. She slipped a single orchid bloom into a filter, nipped it closed and attached it to a black velvet band. Then she put it into a cellophane box and handed it to him with a smile. Florists always smiled, in Rafael's experience – it was professional. But he was also experienced enough to see that this florist found the tall dark man with the imperious profile and the unexpectedly rueful twinkle unusually easy to smile at.

He smiled back, warmed by the first unshadowed friendliness he had encountered for ten days.

'Lucky girl,' she said generously. 'Have a nice evening.'

But the demanding starlet did not seem to think she was lucky. She could not have looked more appalled if he had told her the Martians had landed and he was their leader. She put down her wine glass and pulled at that appalling hair, frowning horribly. Maybe she didn't like parties. But that was no need for her to look at him like that, Rafael thought, irritated.

He said impatiently, 'That's what Brian Paul told me

anyway. He was the guy who sent me up her to collect you.'

She cleared her throat. 'What did he say exactly?' Her voice sounded rusty.

'Penthouse suite. Limo arriving seven-fifteen.'

She jumped and looked at her wrist instinctively. No watch, of course. But the movement dislodged the bath towel a bit. He saw it. She seemed not to notice.

A gentleman would have pointed out that that knot needed to be tightened. But Rafael was not feeling like a gentleman. Partly from irritation. Partly from something else he was not prepared to think about.

She cleared her throat again. This time her voice was stronger.

'I'm afraid there's been a mistake. It's my client who's going to dinner. '

Client? This wasn't the starlet? For some reason he felt disappointed. More than disappointed. He felt it was *wrong*. As if this was the woman he should have been taking to dinner. As if she was lying to him.

Too much time zone jumping and paranoia, Rafael chided himself. He was seeing lies and plots were there couldn't possibly be any. He frowned.

'I'm Cleo Kelly, her agent from London. '

And yes, she did have a British accent, now he came to think about it. Cool and clipped as if she was always in control. Made any red-blooded man want to prove that she wasn't, thought Rafael. It startled him.

To hide it, he said roughly, 'So who's the target market?'

Cleo Kelly was glaring at him. 'My client's a well-known actor. Patti Darren?' For some reason it sounded like a challenge.

He shrugged. 'OK. Where is she?'

She had strange eyes. They did not go with the magenta hair at all. They were wide and startled, and a strange sea colour, on the cusp between blue and green where they met gunmetal grey. Now the strange eyes flared. Just for a moment, he thought she was going to scream– or hit out – or run. He took a step forward to stop her.

And, at once, her eyelids fell and she was saying composedly, 'She went to the gym.'

'She's cutting it fine,' said Rafael with faint disapproval.

He expected his dates to take their time getting ready to go out with him.

He had never realised it before, he thought. But he found this cavalier attitude to the evening rather unpleasant. It felt as if he was being thrown on at the last moment like a shawl against a possible change in the temperature. Any old shawl, at that.

Still, what could you expect if you let yourself be used as Rent a Hunk? Rafael might not like it but he tried to be fair. Struggled to see the funny side. With not much success. He wasn't used to women seeing him as a disposable appendage. He didn't like it.

The woman shrugged. That put a strain on the towel knot, too. She didn't notice that either.

'Don't worry about Patti. She can change in the flicker of an eye. She'll be there by seven-fifteen. I guarantee it.' Her voice was full of private amusement.

He didn't like that either. If he couldn't see the funny side of Patti Darren's casual behaviour, he did not like this sea witch-eyed baggage finding him a source of amusement. She was pretty too, in spite of the pugnacious manner and the violent hair. There was something about her mouth…

'If you'll just go down and wait in the lobby, I'll get her ready and send her along,' said the baggage, urging him towards the door.

He had had an English nanny like her once. She had been pretty, too, in a blonde English rose sort of way. Made no difference. She was a steamroller in a gingham dress. Always sweet, always reasonable, always absolutely certain she was right. As a child, he had never stood a chance against her kindly superiority.

A totally childish fury rose up from nowhere.

That must have been why he did it. There could not have been any other reason. She had given him no encouragement. And it was not the sort of thing he did. Not with women he did not know. Not unless the woman in question was already indicating pretty clearly that she knew the rules of the game and was attracted by the idea of engaging in a civilised bout with him. Which this woman was not. And, anyway, after Suzanne he was off women in a big way.

But still, he did it.

As she herded him towards the door, like that nanny of old, she reached out for the door catch. Rafael, resisting being herded, looked down and saw a smooth, naked arm reaching past him – a smooth, naked shoulder invitingly close. Smiling, firm, briskly assuring him that Patti Darren would be with him in just a few minutes, she seemed completely unaware of how close. How naked.

And he did it. He put out one long forefinger and ran it thoughtfully along the length of her shoulder, from the raised arm to the collarbone.

She stopped as if she had walked into a wall.

Rafael was exultant.

Childish, he told himself. But that little flicker of self-mockery didn't make any difference. Exultant was what he felt. A blow for all men there, he thought, pleased.

And he did the unforgivable. He turned his hand over, so that his knuckles rested against the soft skin, and retraced the path to her upraised arm.

The first touch had been exploration, pure and simple. The second was a caress. No doubt about it. And they both knew it.

He saw awareness of it slam through her. Her eyes – those strange sea-coloured eyes – flared and were suddenly a whole lot greener. Then she juddered as if she had just taken ten thousand volts.

It was too much for the over-strained knot. The bath towel slipped disastrously.

At last – and much, much too late – Rafael's chivalrous instincts kicked in.

As a student, he had won a number of cups for fencing. His lightning reactions were legendary. He called on them now. Without even realising that he was going to do it, he managed to catch the towel, one-handed. And then he just stood there, holding the unravelled knot of towelling together against the shadowed place between her breasts. Their eyes met.

A long, long moment. Neither of them moved.

He was aware of her shock. Of the astonishing softness of the flesh he was not – quite – touching. Of the way her breasts rose and fell with her hurried breathing. Of the way his hand rode on that movement, like a surfer on a powerful tide. Of the rapid beat of the pulse at the base of exposed throat.

Of the silence. Of his own breathing. Of the way his body suddenly, urgently, was no longer under his control.

That shocked him back to normality. Rafael never, ever, lost control. He stepped away, holding her at the length of his arm.

She swallowed. He saw her throat move. The whip of lust flicked him again, harder. He set his teeth and fought it into submission.

'Who *are* you?' she said in a shaken voice. Then, before he could answer, 'No, it doesn't matter.'

'Doesn't it?'

She took hold of the knot and stepped away from him. He saw her eyes flicker, as their hands touched. But she said steadily, 'No. You're taking Patti to the awards. And I've got work to do.'

His hand fell. 'You're not coming too?'

She gave an odd bark of laughter. 'Not a chance.'

'Why?' For some reason he was outraged. And disappointed. 'Won't Patti let you? Is she a difficult employer?'

'You could say that.' She sounded distracted. 'Look, I'm behind. I haven't got her dress ready yet.'

He stared. He did not know much about film and its conventions but something felt wrong here. Weren't agents all-powerful fixers? Would an agent get a client's dress ready?

She was saying agitatedly, 'Look, she'll be back at any moment. Please, just go down to the lobby and wait.'

He had the oddest feeling that if he let her push him out of the penthouse, he would never see her again. And he had to see her again.

'Why don't I wait here?'

She looked horrified. 'She – I – she would never forgive me,' she said with total conviction.

'She *is* a difficult employer.'

'Yes. No. Oh, please, just go.'

'Not until you tell me when I can see you again.'

Her unease intensified. But she did not pretend to be surprised. He liked that.

'Can Rent a Hunk afford to see me again?' she said with a flicker of a smile.

'I can explain...'

But he was not given the opportunity. From outside, the door there came the unmistakeable sound of the elevator arriving.

Her smiled died as if someone had switched it off. She tried valiantly to hide it, but there was no disguising her alarm. Every tense muscle gave her away. Patti Darren must be a real witch, thought Rafael.

The doorbell rang.

A witch who had left her key behind. He turned and flung the door open impatiently. The bellhop stepped back at the expression on Rafael's face.

'Er – more flowers,' he said, holding a large crystal goblet of slender stemmed roses between him and Rafael like a shield.

'Thank you,' said Rafael, not sounding it. He snatched the goblet.

The bellhop retreated without waiting for a tip. Rafael kicked the door shut and put the roses down on a convenient console table.

The pause had given her time to pull herself together. 'Right,' said Cleo Kelly with resolution. 'Time to go. That was too close a shave for me.' It was only by a supreme effort that her voice was not shaking, he thought.

He resisted the urge to take her in his arms and tell her there was nothing to be alarmed about. It was too soon. Beside, he thought, she'd probably break his leg.

Suppressing a grin, he said instead, 'Then tell me when I can see you.'

She hesitated. Then gave an abrupt, expressionless nod.

'OK. Um – some tourist place. What about the Avila Adobe? I'll meet you there tomorrow at ten.' A faint gleam of mischief broke through. 'If you can get up, of course.'

'I can get up.'

Their eyes met. The gleam of mischief died. It was replaced by something a lot more complicated. He felt a blast of pure masculine triumph.

'I'll see you there,' he said roughly.

She nodded.

She did not try to crowd him towards the door this time. In fact, from the stunned look in those sea witch's eyes, he suspected she would not willingly have got within touching distance of him.

Not that she was afraid of him. Of the magnetic field between them, maybe. He was taken aback by that himself. But that little shiver when she looked at him was a long way away from fear.

And he had to wait until tomorrow before he could do anything about it! But when he did…when *they* did…

He had better get out now, Rafael realised. Before his imagination highjacked the evening. She clearly didn't want that.

And he could wait. That was another thing that his fencing opponents had learned. He was a patient man. Very patient, especially when something was important.

And this woman, with her bewitching eyes and her incompetent way with a bath towel, was the most momentous challenge he had encountered for years. Perhaps ever.

'Tomorrow,' he said and closed the door behind him.

# chapter four

Cleo looked at the closed door blankly. *What a mess*, thought her rational mind.

*What a man!* thought everything else.

'Just what I need,' she said aloud, between irony and despair.

She put a hand to her forehead – and realised that Agent Kelly's purple wig was starting to slip. Oh help, she thought. Had he seen that? He'd seen damn near everything else!

Exactly, thought her rational mind as common sense reasserted itself. He never got his eyes high enough to look at your hair.

Yes, that was better. She should hang onto the image of his eyes locked on her breasts. That way, she'd keep the man in perspective. Somehow, she needed to keep the man in perspective.

And yet…And yet… She wandered back to the bathroom, disturbed. She turned on the water again, restarted the whirlpool effect and watched the scented bubbles take over the massive tub. None of it blocked out the tall man with the haughty profile and eyes like hot coals.

Oh yes, when their eyes met, it seemed as if he had reached into her soul and put his mark on it. And when he touched her, she wanted to give him the world.

'Get real,' Cleo told herself, pulling off the wig and squaring up to the mirror with determination. She was shaken. 'The excitement is getting to you. You've never wanted to give a man the world in your life!'

Anyway, what did she know about him? He was a hired escort, that was all.

'Probably as big a flake as I am,' she told her reflection bracingly.

But he had not felt like a flake. He had felt – she closed her eyes, remembering. He had felt like someone you could trust. Rely on, even. A man who knew where he stood and wasn't afraid to tell the world. His own man. Unconsciously, she let out a longing sigh. It was a long time since she had met someone who was his own man.

What if he was not Rent a Hunk, after all? What if the dark and furious stranger was her knight-errant in disguise?

Her eyes flew open. She stared at her reflection. Her eyes were wide and soft. Dreaming, as she had dreamed that night on the fire escape, when the smoky saxophone had spoken of sex and her heart had dreamed of waterfalls and freedom. *A man who loved me…*

'Pull yourself together,' she told the mirror crisply. That look shook her to her foundations. Now was no time to go soft.

In fact, now was no time to do anything at all but get ready, and *fast*. The eyes like hot coals were waiting for her downstairs.

Rafael went back to the lobby, frowning heavily. The chauffeur of the limousine was waiting, leaning against a pillar. He straightened when he saw Rafael and, as he took in the full impact of his expression, grinned broadly.

'Kid give you a bad time?' he said. 'Don't be hard on her. Tonight's going to be tough for her.'

Rafael's expression did not lighten. He was not tempted to confide that her agent had called him Rent a Hunk. So all he said was, 'Oh?'

'She's angling for a comeback,' said the chauffeur knowledgeably. 'Never easy. But she's only twenty-three or something. That's real hard.'

'Terrible,' said Rafael absently. 'Do you know her agent? What's the woman's name?'

But the chauffeur wasn't interested in agents. 'She was one of those child stars. Came from nowhere. Made a television series, two movies and *pfft*,' he made an eloquent slicing motion, 'dead. Black hole time.'

That caught Rafael's attention at least. 'Very graphic,' he said.

'It's a shame what they do to these kids,' the chauffeur said earnestly. 'Treat them like royalty. Then junk them when they're not cute anymore. There are some bad stories.' There was a hint in the upward inflection that the chauffeur could tell more if he was asked.

Rafael did not even notice. He was deep in his own thoughts again. A muscle worked beside his mouth.

Where had that magnetism come from? Her hair was terrible and she looked as if she'd fight you as soon as kiss you. So why had he insisted on meeting her tomorrow? It was crazy. God knows, this was no time to start a relationship, however fleeting.

*Well, that's just as well*, said a cynical voice in his brain. *What's the betting she doesn't turn up?*

The thought of the purple-haired, pugnacious woman not coming to meet him at the Avila Adobe, made Rafael's hands clench at his sides. It was all he could do not to turn round and go straight upstairs again.

To drown out the voice that was telling him to do just that, he turned to the chauffeur.

'Come on. Let's you and I get a beer,' he said curtly. 'She wasn't there, so she hadn't even started dressing. It's going to be a long wait.'

But he underestimated her. He only had to wait another quarter of an hour. That was when Patti Darren made her entrance.

And Rafael was the only man in the bar who did not look up and yearn.

Cleo had practised too assiduously to let the Rafael throw her off her stride for long. The hard-learned discipline was too strong.

She went into the routine on autopilot. Moisturiser. Gold body make-up, everywhere. Suddenly, she was not hard-as-nails actors' agent, Cleo Kelly, city pale and uptight. She was a glittering international babe. She did some loosening exercises, to get her in the mood. Glittering international babes moved as if they had forgotten they were wearing clothes. When they were, of course.

Then the dress. What there was of it! Naomi's fashion student had done her proud. If she got a decent photograph taken this evening, she must make sure that the guy got a name check.

She looked at herself.

Golden skin gleamed through filmy underwater transparency. The skirt swirled. But nothing could disguise that, fundamentally, the dress was hardly there. It was scoop-backed, and slit to the thigh on the right side. And the thing clung. How it clung!

She swallowed. What would Rent a Hunk think when he saw what he was taking to the Diamond Awards? Sea colours, clinging like Greek drapery to the briefest bikini when she was still, floated like seaweed in rock pools the moment she moved a muscle. And when they stirred, they turned transparent.

Cleo stood in front of the mirror and found herself wishing that she could wear black from neck to toe instead. Preferably with a full carnival mask. Anything to keep her from those all-seeing eyes.

It had never occurred to her that she would encounter someone who gave the impression that he could look right down into her soul. Not at the Diamond Awards. Not at any film event. Nor that he would be the last man in the world that she wanted to flaunt herself in front of in tawdry glitter and see-through lace.

She had never cared before, even when her mother sent her

to the Soap Convention in a dress that she had had to tape to keep in place over her breasts. Why tonight? Oh, it was not *fair*.

But she did not have any ankle-length black and time was running out. She made up elaborately, with glitter on her cheekbones and blocks of sea-colour around her eyes. It was as close to a Venetian mask as she could get. Maybe it would be enough.

Anyway, he would have to look hard, she thought, to detect the real features underneath. And nobody else had noticed that Patti Darren and Agent Kelly were one and the same woman. Why should she be afraid of detection by a beach bum who hired himself out as a professional escort?

Except that he did not look like a beach bum. Or behave like one. And his eyes were keen. And intelligent. And he had looked into her soul and started her dreaming... 'No he didn't' she said aloud, furious, 'and he's no magician either. You just loosened up a bit too much. And you fancy him rotten. Get over it.'

She took the twists of tissue out of her hair, newly-washed, scented and blow-dried. Flicked it into a torrent of Renaissance curls, sprayed it with the horridly expensive fixative that made it shine under the lights. Then the jewellery – a thin glimmer of gold lattice work around her throat and up one arm, long earrings that were a fall of glass shards, peacock and midnight-blue and turquoise among rain water clarity of elongated prisms. One of Naomi's colleagues on the faculty had designed the jewellery too. Everything was geared to getting her maximum Press attention.

*And that's what I want. That's what I need. That's what the whole charade is about. An investment. I can't lose my nerve now because Rent a Hunk caught me in a bath towel!*

Her shoes had tiny straps and were achingly high. They made her a good five inches taller than the barefoot girl who opened the door to him. That should help too.

She was Patti Darren, going for the big one. She made a

few more of those magic, loosening passes with her arms, flexed her ankles, her knees, her hips. Told herself to move as if she was dancing naked at dawn. Felt sick. Lifted her chin. Went to the door.

And saw on the console table the oval cellophane box he had brought. She opened it. He had given her an orchid!

She turned it over. The black velvet wristband hardly went with her glitter-dusted skin or the underwater dress. And yet – the little flower keeper was so cleverly designed. The waxy bloom so beautiful, with its ivory petals threaded with green, like veins under a Tudor beauty's skin. The gift so unexpected…

She stopped. Yes, that was it. That was why she wanted to wear it. It was the only thing in this hothouse of luxury and designer gear that was real. Even the baskets of flowers were a pretence, billed to other people, a scam by Mikey's girl-friend at the florist. But this orchid – it was real. It was meant for her and nobody else. And Rent a Hunk had given it to her.

She made up her mind. 'For luck,' she said aloud. She slid it onto her wrist and went to the party.

And it seemed that luck was with her. Rent a Hunk showed no sign of recognising her. If it had not been for the chauffeur standing up when she walked into the bar, she could have walked right past him and he would not have known who she was, thought Cleo. So much for fearing that he would see through her disguise.

Even so, she went into full Patti-Darren-back-from-the-dead mode. It kept him from asking personal questions, at least.

The woman was completely self-absorbed, thought Rafael. When he introduced himself, she nodded but he was not sure she took it in. Patti Darren knew that people were looking at her. That was clear from the start. And she revelled in it.

Fair enough, she did not giggle. That was something, he supposed. But she tossed that magnificent gleaming red hair more than was strictly necessary. And all her gestures were huge, graceful enough but sweeping, as if she were on a stage. He had to dodge a couple of expansive arm movements, embracing her worldwide fans, before they even got into the car. Once inside, she hugged the window, looking out to see who might be lining the boulevards to watch the stretch limo go by. She must be really hungry to be showbiz royalty again, he thought, bored.

The Awards were at one of the big hotels. When they got into the slow-moving queue of limousines, she leaned forward to stare out of the window. The red carpet seemed to fascinate her. It occurred to him that all the hair tossing might be because she was nervous.

'Scared?' he asked with a twinge of sympathy that surprised him.

She stiffened. 'Why should I be scared?' She did not look at him but, for a moment, her soft, easy Hollywood voice took on all the edge of her British agent.

Rafael grinned privately. Obviously, he had hit a nerve there.

He said, 'I don't know Los Angeles but I've been to these ceremonial dinners all over the world. A ballroom full of industry moguls is the same in Rio de Janeiro as LA. It's all about power-broking and money. The guys who do the actual work are a long way down the food chain.'

She turned her head, without tossing her hair for once. She stared at him, as if she had only just clocked that he was there.

'Who did you say you were?'

'Rafael Dourado,' he said patiently.

'*Not* an actor?'

As if the whole world was peopled by actors, he thought, irritated. 'No not an actor.'

'And not in the film industry either?' she said slowly.

It was Rafael's turn to stiffen. 'No.'

'Then what do you do?'

Rafael felt that he had walked into a minefield and so

started inventing rapidly just as the queue finally deposited them in front of the red carpet. An accredited greeter opened the door beside Patti Darren where the banks of photographers were snapping and the crowd was craning. She gave a small shrug and got out.

There was a surprisingly large crowd gathered behind the looped gold braid barriers and they loved her. Or maybe they loved the near dress and the golden body underneath it, he thought cynically.

He had never attended one of these things before. But the form was obvious. He hung back, letting Patti Darren wave and smile. A fan leaned forward and she responded with instinctive professionalism. She gave the man a warm, charming smile but she did not get too close, or let herself get between him and one of the watchful, dinner-jacketed security men.

One of the women behind the barrier called out and she turned, lifting one arm above her head as if she was waving at the stars in the sodium-masked sky above them. The wonderful hair flew. It was obviously a dream of a shot. Rafael heard twenty cameras click at the same time. She laughed aloud, delighted.

He followed her up the red carpet, smiling, sighing inside. It was going to be a long evening, he thought.

Still, if he stuck with it, he could at least get her to reveal the number of her belligerent agent. Just in case Magenta Hair did not make their date tomorrow. That seemed important, somehow. He had to leave LA soon, but he could not leave that question – whatever it was – unexplored. However crazy it sounded.

Then another limousine drove up and the major-domo stepped forward to open the door. Rafael realised that a good escort would now take charge. He sighed, but stepped forward dutifully.

'Very smooth,' he said in her ear. 'Now let's get inside before they eat you.'

He took her arm. And she jerked as if he had burned her. All laughter, all hair tossing stopped dead. Their eyes met.

He heard her little in-drawn breath. But her shock was nothing compared with his own. His brows snapped together like a vice. For a moment, they stood there staring at each other, both tall, both striking. Both turned to stone.

It was another great shot. The loose red hair and golden limbs under the sub-aqua draperies looked all the more exotic against the man's dark tuxedo. Another barrage of camera clicks brought them out of their trance.

Then Patti Darren gathered herself together again. She gave a little breathless laugh and broke that mesmerising eye contact.

Rafael put his arm round her. He had been to a lot of ultra-sophisticated gatherings in his time and famous faces did not faze him. But something was fazing Patti Darren, and in a big way. His hand rested on bare golden skin and there was no disguising it. Under his palm, he could feel that she was shaking. It was very slight but convulsive, as if she wanted to control it and couldn't.

He was pretty sure he knew what it was too. Those eyes! Why had he not looked at her properly before? He had seen the hair tossing and hand waving, the gold-dusted near nudity and the carnival make-up. And he had damn nearly missed the one thing she couldn't change.

Eloquent, watchful eyes the colour of seawater in sunlight.

So, where did the ferocious Cleo Kelly fit in? A relation? A sister maybe? But those weren't like Cleo's eyes. Those *were* Cleo's eyes. A twin?

But if they were twins, why on earth did Cleo pretend to be afraid of the woman she represented?

Anyway, now was no time to demand explanations. He could have punched something, he was so frustrated. But he knew he had to bide his time.

He set his jaw and said with an effort, 'Do photographers worry you?'

'No.' Not loquacious any longer. No more expansive gestures either. She moistened her lips. 'No. But it's been a long time. This evening – well, it's a big deal for me.'

Suddenly he liked Patti Darren a lot more.

'I heard.'

She gave a ghost of a smile. 'Everyone knows everything in this town.'

He shook his head. 'Not me. I'm just off the bus.'

She laughed. Yes, a *lot* more. He liked the way she stopped laughing and looked at him uncertainly too.

'You don't mean it!'

'Sure thing,' drawled Rafael, beginning to enjoy himself. 'Just blew in to town today.'

She digested this. 'Then I'm your first…?' She stopped.

He let the pause lengthen.

Then he said softly, 'Yup.' There was a wealth of innuendo in the syllable.

That ought to get her writhing, he thought. With lust or embarrassment, it didn't matter. Either way, it would be a blow for his self-respect. Rent a Hunk still rankled. And the masquerade more than rankled.

But she surprised him yet again. Her long eyelashes flicked up and she gave him a glare, both barrels, that made him blink.

'Well, I'm *sorry*,' she said on a militantly rising inflection.

He thought he had never heard anyone sound less sorry in his life. On the other hand, she didn't sound like chattery Hollywood Princess Patti Darren either. His eyes narrowed.

But at that moment, they hit the crowded ballroom and all chance of talk was gone.

The Anitra Productions team were already there – the producer with his shark's smile, the tense director, the producer's assistant, power-dressed for the occasion, and an elderly man who was the only one not to rise from his gilt chair when they approached. Rafael did a double take.

'I don't know the old guy,' muttered the girl on his arm. She sounded dissatisfied. 'Maybe he's the money.'

'He's the author.' Rafael was amused. 'Great Latin American novelist. Very distinguished man.'

'Oh!'

He looked down at her, alert. 'What does that mean?'

'Just off the bus and you know more distinguished screen writers than I do?' She sounded more than dissatisfied. She sounded downright suspicious. 'It don't think so.'

But she had no chance to go on. The producer was embracing her, introducing her, arranging the seating. Rafael was placed opposite her. Since the producer did most of the talking, Rafael used the evening to study Patti Darren at work.

He enjoyed it.

She was lot more intelligent than she wanted anyone in this crowd to know. She seemed to chatter all the time but she never said anything about her personal life, or her career since she had left the teen soap, whose name he could not remember. She had an odd, mobile, three-cornered mouth that she used wickedly and with total premeditation. Oh yes, Patti Darren certainly knew what effect she was having at all times.

But if you wanted to know what she was feeling, you looked at her eyes.

They jerked him into awareness every time he looked into them. They seemed to capture light, glittering and shifting, so that you had to concentrate really hard to see through the glamour. But when you did…when you did…

Suddenly an idea occurred to him, so off-the-wall that he could not believe it. And yet, there was something there that felt like truth.

He turned to the power-suited Production Assistant. 'Miss Darren's agent not here?'

The woman smiled. 'She's called. She's been delayed. She'll be joining us later.'

'Ah.'

Looking at Patti Darren's sparkling sea green eyes, Rafael doubted that. His suspicions were hardening.

He said in an idle tone, 'Tell me – I'm new to the film

world. Would an agent double as a maid for one of her clients? Get her dress ready, that sort of thing?'

The production assistant laughed heartily at the idea.

Rafael nodded. His suspicion crystallised into diamond hard certainty.

He did not know what game she was playing. But, whatever it was, she knew exactly what she was doing. And nobody else had noticed a thing, he thought, marvelling.

'I hope your hotel room is OK,' said the production assistant.

He came out of his thoughts. 'What?'

'The room Brian had me book for you.'

'Oh yeah. It's fine, thank you. And thank you for the dinner jacket too.'

'Oh, the tux. No problem. We hire them all the time.'

'Well, I certainly didn't have mine in my overnight bag,' said Rafael laughing.

There was a little silence. Then the woman said slowly, 'You're very good at this, aren't you?'

He was startled. 'Good? At what?'

She waved a hand full of art deco rings. 'Escorting the star.'

Rafael was taken aback. 'What do you mean?'

'You don't take your eyes off her.'

For a moment he was offended. Then he realised that, far more important than offence, it made him uneasy.

'So?' He was not quite defensive.

She smiled. 'It's real impressive. People notice.'

'Notice?' He had not thought of that.

'Look around. Half the columnists here have made a note to self, "Who is Patti Darren's new man?" You'll get some column inches of your own tomorrow.'

'I hope not,' said Rafael, alarmed.

But there was no more time for talk. There was a drum roll and some complicated lighting shifts. The public address system came into life with a prang that made people wince. And the speeches started. All round the room, conversation fell, and a general air of expectation took hold.

Anitra Productions collected its fair share of the little diamond shapes. The seating at the table began to shift as people went up to collect awards. Eventually, Rafael slipped into the seat beside Patti Darren, as her neighbour went to collect a statuette. On her other side, the distinguished author raised a hand in greeting.

'Dourado. Glad to know you. We must talk.'

Patti Darren did not seem to notice.

Rafael extracted his business cards, the old ones with his New York apartment and his e-mail address on them, and put them on the table in front of him. He passed them round the table like a Mississippi gambler dealing from the deck.

A few more statuettes were handed out. Surreptitiously, Rafael looked at his watch. The elegant gilt chairs were supremely uncomfortable.

There was a longer drum roll. The master of ceremonies said, 'And finally…' All around the room, drooping figures straightened hopefully.

'We are proud to have some of the greats of international daytime sagas with us at this, the first Diamonds Awards. Actors who made a seminal contribution to the genre. First…'

The list started. It was clearly not going to be a short one. Shoulders drooped again.

A spotlight travelled round the room, finding the actors as they were named. One by one, they came to their feet, bowed, and said a couple of words into the travelling microphone. An elderly man had to be helped painfully to his feet. He looked bewildered. After him, a woman with bouffant hair lacquered so fiercely it looked as if it would withstand aerial bombardment, flung her arms round her companion and forced him to stand up too. She made an incoherent speech and concluded it with a passionate embrace.

Beside him Patti Darren sniffed. 'Just what she did all the time on "Cotton Candy",' she muttered. 'Bet she's standing on one foot. She always did that too.'

It sounded like the first, purely spontaneous thing she had said all evening. Her disdain was unmistakeable. Rafael looked down at her, amused.

'If you get a name check should I kiss you too?' he murmured.

She sent him a dark look. 'Don't even think about it.'

The urge to tease her was irresistible. 'I wouldn't want to let you down. I'm sure it's part of an escort's duties.'

'Don't let that worry you.'

He kept his face solemn. 'You needn't be afraid. I'll be gentle with you.'

Under the masquerade face paint, her eyes narrowed to slits.

'I don't think so.'

He deliberately misunderstood her. 'But I will. Look, I'll show you…'

She recoiled so fiercely, she nearly fell off her chair.

'Forget it,' she said harshly. 'I was taught to kiss by experts.'

He raised his eyebrows.

'You don't have to show me a thing,' she spat, goaded.

'Now, is that a challenge?' Rafael wondered aloud.

Even in the semi-dark, her look of contempt could have taken his skin off.

'I can do without the macho cracks too.'

And then irony struck, and the spotlight surged over them. For a microsecond, it picked up Patti Darren glaring at him, while Rafael looked down at her, relaxed, appreciative, and deeply amused. Brian Ross and his assistant exchanged startled glances. These two were naturals at the photographic moment!

Patti broke eye contact and then snapped into action. She laughed, all flying hair and wide-eyed charm. The whole table – possibly the whole room – gave a sigh of relief.

The master of ceremonies was saying, '…little plain Jane, Stephanie Salter, who won our hearts in "Snow Mountain".

A nation held its breath, when Josh gave her her first kiss. Now here she is, all grown up and gorgeous. Ladies and gentlemen, back from her home in England where she has stayed too long, Patti Darren.'

The applause sounded genuinely warm. She stood up, acknowledging it with just the right balance of confidence and modesty. There was a murmur as people took in the revealing dress and the spectacular figure. Perhaps the applause intensified.

And then she was sitting down, before it started to die away. Still smiling, she shook her head and waved away the microphone. The applause definitely intensified. With pretty reluctance, she stood up. A technician swung a boom above her head, so that the microphone was in front of her. She leaned forward to talk into it, as if she was an unpractised amateur, Rafael saw. As a performance, it was masterly.

'Thank you,' she said huskily. There was an attractive hint of a catch in her voice. Her eyes sparkled. Were those tears? 'It's so good to be back. It still feels like home among you all.' She spread her hands. 'I can't tell you what this welcome means to me. Thank you. Thank you.'

The applause was deafening. She sank back into her seat, swallowing. The spotlight stayed on her. Cameras clicked.

She sounded so sincere. Looked sincere. Even these fellow professionals – who must surely know how the trick was done, if anyone did – were moved. How could anything be that intense, that emotionally appealing, and be pure illusion?

For it was an illusion. There was no mistaking that. Once the spotlight had moved on, there was no hint of tears in the eyes she turned on him.

Oh yes, she knew *exactly* what she was doing, thought Rafael. She could manipulate stone if she wanted to. For some reason, that made him furious. But maybe that was because he felt that she'd had him dancing to her tune as well.

*You can't take your eyes off her!*

Nobody manipulated Rafael Gonçalves Dourado. *Nobody.*

He leaned forward and put his lips to her ear. All around, grateful photographers snapped the tall handsome man whispering to the gorgeous red head back from the past.

They did not hear what he said, of course.

'You're *good*,' he murmured. His breath stirred some of the shining fronds about her brow. 'You're really good.'

She bent her head. To all the world, it must look as if she enjoyed the sensation of his breath playing over her exposed neck. But there was not a hint of sensual appreciation in the husky voice. It was raw triumph when she said, 'You have no idea how good.'

'I'm beginning to.' And, as she smiled away from him, carefully misty-eyed, he added one deliberate, devastating word. 'Cleo.'

## chapter five

For a moment, she pretended she had not registered what he said. She kept her smile in place and her eyes misty. While her brain went into hyper drive.

So she did not answer him. He did not like that.

He slid an arm along the back of her chair and whispered, 'Did you hear what I said?'

She swallowed, still looking away. 'Oh yes.'

'And?'

'And nothing.'

'You mean, I can stand up here and tell this whole room that you're leading a double life?'

He sounded incredulous. Also amused. Damn him. *Damn him.*

'I can't stop you,' Cleo told herself as much as him.

She sniffed the orchid at her wrist, as if that was the only thing in the world that interested her. Of course, the silly thing had no smell. His eyes mocked her, telling her he knew that.

'Aren't you even going to try?' It was a jibe.

She looked at him then. 'Blackmail, Mr...?'

His brows twitched together in that nutcracker frown she was coming to know. 'Dourado. Rafael Gonçalves Dourado,' he said with great deliberation.

'Mr Dourado.' She inclined her head.

'Oh, you'd better call me Rafael.'

The look she sent him was a calculated insult. 'Why would I want to do that?'

His eyes were very dark and very angry. 'Because it pays to keep your blackmailer sweet,' he told her affably.

*I will not get the shivers. I will not let him see how much this matters to me.*

'I'll take your word for it.' Contempt dripped. 'I've never been blackmailed before.'

He gave a soft, unamused chuckle. 'You amaze me.' He touched her cheek, quite as if he owned her. 'Oh, and you'd better be careful,' he said, preparing to turn away.

Cleo sat up straight so fast that her draperies nearly tore under the strain. 'Are you threatening me?'

He did a very good wounded-to-the-heart. 'Just a friendly warning.'

'Oh?'

'When you get mad,' he said pleasurably, 'your accent goes very British. Very purple-haired harridan.'

She was dismayed. And not quick enough to hide it.

Rafael picked it up, of course. She saw the flicker of triumph in his eyes. She decided she hated him.

He said softly, 'Careful. Someone might notice.'

'Someone already has,' she said dryly.

'Ah, but you can trust my discretion.'

She thought she did not trust one thing about him. Her chin lifted. 'Really!'

'Oh yes.'

'Convince me.'

He gave her a wonderful smile, all flashing eyes and deeply sensual intent. In spite of herself, Cleo felt her insides turn over. Lust, she told herself. Simple lust. Ignore it and it will go away. She did not even like the man, for Heaven's sake. She turned her shoulder, smiling blindly round the room.

'I have more to gain by keeping your secrets than by telling,' he explained. His voice dropped intimately. 'Much more.'

She swallowed.

'Mr Dourado…' She didn't know what she was going to say. Not plead. Definitely not plead. Maybe appeal to his better nature?

But he interrupted her. 'Rafael.'

She was not going to call him Rafael for all the star

parts in the studios. She said hastily, 'We can't talk about this now.'

'I agree.'

She was surprised. 'Oh?'

'I get to take you home,' he reminded her softly. It sounded more like a promise than a threat.

Startled, Cleo turned her head unguardedly. He was looking at her mouth.

She wished he wouldn't. It unsettled her. On the other hand, she felt sheer shameful triumph that she could make him look like that. Rafael Dourado might think he had got her where he wanted her, but Cleo could see hunger behind the mockery. *Yes!* she thought. And that unsettled her even more.

This is no time for getting randy, she scolded herself. Especially over an unprincipled Rent a Hunk with a sideline in blackmail. You've got a job to do here. Keep your mind on it. Sparkle, dammit. *Sparkle*.

She turned deliberately to the distinguished author and squared her shoulders. *Sparkle hard!*

'I'm sorry I haven't read your book,' she told him. Experience had taught her that it was best to be straight with authors. A short sharp shock and then they forgot about it. 'What I saw of the screenplay looks great. But I know it's not the same thing at all. I'll buy a copy tomorrow.'

He face creased into a thousand leathery lines. 'I will send you one.'

She was genuinely flustered. 'Oh no. I wasn't hinting.'

'It will be a pleasure. You are just what I imagined for my Vanessa.'

From her other side, Rent a Hunk raised those fierce eyebrows. 'A virginal English bluestocking? Really?'

Cleo became conscious of the minimal dress suddenly and glared at him. Blast the man! Up to then, she had put the way he looked at her out of her mind for a good sixty seconds. Now she felt hot again, as if he was undressing her with his eyes. Instead of which, he was leaning forward politely to hear what the distinguished author was saying and not even looking at her.

So why did her breasts start as if he was staring straight down her front?

*Look at me,* something inside her screamed. Had she gone mad?

'You've read "Cloud Orchid"?' The author was polite but he sounded sceptical.

Rent a Hunk grinned and said something in Spanish.

The author pursed his lips. 'Quoting his work back to a writer is very effective,' he observed dryly. 'Nothing is so flattering as the hint that one has touched another person.'

'Is is flattery if I mean it?' asked Rent a Hunk, his eyes dancing.

Cleo thought, *What would I do if he said that to me?* And her mouth dried. He was a self-confessed blackmailer. And here she was, lurching all too easily into fantasy.

'Do you?' The distinguished author sounded honestly puzzled.

'I recognise those people in "Cloud Orchid". God help me, some of them are in my family.'

'Really?'

'Yes. For them, life stopped in 1920, when men were men and women were grateful. No well brought up person ever mentioned money. And you dressed for dinner. You could be in the African bush after a lion or halfway up the Amazon chasing butterflies. But you still dressed for dinner.'

Everyone laughed.

'And that's what your family did?' That was the director, intrigued.

'My Great Aunt still does. Rubies and silk, every night, though half the time she lives in the Amazon jungle.'

Cleo's eyes narrowed. So Rent a Hunk's family were rich, were they? He was turning out to be more and more unexpected.

More than unexpected. When he looked at her, even just a

half-glance as he looked round the table, she felt as if a flame-thrower had flared across her exposed flesh. And that feeling was not just unexpected. That was brand new.

*Not now*, she thought in agony. *Please, please, please, not now. Not when I've nearly got everything under control. Don't let me fall for a man I can't trust. Don't let me fall for Rent a Hunk.*

It is not easy to avoid a man sitting next to you, but Cleo did her best. She did not look at him for the rest of the evening. She did not speak to him if she could help it. If she had to answer a question of his, she spoke at large, dragging anyone into the conversation to help her out, from distinguished author to hard-bitten producer.

They were a bit surprised sometimes but no one resisted. They did not know what she was doing, of course. But he did. He did.

She began to look forward to the drive home in the chauffeured limousine with mingled alarm and militancy.

Anitra Productions were very pleased with her. 'I look forward to working with you,' said the director, as they parted.

'Should be great coverage from tonight,' said the production assistant.

'See you in Brazil,' Brian Cross said to Cleo and Rafael impartially, shaking hands outside the hotel.

It gave her the perfect opportunity to open hostilities with a round of her own.

'Sounds as if he's thinking of taking you on as a permanent escort,' said Cleo, settling into the back seat.

Rafael smiled. 'Does it?'

'Do you want me to give you my endorsement?' she said lightly. 'Is that the price of your silence? I'll tell Brian Ross that you turned up on time and kept your hands off me, if you like.'

He turned his head, laughing gently. 'You know better than that.'

Her eyes faltered. 'Do I?'

'The price of my silence comes a lot higher.'

She swallowed. He couldn't be saying what she thought he was saying. Could he?

Well, if he was, it was about time somebody told him that macho piracy was out-of-date.

She said crisply, 'I've been an actor most of my life and I've never hit the casting couch in all that time. I'm not falling onto it now. Publish and be damned.'

He laughed but differently. It sounded rueful. And very, very sexy.

*Oh help. It's not fair. No one should be such a heel and sound so – warm.*

'I concede,' he said cheerfully.

Too cheerfully, thought Cleo. This was not a man who let other people beat him. She suspected that he had let her win what he intended to be the first game in a long, long match. Well, he would find out his mistake. She had a life to run. There was no room for a challenging stranger. Especially not one who made her feel as if she could not run a trip to the grocery store.

She did not say so though. One of the things she had learned in television was that you did not pick a fight until you had to. So instead, she tipped back her head against the cushions with a deep sigh.

'I'm wiped.'

'Want me to carry you up to your room?' he said, amused.

It was instantly erotic.

Cleo's eyes flew open. 'No.' She sat up straight and put her knees together. 'You don't need to see me to my room. You must be tired too. Take the limo back to your hotel. I'm sure Brian would want you to.'

He returned a non-committal answer. But when they got to the hotel, he sent the limousine away and took her through the lobby, one hand under her arm.

Another great entrance, thought Cleo, wishing she had appreciated the stares and the whispers as much as she had this afternoon. She tried not to look as tense as she felt. She did not pull her arm away from him but it was a close run thing. At the block of elevators, she turned to him with a firm smile and her hand out.

'Thank you for seeing me home.' Her eyes dared him to kiss her.

His mouth twitched.

She thought, *Oh heck, he's going to. I should have known he wouldn't resist a challenge.*

Just then, salvation came. Well, salvation of a sort.

A tough-looking woman approached. It was a motley crowd in the late-night lobby, but even so, she looked out of place in a five star hotel. She had studs in her nose and rings in her eyebrows and was carrying twenty pounds of excess weight. She looked belligerent. Rafael moved forward discreetly to put his body between the newcomer and Cleo. But when the woman squared up to them, her belligerence crumbled. For a moment, there were even tears in her eyes.

'Why didn't you tell them?' she said in a choking voice.

Cleo pinned a brilliant smile to her lips. 'Hello Jill. I take it you saw the awards ceremony on TV?'

'Why didn't you *say* something?'

It felt as if her smile was setting hard. 'Get real, Jill.'

'You were the one who said we had to do something. You were the one who said we had to stand up and be counted.'

This was a nightmare.

'And so I will,' Cleo said hurriedly.

'I don't believe you. You had the chance tonight. Perfect chance. Spotlight on you. Everyone looking. It would have been all over the papers tomorrow…' She broke off, her voice cracking.

Cleo fished out a handkerchief from her tiny purse and stuffed it into the woman's hand.

She said in a softer voice, 'Oh Jill, it wouldn't, you know. It will take a really well planned campaign. We need professional advice, PR, lawyers. And it's going to take time.'

The tough woman blew her nose on the napkin. 'It's already taken sixty years,' she said desolately. 'How much longer?'

'We're getting there…'

'That's what they told Jackie Coogan,' the woman said bitterly. She turned her back pointedly and walked away.

Cleo felt as if she had been winded. She put a hand to her side, looking after the retreating figure with a frustrated expression. 'Damn!' she said under her breath.

'Congratulations,' said Rafael, moving in front of her.

She jumped. 'What?'

'I was congratulating you on the first spontaneous emotion you've had all evening.'

Cleo was no fool. She saw the trap. He wanted her to deny it – and then he would tie her up in knots over the exact nature of the spontaneous emotions she could lay claim to.

She sidestepped neatly. 'Very funny.'

'No, it's not funny. It's sad.' He glanced down at her. 'Who's Jackie Coogan?'

She looked at him suspiciously. 'Are you sending me up?'

He shook his head. 'Not when you've hit an honest streak at last.'

He thought she flushed slightly under the heavy make-up. She shrugged quickly and punched the elevator button.

The doors opened silently. They both got in.

'Oh, well then. If you really want to know, Jackie Coogan was the first famous child star. Back in the twenties, when the industry was new. He got ripped off by everybody – parents, parents' partners, business managers, the works. Made a fortune and never got his hands on any of it. Ended up suing the pants off them. But, of course, the money had all gone by then. It ended up with the State of California setting up a thing called "Coogan's Law" which is supposed to protect the earnings of child actors for when they grow up.'

'Sounds a good thing.'

'In principle,' she agreed sombrely. 'Trouble is, most times it doesn't work. It's out-of-date. It's only enacted in a handful of States anyway. Clever accountants know how to get round it. You don't know how many former child stars there are out there on the scrap heap now that they aren't cute any more.'

'Like your friend, Jill?'

She shook her head. 'Jill is one of the lucky ones. Works in wardrobe. She's got her problems but at least she can make the rent. Some of them can't. They missed out on education while they were filming. They have high expectations, no discipline and all-too-often, a star-status drug habit. And nobody wants to know.'

Rafael looked at her curiously. This was spontaneous feeling with a vengeance.

'You care about these people.' He shook his head. It seemed out of character to the woman he had seen so far. She might have two parts to her personality, but they had both seemed equally self-absorbed. 'But why?'

'I'm very nearly one of them,' she said curtly. Then bit her lip, as if she wished she had not said it.

They reached the penthouse and got out. She flipped open her purse for the card to unlock her room.

He said ironically, 'Oh sure. You look like a down-and-out with a drug habit.'

The glance she sent him was unreadable. 'You don't want to judge by appearances in this town.'

'You mean it's back to the homeless shelter tomorrow?' he mocked.

She did not smile. She shivered noticeably. 'No. And I don't do drugs either. But there are other things…'

He waited.

She stopped rummaging in her purse. At last, she said slowly, almost to herself, 'When I was thirteen I was on the cover of *Time* magazine. The country voted on who should give me my first kiss. I was earning a bomb. I never went to school. I worked eighteen hours a day, then crashed out every couple of months. I was the worst-educated millionaire in the history of the world.'

Rafael drew a shocked breath. She did not seem to hear.

'OK, I don't live in a shelter for the homeless. I don't turn over stores for the price of the next fix, either. But, God help me, I might have done.' She looked up at him, her eyes suddenly fierce. 'I've been lucky. And if you want to know why I care, that's it. Because there, but for the grace of God, go I.'

She was shaking. Rafael took the purse away from her and opened the door. She went inside as if she was in a dream.

He followed her. Well, it was what he had planned, as soon as he saw what she was doing. Nobody manipulated Rafael Dourado.

Except now, he did not want to make a move on her. Crazily, he found himself wanting to look after her.

He said. 'You're cold.'

She jumped. Then realised that she was grasping her arms. She smiled.

'Yes, I suppose I am. Mad, isn't it? If I were at home, I'd be sitting on the fire escape to get cool. That's five star air conditioning for you.'

His eyebrows rose.

She thought, *Oh heck, he's going to point out that if I wear next to nothing, what else can I expect?* She could feel the heat start under her skin.

But all he said was, 'You live in LA? You're not from Britain, after all?'

Thankfully she pressed a hand to her cheek. 'No,' she said distractedly. 'Well, originally. My parents are British. My dad went back a long time ago.'

Which left a whole world of disasters unexplored! She thanked Heaven he could not guess at them.

Under her fingers, the glamorous gold-dust make-up felt like a snakeskin ready to be shed. She could see herself reflected in the mirror behind him. Now that the excitement was over, she could see the tawdriness of her image all too clearly, like a circus performer out of the big ring. The glitter looked brittle and under the dramatic paint, her eyes looked feverish.

She recoiled. 'I need a shower.'

'Don't let me stop you.'

That was when she realised that he had talked his way into her suite without her putting up so much as a token resistance. Without her even noticing!

Cleo shivered again and this time it had nothing to do with the air conditioning. She stopped huddling and stood up straight.

'Yes, I will when you've left.' She yawned ostentatiously, and held out her hand. 'Thank you for your company tonight.' He did not take it.

'The night's still young.' He strolled over to the bar. 'Drink?' He opened the fridge. 'I see you've been hitting the champagne.'

But not very much of it. And only one glass was used too. He lifted it up to the light.

'Secret drinker? I saw you weren't taking anything but water at dinner.'

She looked annoyed. 'I noticed you watching. Didn't realise you were doing an alcohol audit.'

'You know why I was watching you.' He lifted two glasses down from the rack and started to pour the wine. Across the counter, he gave her that long slow smile of his that never failed.

Only this time, it didn't seem to be working its usual magic. She hesitated a moment, then sat on an over-stuffed arm of a sofa and clasped her hands round one knee. She put her head to one side, as if considering him.

'That's a rotten thing to say,' she told him calmly. 'There are only three possible answers to that. And I don't like any of them.'

He was so taken aback, the bottle jerked, splashing cham-

pagne on the gleaming counter top. He *never* splashed wine.
'What?'

She was looking amused. Wary but amused. Then, to his
affronted amazement, she listed the possibilities. She even
ticked them off on her fingers.

'"OK, why were you watching me?" is coy. "No I don't
know," is a lie. Well, half a lie. "Sure, get your clothes off,"
is not my style.'

Rafael could not think of one single thing to say.

Cleo saw it. Smiled. 'Try another tack,' she advised,
holding out her hand for her champagne.

It took him a moment to realise it, but that was when he
saw that he had won this bout too. Even though it did not feel
like it, he thought ruefully. She was so pleased with herself
for her riposte, that she had missed her chance to fling him
out. Now he was over the threshold and entrenched. She had
even tacitly accepted that they were going to share a drink
together.

'Obviously I underestimated you,' he said mildly, hiding
his glee. He strolled round the bar and gave her the glass.
'Which tack do you suggest?'

She surprised him again. 'Well, you can try telling me what
you're really doing here. I was watching you too, you know.
You're way more sophisticated than you want me to think.
And, from what you were saying to our author, you've obviously got a serious reading habit – in the original language,
too! Does that add up to a career as a male escort? I don't
think so.'

He sat on the deep chair opposite her, very much at his ease.

'You're very hidebound,' he said amused. 'What do you
think is the ideal *resumé* for a male escort then?'

She was surprised in to a choke of laughter. He liked
the husky note to it. They smiled at each other, suddenly
mutually pleased.

She let herself flop off the arm into the cushiony embrace
of the sofa. The orchid on her wrist was like an exotic

manacle. His orchid. Her shoulders gleamed in the soft lamp-light. He saw tiny individual gold sparkles as she moved.

How far had she gone with that gold dust stuff? If he took that apology for a dress off her now, would she glitter all over? Or just those places where she thought the dress might dip and part? And where were those places? The thought of gold-dusted nipples made his head spin. He clamped down hard on the urgent distraction that his body was offering him. Not yet, he thought. Not yet.

She stretched one arm – her glittering, gold-dusted, orchid-manacled arm – along the back of the sofa and looked at him gravely over the top of her champagne glass.

'You know what you're doing, don't you?' she said, suddenly serious.

It was what the production assistant had said to him. Just before she said, *Can't take your eyes off her.* Somehow, that didn't seem such an insult anymore.

Rafael stretched his legs out in front of him. 'That sounds like another of those questions with only three answers,' he said lazily.

She inclined her head, acknowledging a hit. The wonderful red hair waved and curled, flowing around her shoulders like something out of a Florentine painting. She seemed quite unaware of it.

'I mean, you know how to play the game.'

'Which game? There are so many.'

'Are there?' She was dry. 'I mean the one that's going on here now. Tease. Invite. Retreat. Advance.'

This time when their eyes met, neither was smiling.

Rafael thought, *This sounds honest. But then, this woman is a game-player par excellence. Maybe I haven't won any points off her at all. Maybe I'm supposed to stay and seduce her. She was the one who demanded Rent a Hunk after all. Maybe that was always part of the deal.*

He remembered, uncomfortably, that the producer had certainly thought so. Why else had he told him to 'show her a good time, know what I mean?' That air of false heartiness should have been all the clue he needed.

It was a sour note. But Rafael found it did not make an ounce of difference. He looked at her and he wanted her. Chameleon. Siren. Diamond-hard agent. Exuberant starlet. He did not trust her an inch. And he wanted them all.

He said very quietly, 'Who's retreating?'

He saw her eyes flare. She looked away quickly, as if she knew her eyes gave her away. But not quickly enough. He put down his champagne glass untasted and stood up.

'Are you going to tell me your secrets?' He did not know why he said it and it brought her off the sofa like a rocket.

'Thank you for bringing me home,' she was saying rapidly. She did not even try to meet his eyes. 'Very kind of you. I'm tired now, though. You have to go.'

He took a step forward.

Off the sofa like a rocket – and into his arms.

For a first kiss, it was spectacular. When he lifted his head, they were both shaking.

She drew a harsh breath. 'Oh yes, you know what you're doing all right,' she said grimly.

But she did not step out of his arms. And, in that flimsy dress, she had to know what his body was clamouring for as urgently as he did.

He had a code. It was strained to near breaking point but still he had a code.

'Do you want me to go?' His voice was ragged.

'I…' So was hers. Worse. 'Yes. No. I don't know.'

He took her face between his hands. He did not trust her. He did not trust any woman, and she had proved herself as tricky as they come. And yet, when he looked into her eyes, under the wild alien make-up, they were green and bewildered. And hungry. That hunger was the undoing of him.

He said harshly, 'Tell me something real.'

She jerked in his arms, her eyes darkening. 'What do you mean?'

'Why the double life?'

Cleo hesitated for a moment, torn. How much could she afford to tell him? How much could she afford to give away and still feel herself?

Then she shrugged. Rent a Hunk would be gone tomorrow. That was the whole point. She was not giving away anything to anyone who knew her. Or who would come back.

'I haven't worked – well, not as an actress – for five years. Agents lose interest in that time.'

Even with the minimal risk, she was not going to tell him about her mother. Or the games Margaret had played with her daughter's career. Or the debts.

She went on, 'But if I'm realistic about a comeback, I have to have someone to represent me. Casting directors, producers – they don't talk to the meat.'

Rafael was momentarily shocked out of his suspicion. 'Is that how you see yourself? The meat?'

'It's what I am.' The bitterness died as quickly as it had flared up. Cleo sounded resigned. 'It pays not to forget it.'

'Then why on earth don't you walk away? Get a real job? Something that gives you self-respect?'

'And regular hours? And a pension plan? Yeah, sure. Dream on.'

'Well?'

Cleo sighed. She said in a practical tone. 'You have no idea how bad my education was. I'm trying to put that right now. But it's a long slow business putting yourself through college. I'm older than most of them. And I still have to eat. In the short term, acting is the only way I'm going to make any money. It's the only thing I know.'

'I see.'

It was clear that he didn't. Probably just as well. She didn't want anyone seeing her too clearly. Not until she had freed herself from debt and the effects of Margaret's ruinous course anyway.

She danced in his arms, touching her tongue tip to her upper lip naughtily. She felt him react and smiled. *Serve him right for watching her mouth all the time.*

She gave a soft, pleased laugh.

Rafael thought, *You've just lied to me. And you think I don't know.*

The woman was a chameleon. She was eager and *blasé* by turns. Young and fresh as a water nymph one minute, then as knowing as a siren. Heedless and wary. Laughing and yet full of some implacable purpose. Overtly sexy – and yet she trembled like a frightened doe when he touched her.

How much was real and how much was clever, clever acting? Rafael did not like that one bit. Suzanne had been a liar but at least she had been a consistent liar. With this woman, you never knew where you were. And that seemed to be the way she wanted it. Was it a marketing ploy to keep the film company interested? Or – he liked this idea even less – one of the men at the party tonight. Or did she just like staying an enigma?

*Well, not with me, darling,* he thought. *I've deduced one of your secrets. And I'm going to find out the rest. Every last one.*

He looked at that tremulous, sensual mouth and thought about secrets. As he had looked at it all through the evening, feeling as if he was walking on hot coals until he tasted it.

'Don't,' said Cleo, nearly voiceless. 'I don't do stuff like this.'

He did not take his eyes off her mouth. 'Like what?'

'I told you. No casting couches.' She swallowed. 'Please.'

He let her go. It was so sudden she staggered on her crazy heels. But he flung his arms wide, not catching her.

'See? No pressure.'

'Oh, this is no pressure, is it?' she said, trying to make a joke of it. But her eyes gave her away. They were almost as hungry as his own.

She ran her tongue nervously along her lower lip. Rafael closed his eyes to shut out temptation. His jaw was clenched so hard that he could almost hear it. It did nothing to stop the rioting demand of his body.

'It's the best I can do at the moment,' he said with wry honesty.

She went totally still. Even from where he stood, not touching her, he could feel the tension in her. Almost hear the blood thundering. His blood? Hers?

The heavily outlined eyes lifted. Pound for pound, her make-up probably weighed as much as that outrage of a dress. Outrage, provocation, curiosity – that's what she had laid out for tonight. And by God she had got it. From him and…

'Every man in the room wanted you tonight,' Rafael said harshly.

She jumped. He saw that she did not believe him.

He was incredulous. 'That's what you wanted, wasn't it?'

She shook her head violently. 'No. No, of course not. I told you…'

'You don't do meaningless sex,' he said wearily. It was like a pain inside him. 'I know. You don't have to tell me again.'

She gave a sudden, unexpected snort of laughter. 'Oh, meaningless sex is fine. It's the meaningful stuff I don't like. The thing where sex is only half of a bargain.'

Their eyes locked.

His body did a double take, like a runner that stumbles and then picks himself up, running faster than ever. He thought, *You can do this after all!*

As if he was laying claim to her, he said gently, 'Patti. Cleo. Your name is Cleopatra, isn't it?'

Her lashes flickered. 'Yes.'

'Does anyone else know that?'

This time her eyes flared, wide and startled, and just a little alarmed.

'No,' she said at last.

He believed her.

'Well, except for my parents. Though they've probably

forgotten. My mother always calls me Patti anyway. My mother still…'

But he did not want to know about her mother. He wanted to know about her. All. Everything. Every last secret place. Every nerve and reflex.

He put his hands on her, claiming her.

She shivered but stood quietly in his hold like a gentled filly. He ran his finger over her warm and naked shoulder blades and watched her lips part.

'Tomorrow,' he said unevenly, 'you'll tell me what tonight was all about. For now…'

He pushed her hair back from her painted face. His fingers shook.

'Yes.' It was a breath, a sigh. A surrender.

Total, astonishing, voluptuous surrender as if she had been waiting for this moment all evening. Maybe all her life. As if she was sharing a burden she had carried for too long. As if the chameleon had come to rest in the right place and was the right colour at last.

Rafael found that he did not care why she was playing her game of double identity after all.

He ran his hands slowly down her spine. There was a lot of it before he got to the first fastening. And by the time he had got to that first fastening, she was already clenching in a tiny climax. She fell against him, shuddering without reserve.

He felt humbled.

'Hey,' he said gently. 'I'm good. But I'm not that good. You have been off the meaningless sex for too long.'

She tried to respond in kind. *Keep it light,* she told herself, though she felt as if her body was melting, flowing away from her to embrace him. *Keep it light.* 'I don't know how that happened.'

'I do.' There was a smile in his voice.

She moistened her lips. 'I had a drink somewhere.'

'Forget it. You won't be needing it,' said Rafael with confidence.

The dress was astonishingly complicated to unfasten. Or maybe that's because his hands were shaking so much, they were clumsy. Rafael was never clumsy. Just like he never spilled champagne. Tonight was a first on a number of fronts.

Her skin felt like fire. But she stood so still. Almost as if she did not believe what was happening to her.

Come on, Rafael told himself. A Hollywood Princess? Even one who's been out of the limelight for a few years? She must know plenty. She even told you – she prefers sex to be meaningless.

Certainly, when the dress fell away, it left her naked. And he was right. Her nipples had had the gold dust treatment too.

'Cute,' he said in a strangled voice.

He touched a gentle finger to them. She drew in a sharp breath and stood still, quivering. He saw the tip of her tongue. Watched her eyes glaze. So that was what she wanted! Very, very slowly, he stroked her until her head went back and she cried out.

In the silence that followed, they stared at each other. Cleo looked dazed.

Then she began to pluck at his jacket. Her fingers seemed to have no strength and she made a total mess of unbuttoning his shirt. In the end, Rafael could not bear it. He pulled the thing over his head and flung it away before hauling her against him.

She gasped as if his naked skin burned her. She was starting those little convulsive tremors again.

'Bed,' he said while he could still say anything.

Her eyes looked dazed. He had seen people like that lost in the jungle, turning dumbly to their guide to get them out alive. He thought quickly, *What's going on here?* But then she started to unzip his pants and he forgot everything but the imminent need to get her somewhere where they weren't going to kick over the furniture.

He picked her up. It seemed the quickest.

It made her gasp and tremble harder.

'You,' said Rafael, 'have got the lowest flashpoint of any woman I've ever met.'

She flinched. At once he thought, *Wrong!* But she was not hurt. She had put her arms round him and found the diskette taped to his side.

'What's that?'

'My insurance policy.'

He carried her into the bedroom.

'I don't understand.'

'Good.' His voice was ragged. 'I don't want you to understand. I want you to concentrate.'

And she did. Oh, she did.

Somewhere in the early hours of the morning, when they were both spent and she was lying with her red hair tumbled all across his chest, he said, 'So you always carry condoms around with you?'

'Staple. What every woman should have in her overnight bag,' she said, She was punching her weight again, or nearly. 'After toothpaste and nail polish remover.'

He reared up indignantly. *'After?'*

She sucked her teeth naughtily. 'There are no alternatives to toothpaste,' she pointed out.

He eyed her. 'And the alternative to condoms?'

'Abstinence,' she said coolly. 'Or perverted practices.'

His eyes gleamed. 'I remember. Best meaningless sex I've ever had.'

She looked away.

There it was again. Just when he thought he knew everything there was to know about this chameleon of his, she changed again. For a moment, in the soft bedside lighting, she looked young and awkward. Almost – if it had not been ridiculous – *shy*.

He took her in his arms and gathered her against him.

'Cleo…'

'I'm glad it came up to expectations.' Her voice was brittle. Rafael was so tired he was nearly hallucinating. He could feel sleep curling round him, touching and retreating. He could not have sworn that he had not fallen asleep a couple of times during this conversation already. But he did not like that brittle voice.

He made a heroic struggle to concentrate.

'Are you all right?'

'Are you asking me if it was good for me?'

He liked that voice even less. 'I'm asking you if you had what you wanted?'

'You said it. Olympic-class, meaningless sex.'

No, that voice was really bad. Alarmed, Rafael tried to make her look at him. He did not succeed.

'That was what you wanted, right?'

'What does any twenty-first century woman want?' she countered.

There was a little pause. Then he sighed and hauled himself up even higher in the bed. This was important. He could not afford to fall asleep now.

'What about passion?' he said gravely.

She flinched. He felt it right through him, as if he had jabbed a knife into his own side.

But she said in a cool little voice, 'Passion is an illusion. I like my sex without the fairy stories, thank you.'

She did not physically remove herself from his arms. But he could feel the distance as if she were on a boat sailing rapidly out of sight. He knew he ought to do something about it – *had* to do something, say something…

But his will was not enough to sustain him any longer. His eyelids fluttered once, twice. Fell. He slumped back among the pillows.

'We'll talk about it in the morning,' he mumbled.

But in the morning, she was gone.

## chapter six

She had cleared out every sign of her occupation from the suite. When he called the desk, they told him that the room was his until noon but, yes, Ms Darren had already checked out.

'She had a flight to London,' they said, clearly sympathetic to the one-night stand left behind. 'But...' encouragingly, '...breakfast is paid for.'

'Thank you,' said Rafael between his teeth.

He was fairly certain that Cleo did not have a flight to anywhere. She had disappeared back into the suburban sprawl of Los Angeles. To say so would be a betrayal, he thought. So he did not, even though she had felt no similar respect for him. But his horrible courtesy froze the telephone line.

'She dumped him. Don't blame her,' said the desk clerk with feeling, returning the phone to its cradle.

But room service reported back that the guy was a dish and the Darren chick had to be out of her mind. In fact, room service helped him work the state-of-the-art phone and finish off the croissants while he tried Directory Enquiries.

He drew a blank. No one was listed as Cleopatra Kelly. Or Darren for that matter.

Well, it meant that he would have to go back to Anitra Productions. That shouldn't prove too difficult. The production assistant had already noticed that he couldn't keep his eyes off Cleo. She probably wasn't alone.

Rafael lobbed a wilting flower arrangement at the mirror behind the bar. It splatted very satisfyingly. It was not much but it made him feel marginally better. Briefly, furiously, he wondered what had happened to his orchid on her wrist last night. Torn to shreds in that bed, presumably. For a moment, he could have hit someone.

But that was pointless. He turned away, thinking, shooting his cuffs. Then he remembered. The hired tuxedo would have to be returned. All he had to do was take it back to the production office, convince the romantic production assistant that his heart was breaking and, Bingo, Cleo's phone number would be his. He swung the jacket over his shoulder and he began to whistle softly.

It went against the grain to lie like she had done. But – well, he had said they would talk in the morning. It was only good manners to wait for his half of the dialogue. He was going to find her and point that out.

He surveyed his image, in the vegetation-stained mirror. 'My heart is breaking,' he announced experimentally. It did not sound convincing.

He took a cab back to the hotel Anitra had booked him into. He was still simmering but, underneath, he knew he was worried. OK, she was a chameleon, and he couldn't expect her to behave rationally. But what sort of woman takes off after a night like that without leaving so much as a note?

Matt Gottlieb's warning words echoed unpleasantly, *Eric said that the week before he died that girls kept coming on to him, out of nowhere. So watch new people. Mistrust coincidence.*

She hadn't come on to him. She had said that she did not do things like that…

But she had still done it, hadn't she? They had fallen into bed as if they were starving, both of them. Cleo Kelly, or Darren, or whatever she was called, really was about the biggest coincidence he could think of.

And why had she not left him a message? He had hunted. Then the obliging room service had hunted, in case Rafael was being stupid and could not see what was staring him in the face. No note.

He found his precious insurance diskette lobbed halfway across the bedroom floor. But no note anywhere.

Did that mean that he had meant nothing to her after all? That he was as disposable as last night's condom? That was a bad thought.

Even worse – had he hurt her somehow? Under the gold dust and war paint there might just be a vulnerable woman. He thought he had seen her peep out several times last night. No matter how bravely Cleo boasted the virtues of meaningless sex, he knew different.

Or did he? Rafael shut his eyes briefly. *I don't do stuff like this.* That was before she decided she had to be cool, of course, and had started pretending again. Oh, she knew how to lie and evade and pretend until a man did not know whether he was on his head or his heels.

But there were some things Rafael was hanging on to. For all the fire last night, she had not made love in a long time. He was an experienced man and he knew the signs. Little awkwardnesses. Moments of astonishment, quickly hidden. Dismay, even, when her body's response, like thunder to lightning, was fiercer than she wanted and way, way out of her control.

Oh yes, Cleo was out of practice, he thought. He felt hot and hard again, just thinking about what they had done to each other last night. But what had him on the rack this morning was that she was too unpractised to realise how rare it was. Or how proud he had felt when she had abandoned herself to him.

Rafael shifted angrily in the back of the cab. Proud! Nonsense! Anyone would think he was hurt by her flight. Of course he was not hurt. Of course he was not. It was a question of courtesy, that was all. She had every right to walk out on a one-night stand if she wanted to. But she should have had the courtesy to…

Who was he fooling? He was hurt. He thought he had changed the world for her last night. She had changed his. He was only just coming to realise it. He did not want it, but he knew it was true.

And she had *left*.

*Maybe I was the only one it happened to*, thought Rafael, wearily.

And then he thought – she came into my arms as if she was sharing a burden. I didn't imagine that. She let down her guard with me, long before the physical fireworks. And I don't think she's let down her guard with anyone ever. She *did* feel something.

Oh yes, she had felt something, his Cleo. Even if she was not admitting it this morning. Even if she didn't *know*. Last night she had been naked to her soul.

Then, suddenly, he remembered. She had never told anyone else that her name was Cleopatra. *But she told me*, he thought. It felt as if a vice round his heart had been released.

He gave a long sigh. And began to smile.

*I know you. Better than you think. Better than anyone else does. When I find you, my Cleo, you're going to admit it. And I'm going to find you today.*

But when he got to the hotel, his plans all stood on their head.

Because his room had been ransacked. More than ransacked.

'Can you give us a list of what's missing, sir?' said the young policeman.

*He was a lot more excited than the police usually were about hotel break-ins*, thought Rafael.

'Some diskettes.' All of them actually. This time, they had found his hiding place. Except the one that Cleo had bowled away across the carpet last night. Thank God for insurance. Thank God, too, that he had not been here. He remembered Eric's fate – the diabetic who didn't drink, found dead after partying too hard! .

'When did this happen?'

'Between six and eight yesterday evening as far as we can tell.'

'Just as well I didn't come back last night.' *Cleo, you not only changed my world, you may just have saved me from a nasty beating. Even my life.* 'I'm surprised they didn't take the laptop.'

He went over to it just as the policeman's boss said sharply, 'I wouldn't touch that, sir.'

Rafael's hand fell. 'Oh sorry. Fingerprints?'

'No, sir. We're waiting for the explosives guys. We think your computer may be booby-trapped. Like – real fire-bomb stuff.'

Rafael stood stock-still.

'Can you think of anyone who might want to harm you, sir?'

He swallowed.

*Toussaint.* Paul-Henri, damn his eyes. He hadn't really believed it. Not in his heart of hearts. He had taken all those precautions because he was stubborn and because he was careful. Determined to prove to the world that Paul-Henri's research was phoney, he had not really thought about anything else.

But was Matt Gottlieb right after all? Was Paul-Henri more than a fraud and a greedy cheat? Was he a murderer? And, if so, what could Rafael do about it? He had no *proof*.

'Yes, I can think of someone,' said Rafael in a still voice.

He told them everything.

Thank God for George's diner. And for classes. And even for her mother, calling in from the clinic that her credit card had been eaten and she needed money fast.

Thank God for anything that took her mind off Rafael Gonçalves Dourado. The man had marked her.

Not literally, of course. He had been an exquisitely controlled lover. Alert to her every need, including time. He had lured and led her, sure. But never pushed. If he got carried away – and he had, oh yes he *had* – it was only after making sure that she was ready. He had not done one thing she had not been begging for.

Yet this morning, her unaccustomed body felt stiff. And – not exactly sore but – well, tender. Cleo made a face at the feeble word. What could you expect if you went at it like a steam train after years of abstinence, she told herself bracingly.

But this new tenderness was not just physical, and she knew it. For a moment, last night, she had felt as if the dream was within her grasp. When he brushed her hair aside she had felt – cherished.

An illusion, of course. But she had shut her eyes hard, concentrating on the fantasy of freedom and a knight-errant and love. Even the waterfall. Well, what was the point of having a fantasy if you didn't take it the whole way?

Leaving this morning had been the hardest thing she had ever done. But there was no room for fantasy in her life at the moment. And she knew it.

'Bad timing,' she said aloud. 'Horrible, horrible timing. I was not myself.'

That's what she went on saying. *I was not myself.* It became her litany.

She did a deal with her professor over the schoolwork she would miss while she was on location. She got her visa. She called Jill and persuaded her to dump the nose rings for a month and fill in for her at George's diner.

She even borrowed George's car and went up to the Braybourn Clinic to get Margaret. She had to break the news that the Patti Darren rocket was flying again – and Margaret was jettisoned.

'Be strong,' she told herself. 'This had to happen. It's long overdue. You can handle it.'

But Margaret did not take it in. Would not take it in.

'How exciting, darling. I don't remember Brian Ross. But I'll put in a call to him at once.'

Cleo breathed carefully. 'Don't you understand, mother? It has nothing to do with you. The contract is already signed.'

'Don't be silly, darling. And don't call me mother. It's not professional.'

'Our professional relationship is over,' said Cleo, made brutal by despair.

But Margaret was fussing with her matching luggage and the glossy carrier bag of designer lotions she had purchased at the clinic and did not hear. Or rather, refused to hear.

She refused to hear all the way back to LA.

In the end, Cleo took her to her apartment block, unloaded the cases on the steps, and stood in front of her, hands on hips.

'Listen to me, mother. This is the last time I'll say it. *You're off my case*. I'm not discussing it and I'm not changing my mind.'

For the first time, Margaret gave a flicker of awareness that she knew what Cleo was talking about. 'You'll have to. You get paid through me.'

'No mother,' said Cleo sadly. 'Not anymore.'

That shook Margaret as nothing else had done. 'But…'

'*No.*'

'But you don't understand. They'll know you've got a job. They'll expect…'

Cleo felt a hand clutch at her heart. 'Who? Who will expect? Expect what?'

But she knew. Of course she knew. She'd just been pretending.

'Is this about the man in dark glasses? The debt collector?'

'I don't know what you mean,' said Margaret unconvincingly.

'You've been gambling again, haven't you? You've hit your limit. That's why your credit card was destroyed. What have you done?'

'I needed funding…'

'What have you *done*?'

It all came out then. Standing on the steps in the bright sun, surrounded by pots of flame-coloured geraniums, with Margaret alternately hectoring and pleading, it all came out. She had given her marker to a man who ran an illegal casino. And now it was payback time. That was why she had taken off to the hills for her latest bout of cosmetic surgery.

'You're sick,' said Cleo. She felt as if she were drowning.

'I have to look my best. You know what this town is like. An agent...'

'You're not an agent, mother.' Cleo was nearly screaming.

'But you need me.'

They glared at each other. Cleo closed her eyes briefly. And out of her memory came the clear, crisp tone of the man who had woken her senses. *Why on earth don't you walk away? Find something that gives you some respect?*

Yes, she thought. That's what I have to do. Me and Margaret both.

'I can't cope with this,' she said at last. 'You need help. And I'm not qualified to give it.'

'We'll get through this,' Margaret said, eager again now she thought she was getting her own way. 'We always have. We're a good team.'

Cleo's heart hurt. 'No, we aren't. I can't help you.'

'But...'

'Get some help, mother. Gamblers Anonymous. I don't know if there's a support group for addicts to facelifts but if there is, you qualify. Find them. Find a doctor. Anyone. I'm not playing the game anymore.'

She turned on her heel and walked to the car.

Margaret said, incredibly, with all the old maternal authority, 'Patti Darren, get your butt back here.'

Cleo looked at her levelly across the bonnet of George's car.

'It's over mother. And my name is Cleo.' Her heart lifted, suddenly, in spite of the awfulness. For a moment, she almost felt as if Rafael was there with her, standing just behind her shoulder. That, if she wanted, she could tilt back and lean against his strength and know she was loved. She said softly, 'In fact, my name is Cleopatra.'

And knew that she had won a victory.


'Well,' said the senior detective, 'I'm not saying you're wrong. I'm saying we can't do anything about it.'

Rafael was not surprised.

'We can put it all on file, of course. Put a note out to Interpol records, too. But – a guy uses a hit man, it's difficult to prove, Professor. Especially a guy like this one. Mr Toussaint...' He did not even attempt the French pronunciation, '...is a real operator, you know. Seems to know everybody who is anybody. And not just in medicine.'

'I know,' said Rafael, depressed. 'I thought I had good contacts. But he makes me look like an amateur.'

The senior detective smiled. His researches were thorough. He did not say that he knew that Rafael was the son of a mega-rich Brazilian family, as well as being a noted figure in the world of medical research. Normally, rich men were a pain to a hard-working policeman. But Rafael was a man with a real problem, and he wasn't expecting the police department to clear up his mess. The detective warmed to him.

'Want some advice?'

'Anything.'

'You're on the right track. Make those international guys do the business.'

'You mean, keep trying to get the academic journals to re-examine Toussaint's results?'

'Yeah. That's the only way you can do it. Fight him with facts. Only it's gonna take time, right?'

'Yes.'

'So, drop out of sight. Disguise. False name. Whatever it takes.'

'But if I do that, I can't keep in touch with the journals.'

The detective lost interest. Rich men never took advice. How come he had forgotten that?

'Best I can think of.'

Rafael nodded.

'Look, sir. You want anyone, anywhere, to arrest Toussaint for conspiracy to murder, you gotta have proof. And to get that, you gotta stay alive. Check?'

'Yeah,' said Rafael, resigned. 'Check.'

He knew the man was right. So he wasn't going to find his Cleo this time round. Unless…

She'd be going to Ruprechago, wouldn't she? She was in this film, after all. At some point, she'd have to be on location in the Amazon, surely?

It was a sporting chance, anyway. The best he'd got. And he could drop out of sight in Ruprechago, as he could nowhere else in the world.

He gave the senior detective a sudden, blinding smile. 'Check.'


Cleo had been on location before, but never to anywhere like this. The first time she saw the house at Ruprechago, she nearly turned and fled. It was quite simply menacing.

'Boy, oh boy! Dracula hits the jungle,' said Ed Brandon, the male lead, as they drove up the dirt track from the plane.

The four-wheel drive bucked like a bronco over ruts as deep as Atlantic waves. Cleo was feeling distinctly seasick. But the sensation she got from her first sight of the brooding mansion had nothing to do with her digestive reflexes. It was more like fear.

It had originally been designed as an impressive plantation house. It was all there – the columns, the long windows, the huge double-height veranda. But at some point, it looked as if the jungle had started to overwhelm it. Almost a third of the façade was overgrown with darkly waving creeper. Such paintwork as was visible had not so much faded as ossified, so it was no longer white but a queer bone colour.

Inside, it was not so different. The ceilings were high and supplied with old-fashioned rotary fans that kept up a perpetual soft purr. But the circulation they induced was not enough to stir the heavy velvet curtains. The floors, the staircase, most of the furniture, were oak and polished until they shone like a mirror. Cleo tried to convince herself that the sweet herbal smell that followed her round the house was lavender and beeswax in the polish. But she had the nastiest feeling that it was the jungle encroaching, unseen, into every corner of the place.

But the servants were friendly and open – well, all but one, and he was hardly ever there. He just hung around in the garden, in his sloppy white shirt and loose trousers, with a straw hat pulled over his face, as if he was trying to mask his features. She could feel him watching her too.

But as far as Anitra Productions were concerned, Ruprechago was Paradise incarnate. The servants were helpful. The newly restored salon was a work of art. And the owners were *away*.

The distinguished author was in raptures too. He kept going round, patting tasselled lampshades and fat cushions, murmuring, 'Perfect. Perfect.'

Cleo tried to forget that the place made her uneasy. Everyone else was happy enough. But then, everyone else already knew each other. They were a tight knit team already and they looked on her with suspicion.

So, when, after a particularly bad night she said, 'This place gives me the creeps,' she could almost feel them start to back away.

'But it's so authentic,' said Michelle Latimer. 'It even has real jungle on the doorstep. And its own waterfall. Pity there isn't a waterfall in the book.'

She was the Big Star and had come laden with the original novel in three languages and every academic study of the author she could find. Given half a chance, she would launch into a literary history lecture at every break in filming. As the only other actress on set, she was particularly determined to squash the newcomer.

'Waterfall's great but have you seen that drop? And the house is a bit decayed,' allowed Ed Brandon. He was younger, not quite a Big Star yet. He had been hired for his looks and didn't care. He raised a careless eyebrow at Cleo across the energy drink that was shipped in for him. 'Just general creeps? Or did something spook you out?'

There was a pause. Everyone else looked bored. Cleo looked at the mango on her plate as if she had never seen the fruit before.

She felt a fool. That man in the garden was not quite a servant – she had never seen him actually *doing* anything.

She muttered, 'I went for a walk and one of the servants followed me. He wears a huge floppy hat. You never get a good look at him.'

Ed said kindly, 'Probably just shy.'

Michelle was superior. 'Or trying to stop you doing anything dangerous. This place is pretty remote, you know. They don't want you falling down into the ravine or impaling yourself on a poisonous plant.'

'But does he have to watch me like that?'

'The servants are here for all of us, you know,' Michelle said sharply. 'Heaven preserve me from Comeback Kids!'

Cleo bit her lip and said no more. But she knew that she was right. There was only one person those shadowed eyes followed round the garden.

And one night, when she went into the room she had been allotted, she had been certain there was someone there. The mosquito net round the bed was moving, very slightly, as if someone had brushed against it. She tried to tell herself that it was the ceiling fan. But she knew that fan was too high even to stir the cobwebs in their corners. It would not make the mosquito net shiver like that. But when she had called out, 'Anyone here?' no one had answered. And there had not been anyone on the balcony when she looked.

She had taken her new keepsake to bed. She knew she was a fool, but the dried petals, halfway between paper and silk, somehow made her feel safe. She did not say anything more about the tall peasant who never seemed to do any work or look anyone in the eye – but was always there. She just locked her door at night and kept a watchful eye.

She made sure none of the rest of the crew ever had the chance to call her a Comeback Kid again either.

She was word perfect. She read all Michelle's books and more. She became such a perfectionist about her costume that the wardrobe girls started to hate her. And she acted her socks off.

The rest of my tuition fees, she kept telling herself. That's what I'm doing it for. This is my passport to professional qual- ifications and a better life.

But she knew it wasn't. She knew that Margaret was on the edge of disaster. This time it was not just bankruptcy. This time it was creditors who collected with baseball bats and guns. Cleo knew that, in the end, she could not let that happen.

In the end, that was where the money would go. Where it had always gone. Into the bottomless well that funded Margaret Darren's fantasy life.

Margaret called. Often. That was another reason the production team started to hate her. Her mother called all the time and she wouldn't take the call.

'She's a hard witch,' said the chief make-up expert to the assistant director, after Cleo had taken a stand on blusher.

'No, porcelain. Porcelain. He says that Amanda has skin that is as pale as finest English porcelain. She's not an apple- cheeked farm girl. Take that rubbish away.'

So the make-up girl hated her too.

'Hard witch, she surely is,' said the assistant director. He approved. He did not care how hard-hearted actresses were, as long as they turned up on time and didn't spoil his shot. The Comeback Kid qualified on both counts.

And Cleo, overhearing, laughed in their faces.

He toasted her with his beer can. 'Reinforced steel to the toenails.'

Cleo inclined her head. 'Thank you.'

She didn't care, she told herself. It did not make any difference to her what these people thought of her. She was here to do a job and get out. She need never see any of them again.

Just like she was never going to see Rent-a-Hunk again. It did not matter what he thought of her either.

But when she was drifting off to sleep at night, she sometimes brought herself awake with a start, as the dream hit. In the dream, she was telling him *why*. Why she needed the job. Why she had been nearly naked at the Awards. Why she had demanded an escort that night. It was a long whimpering babble of excuses.

And the man in her dream held her head between his hands and whispered into her mouth, 'Tell the truth. Tell the truth *now*.'

So, the next morning, there were dark shadows under her eyes to be blanked out before the porcelain complexion could be applied and the make-up girl hated her even more. But Cleo was never late for her call.

Eventually, they began to come to the end of shooting. Costumes and props that wouldn't be needed again were shipped out from the private airstrip. Actors with no more scenes left. Michelle went to Rio for a holiday on her way back to Hollywood. In the end, only three of the cast were left. The director was looking tense and the refreshment breaks were perfunctory.

And then, the light plane returned from ferrying stuff to Manaus and brought with it an unscheduled passenger.

'Margaret,' said Cleo, her heart sinking to her buttoned Victorian boots. 'What are you doing here?'

They were shooting on the terrace and her mother arrived during one of the brief breaks. She still looked more like a film star than Cleo did. But she was not as confident as usual.

'I've had a great offer. I need to talk to you about it.'

But the director summoned Cleo back to work and Margaret had to wait until the next scene. Cleo was in the kitchen annex that had been turned into a make-up area, when Margaret tracked her down.

And it rapidly emerged that Margaret had convinced herself that she was in charge of Cleo's career all over again. Especially as she had never got to meet the mysterious Ms Kelly who Cleo claimed was her agent these days. And neither had any of Margaret's contacts.

'You're being taken for a ride by a celebrity chaser, darling,' Margaret said airily. 'Nobody knows her. She hasn't got any other clients. You can't afford to let an amateur mess with your career. Kindness can go too far.'

'You travelled all the way up the Amazon to say that?' said Cleo wearily.

She tipped her head back, as the make-up girl carefully outlined her eyes. In the mirror, she could see the girl's expression at the word 'kindness'. Over the last six weeks, the Comeback Kid had acquired a reputation for a lot of things – hard work, intense concentration, edgy temperament. Kindness was not among them.

'Get out, Margaret,' she said unemotionally.

Margaret took no notice. Like mother, like daughter, thought the make-up girl. She did not know which of the Darren witches she loathed more.

Margaret took another turn round the tiny room, tapping her teeth with one gold-painted nail. 'I've had an e-mail from Tom. He needs a signature.'

Cleo did not need to ask Tom who? She already knew. Her heart lurched sickly with the memory.

She said as steadily as she could manage, 'Tom de Lacey makes the sort of movies I'd pay good money not to see, let alone take part in.' She stared at the ceiling and hardly moved her lips but it did not detract from the force of feeling there.

'We can't keep him hanging about,' announced Margaret, unheeding.

She was prowling backwards and forwards in front of the unoccupied make-up bays. She sent a scatter of brushes and make-up sticks and cotton wool on to the floor with her flying draperies. She did not notice that either.

'He has the rest of the film to cast,' she said in a reproachful tone.

Cleo started to frown and quickly stopped herself. Inside she was beginning to shake. She must not let it out. If her canvas started to tremble, the make-up girl would not be able to do her job properly.

'Well, he is not casting me,' she said flatly, as if the very thought did not want to make her retch. 'Go away, Margaret. I'm on set in five minutes.'

Her mother seemed to take that on board at least. 'This is no time to be temperamental,' she scolded.

'Too right.' Cleo was ironic. 'So go away and stop giving me the heebie-jeebies.'

'How many other offers do you think you've had?'

The make-up girl bent over Cleo's perfect brow with intense concentration suddenly. Actors never admitted that they had no jobs in the pipeline. The past, yes. They would ruefully confess to a bad year or a bad decade even. They could afford to admit to that. But no one ever stood up and said in front of someone else in the business, however remote from casting they might be, that they were short of work *now*. Margaret Darren was breaking one of the two immutable Laws of Hollywood when she did that.

Cleo waited until the make-up girl had finished turning her into a pearly-skinned beauty and then sat up very straight. Her remarkable eyes, emphasised by skilful shadowing, were the colour of a sunlit sky. They snapped with fury.

'Can it, mother,' she said curtly.

Margaret stiffened. Not at the brisk command, thought the make-up girl with glee. At the *word*. She knew the type. Margaret Darren would not normally acknowledge that she was anyone's mother, let alone that of a twenty-three-year-old former child star who was now turning into an alarmingly voluptuous woman.

Cleo stood up and shook out her lacy crinoline. She looked like a caged long jumper in the swinging skirts.

'Walk to the set with me,' she said, taking her mother's elbow in a steely grip.

Margaret looked eager and affronted in equal measure. She clipped along beside Cleo, her high heels pattering like raindrops on the polished wooden floor. Margaret had to take two steps to match her daughter's one.

'Now listen to me,' Cleo said in a virulent undertone. 'This is my last movie. I've told you again and again. Believe it.'

'But everyone says how brilliant you are…'

'Rubbish. No one has said anything to you about my performance and you know it. And if I ever did do another film, it would not be Tom de Lacey's bit of nastiness.'

'It has wonderful production values,' protested Margaret, panting a little at the pace.

'It's high-gloss porn,' said Cleo brutally.

There was a half-second when Margaret did not say anything at all. Then she gave a high, artificial laugh.

'Are you saying you're a prude? A modern girl like you?'

'No, of course not.' Cleo stopped dead suddenly, so that Margaret skittered into her. She brushed her mother aside. 'Did you see someone?'

'Someone?' Margaret was bewildered.

'Tall guy. In those loose trousers and smock thing. He always seem to be around.'

'He'll be a servant. It's his job.'

'No I mean, around *me.*'

'A fan,' said Margaret, complacent. 'He loved you in "Snow Mountain" and now he wants your autograph.'

'Mother, get real. We're as near as can be to the middle of the jungle. I haven't even seen a television here. The whole world didn't watch "Snow Mountain", you know.'

'I don't know why you're so determined to play down your success…'

'Because it was a long time ago and I'm not the same

person,' said Cleo crisply. 'Now, take the next plane back to LA. I've got work to do.'

'I'll leave Tom's script in your room then,' said Margaret. 'We'll talk later.'

It was as if the whole of their conversation had not taken place. It was horribly familiar and it drove Cleo wild. She made an explosive noise and stomped back to the set.

She told herself that she was in a temper. That she had every right to be in a temper.

But she knew it was more that that. She could feel the cold hand of inevitability closing round her, squeezing the life out of her.

*God help me. I'm all out of options.*

## chapter seven

Rafael stood in the shadows and watched her go.

It looked as if that conversation he had overheard was right. Cleo-Patti-Cleopatra was one tough cookie! She had not had so much as a smile for her mother. She had not kissed her or put an arm round her either. Another change of colour for the chameleon! Or was it?

Why had she left him that morning, without waking him up to goodbye, without so much as a note? Surely she hadn't lured him to stay overnight so that someone else could search his room? Surely that wasn't possible?

But she had told him almost nothing about herself. Certainly not enough for him to find her. OK, she had let him think that it was his idea to make love to her. But he could not forget that, in the end, she had not taken much persuading. And she was a professional actress. He had seen how good at those Awards.

What if he had fallen for a beautiful face and a skilful performance? *Again!*

Every way he turned, he found himself arguing the opposite. He did not know what to believe and he was furious about it. Furious with her. Even more furious with himself.

So furious, in fact, that sometimes he almost forgot that he had to keep out of sight.

When he first arrived back at Ruprechago, he had had every intention of telling the Anitra Production Company that a member of the family was in residence after all. But then Maria told him that people had been asking about Ruprechago at Manaus airport. Even the doctor in his jungle clinic up-river reported that someone had wandered in from a tourist wildlife group party and asked whether Rafael Gonçalves

Dourado was back home just now.

Dr David had said 'No'. He thought it was the truth, after all. Rafael rode off down the ravine to the settlement to find out more about the curious tourist and came back to Ruprechago three days later, thoughtful. That was when he took a rapid decision and turned himself into one of his own gardeners.

He swore the household to secrecy but, even so, it was a hard task not to unmask himself to Cleo.

From the moment she arrived, he watched her. His heart burned to know the truth. Was she, could she, be working for Paul-Henri? She had told Rafael she needed money, after all. And he sometimes thought she was capable of anything, watching the way she drove herself, uncaring whether others liked or hated her.

And yet…

*No one but me knows she is called Cleopatra.*

Surely that counted for something?

He was almost certain that she knew he was watching her too. Twice he nearly came out of the shadows and challenged her. But… But…

And then someone searched his study. Not very expertly but it was clear what they were looking for – diskettes!

After that, of course, unmasking to anyone was impossible. So Rafael watched the filming and got more and more bad tempered. Now that she had got the part, the chattering starlet fell away like a snake's discarded skin. On set, she was professional. Off, she was remote. Except when she lashed out because something did not come up to her high standards. She made friends with nobody. He could see that she was playing the Victorian Miss to perfection – ruthless, calculated perfection. No hint of passion anywhere at all.

What had happened to his abandoned golden lover? Had she just been another part too?

*Will the real Cleopatra please stand up?*

My judgement is really shot, he thought savagely. First

Suzanne. Now a professional illusionist.

But he still ached for the professional illusionist. That did nothing for his temper either.

There were only two days of filming left and the tension was palpable. The director looked as if he was not sleeping. Cleo was concentrating so hard, she did not even bother to insist that Margaret left. When her mother told her that she had managed to borrow the room of one of the actors who had left, Cleo just shrugged and said, 'Keep out of my way.'

Margaret didn't, of course. So, after breakfast, when she was not needed on a take, Cleo retreated to the study. It was in a separate building in the garden. Once they had stopped using it to film, nobody came there. Margaret would not find it.

The room was faintly musty, with threadbare rugs on a stone floor and more glass cases of butterflies than books on the shelves. The shelves were mahogany and looked as if they have been carved for a Victorian museum's library. She took a book down and the illusion evaporated at once. The book smelled faintly vegetable as if it was turning back into the jungle. Like everything else in this house.

She shuddered and pushed it back into place.

A voice said behind her sharply, 'What are you doing here?'

She whirled and her skirts rocked. She was already in her Victorian crinoline, waiting for her first scene.

It was him. It was *him*. Taller than the rest, just as she had thought. Not just taller. Broad-shouldered, deep chested. Under the loose cotton clothes, there was a long-limbed body that was totally unlike all the other people who lived here. And he spoke English!

'Who *are* you?' Her voice was not wholly steady.

He pulled the disreputable floppy sunhat lower over his brows. 'What are you doing here? They are not filming in this room.' His voice was gruff and suspicious.

'I was…' She swallowed. 'I was looking for some privacy.'

'Is that all you were looking for?'

She stared. 'What?'

'You've been here before, haven't you?'

'Well, yes…' She had been in the scene in the study.

He said something that was not in English at all. Cleo was glad. He sounded angry. More than angry. As if he wanted to lay into an enemy. And she were the enemy.

She quailed. But Cleo was no coward. She lifted her chin and said in the cold, hard voice that usually got results, 'I'll ask again. Who are you?'

She had the feeling of dark eyes boring into her, like one of those pins through the poor butterflies. For a moment, the silence between them was molten with possibilities. Then he flung the door open.

'A fool,' he spat out.

And, before she could demand an explanation, an apology – or even that he took his hat off indoors – he had gone.

She put her hands together. The palms were sweaty, as they so often were in this humid place. And they were trembling. That was new.

'Get a grip,' she told herself aloud. 'Get a grip. This is the last day. You've held it together so far. You can't blow apart this close to the finishing line.'

But the day didn't get any better. The more hampers that were packed and moved out to the airstrip, the more tempers frayed. Once the director had to stop filming the exterior of the house, because the plane took off and came into shot and Cleo thought he would explode.

'Take five,' he yelled, and flung his baseball cap on the floor.

Everyone went inside where there were cool drinks and an ice machine.

Cleo followed, rotating her right shoulder. She could feel the day's tension all the way up from her knees to her temples, but it was her neck that hurt the most. Everyone one else was high on the prospect of reaching the end and going home. But she was – well, it was almost as if she was waiting for something terrible to happen.

Nonsense, of course, she told herself firmly. But as she trod wearily into the drawing room, the long shadows blinded her for a moment. There was a rustle. A slightly surreptitious rustle. She whipped round. *Him*.

But the voice that spoke was not angry, accented, male. It was bright and slightly mad in every way there was, and was even less welcome.

'About that script…'

Cleo glared at the shadow that was slowly forming itself into her mother.

'I told you,' she said fiercely. 'Forget it. I'm too prudish, if that's what you want to call it. Anyway, I'm not taking my clothes off for a sleaze ball like Tom de Lacey.'

Margaret worked a bit more on a light laugh. It sounded nervous. 'A lot of people think highly of him.'

'He makes showy trash that pays,' said Cleo. 'Of course they think highly of him.'

Margaret began to look nervous. 'I promised him you'd read the script.'

'Read it last night.' Cleo spied the drinks table and homed in on homemade lemonade as if it were nectar. 'It's trash,' she said over her shoulder.

'Well, if you read it last night, you can't have given it a fair chance. Your mind's full of this movie…'

'I gave it all the chance it deserved,' said Cleo grimly. 'The answer's still no. Even more, no.'

Margaret's nervousness grew. 'Well, you should at least talk to him. Maybe something can be done with the script…'

'No!' Cleo said with finality.

Margaret had made a career out of not recognising finality. 'You have to. I sort of promised.'

Cleo swallowed her lemonade and poured another glass. She was frowning.

'Why? Do you owe him money? Tell me the truth.'

Margaret looked at the open French windows that led onto the terrace as if they were an escape route she badly needed. 'Not exactly,' she said airily. 'Well, you know… How pretty those bushes are.' She dived outside.

Cleo sighed and pressed the cool glass to her perspiring forehead. And followed. The air was like hot marshmallow. It always made Cleo stop and change the rhythm of her breathing. Today, it nearly choked her.

When she had adjusted to the suffocating humidity she looked down at her mother. 'What does that mean?'

Put out of earshot of the others, Margaret was more than willing to own up. 'Well, I will – owe him money, I mean – if you don't at least *talk* to him.'

Cleo clenched her teeth. She felt the tension it put on her jaw and released it at once. She yawned a couple of times, impatiently. It was supposed to loosen the tense muscles. It didn't do a thing for her this time.

'What harm would it do, just to listen to what he has to say?' Margaret wheedled.

'Oh for goodness sake…'

Cleo rounded on her, the crinoline swinging like a boom. Margaret stepped back instinctively.

'Have you *no* sense? Can't you just see the publicity? Terry from "Snow Mountain" in raunchy rave-up. I could write the copy right now.'

Margaret blinked, genuinely taken aback. 'Well, would it be so bad? They say there's no such thing as bad publicity and…'

Cleo thought, I *am a professional. I can handle this*.

But she didn't feel as if she was handling it. *Oh, my knight-errant, where are you when I need you?*

She lent against one of the bone-white pillars. It felt clammy under her hand. She could hardly breathe. Her ribcage felt too tight.

'How much are you in to Tom de Lacey for?' she said, fighting down nausea.

Margaret told her.

Cleo heard the figure but she could not believe it. She shook her head. It made no sense.

'You *can't* have spent that much on plastic surgery. You'd have a bionic clone for that. And no casino would let you run up that much. So *how?* '

Margaret had run out of arguments. She just looked at Cleo in silence. That silence was more convincing than any protestations would have been. Crazy though the sum was, Cleo found she believed it. She wished she didn't.

'So, let's get this clear.' He heart was thundering so hard, she thought it would deafen her. 'Either I do my stuff in Tom de Lacey's sewer, or you...or you what? Bankruptcy? Jail? What?'

Margaret shivered. 'The people Tom works with don't bother with the law.' There were no histrionics about the miserable statement.

Cleo felt cold sweat break out all along her spine.

*Don't give in. You can't afford to give in again. This is make or break time. But, God help me, she is my mother.*

She wanted to shake her fists at the sky and scream, 'It's not fair. I can't cope with this.' But that would not do any good. Margaret was not going to go away and get a life, not without help. And, even if she did, someone would have to pay off Tom de Lacey. Margaret was not going to be able to do it for years, if ever.

There went the tuition fees. Again.

Cleo knew that she was starting to shake inside. It had to stay inside. She had a critical scene to shoot and today was supposed to be their last. There was no room for error. She could not afford a heavy emotional battle to distract her. She could not afford even to *think* about this until the film was over.

She said flatly, 'I'm not arguing. I'm not doing sleaze and you'll never be my agent again. Go home. We'll talk about your money problems when I get back.'

'But…'

'Mother,' said Cleo in a low voice, 'I am hanging onto my cool by a thread here. If you don't want me to break down and blow my reputation, GET OUT.'

Margaret went at last.

Cleo did neck exercises and repeated, 'I'm a professional. I can handle this.' It was becoming a mantra.

By three in the afternoon, the tropical garden was sweltering. Even the insects had given up chirruping. They were too exhausted.

So were the actors. So were the crew. The boom was slippery with sweat and the external casing of the camera was too hot to touch. The director had called 'Cut' three times because Ed Brandon's make-up kept melting and running into his eyes. Then the Victorian virgin, overwhelmed by jungle excess, leaned forward to take her Marquis by the hand and everyone could see the damp stains under her arms.

'Oh, this is too much!' yelled the director. '*Cut!*'

The actors slipped out of character at once. They looked towards the camera apprehensively.

'Now what?' muttered Roger Terry. He was playing the Marquis and was one of only two of the twenty odd people present not to know about the shameful armpits.

He snapped his fingers. Someone put a glass of ice-cold water into his hand. He drank gratefully.

Ed Brandon winked at one of the make-up girls and she darted out with cotton wool and powder to blot him back to perfection.

Only Cleo stayed in character and did not move. She felt that if she moved, she would splinter into a thousand pieces. Her character had dispensed with her sunhat and, after five takes, Cleo was feeling as if she was three inches off the ground and floating.

The director went into a huddle with the director of photography and the head of wardrobe. The sun was like a giant pressing down on a saucepan lid. The trees began to waver.

For a moment, she thought she saw Rent a Hunk in the lea of a giant hibiscus. She put up a hand to shield her eyes, searching.

But he was not there, of course. It would have been no good if he had been. He was just a would-be actor doing escort service, not the white knight she needed.

Anyway, no one was under the hibiscus. It was just shadows and the shimmering air.

*I must be completely spaced out. Oh, will this day never end?*

Rafael stood behind the chair of the distinguished author. He pretended to be adjusting the tall sun umbrella. However cavalier the director was to his actors, he was doing his best to keep the old man comfortable.

They both looked up the hill. The scene was surreal. All the machinery and twenty-first century technicians, stripped as far as they dared to minimise the heat. Beyond them, the actors – two men in formal nineteenth-century suits, with wing collars and waistcoats – and expressions of profound discomfort – sat at a small table. The table was covered with a starched white linen cloth and bore a silver teapot and delicate rose-scattered china. The whole was presided over by a society beauty in a pale crinoline.

'That's Patti Darren,' said the distinguished author in careful Portuguese, courteous to the man he assumed was a servant and local. He was happily unaware of Rafael's silent fury. 'Did you see the photographs of her at the Diamond Awards? They were in lots of the magazines that the make-up girls brought. Looks different now, doesn't she?'

'She would. She's got clothes on,' said Rafael, with bite.

The distinguished author looked round. He was wrinkled as a tortoise, slow and acute.

'You know her?'

'No,' said Rafael, not taking his eyes off her. They were hard.

'She is not easy to know,' agreed the distinguished author craftily. 'Even though she is so young.'

Rafael gave a harsh laugh. 'Don't let the china doll looks fool you, Maestro. That's a woman who knows exactly what she's doing.'

The distinguished author mulled that over. 'It sounds as if you think she is a Machiavelli,' he said, amused.

'I know she is,' said Rafael levelly.

The writer turned fully round on his canvas chair to look at him. He said slowly, 'She has a mother. Have you met her? Very elegant, very animated?'

'If you mean Cruella de Vil on speed, I've seen her. She arrived yesterday.'

'I sat next to her at supper last night.' The distinguished author hesitated. 'They are not very alike, I think.'

'Seem pretty similar to me.' Rafael was cynical. 'They both get what they want, don't they? And don't care much how they do it, by the sound of it.'

'Do they?'

'Oh yes. Cleo may not rant and rave like her Mama but she's an operator all right. A deep, deep operator.'

The writer looked interested. 'Cleo? Is that her real name? You must have talked to her a lot. She has not told anyone else her real name, I think.'

That was when Rafael remembered he was supposed to be a gardener. He muttered something about what they said in the kitchen, and melted back among the trees.

The armpit disaster was resolved. 'Let it stay,' said the distinguished author, consulted at last. 'That is what must have happened in real life. And this is a girl who is losing all her inhibitions in the excessive atmosphere of the jungle.'

Cleo was dizzy with relief. At least, she did not have to undergo another costume change and make-up repair. She flung herself into losing her inhibitions with eye-watering intensity.

*It must have been OK*, she thought. At least, there was that little silence at the end of the scene that meant people had been shaken. And the director did not call for yet another take. Although that could be time pressure, of course.

She went for a shower and her final costume change.

At least she got out of her Victorian skirts. The virginal daughter of the house, having been seduced by the visiting Marquis, had taken to walking around in breeches to advertise that she was a fallen woman.

*Let's hear it for fallen women*, thought Cleo, slipping her arms gratefully into a loose linen shirt. The breeches were cool too, made of some sort of crisp cotton. Her hair had been clipped back in a severe plait and her face was cleverly made-up to look as if she had been out in the sun.

No more porcelain doll, with her curls and her pallor. This was a woman about to confront the man who had ruined her life. A woman on the edge of madness.

Margaret put her head round the door.

Today would be a good day to do madness, thought Cleo dryly.

But Margaret was not talking about sleazy parts in worse movies. Margaret was being very circumspect.

'There's a seat on the plane that's leaving this evening, darling. I could take it. But it's supposed to be yours.'

'Use it,' said Cleo. 'God knows when I'll be finished here.'

'And I – er – think I'll go straight on to London. See the family.'

*Keep out of Tom de Lacey's way,* interpreted Cleo.

Aloud she said, 'Good idea. If you see Dad, give him my love.'

'And you'll think about…'

'I'll find a way to clear the debt,' she said wearily. 'I'll call you.'

One of the few remaining assistants pushed past Margaret. 'On set in five,' he said. 'OK?'

Margaret gave her a wave and left.

The scene was at the very edge of the cultivated garden. Beyond the lawns and hibiscus trees, there was the rumble of Ruprechago's waterfall and the jungle began.

The water cascaded down into a river, the servants had told her. You could not see it, because of the dense trees in the ravine. All you could see were great banyans, as tall as several houses, with lianas as thick as ships' hawsers. They spoke of huge leaved trees where orchids lodged, seemingly growing out of mid-air. They spoke of parrots with poisonous bites, blood-sucking bats and plants so toxic that just to brush against them was enough to make you hallucinate for days.

The jungle was dangerous, they said. People went up the little tributary of the Amazon and were never heard of again. Up here, on the escarpment, with the lawns mowed daily, you did not realise it. But Ruprechago was a wild place.

Cleo stood on a small viewing platform looking at the waterfall and she sighed. That dense green tree cover below looked inviting. Losing herself up the Amazon sounded the best option anyone was offering.

Maybe tomorrow, she thought. Maybe I can take off and get lost tomorrow.

But today, the director needed poor betrayed Amanda, emerging from the green shadows, to come face-to-face with her betrayer.

They did it four times. Five. And again. And again. Cleo lost count.

The plane, presumably with Margaret on board, took off from the estate airstrip and hit the sky in shot, spoiling another take.

Again.

The Marquis forgot his words.

Again.

Cleo's fake blow went out of control and connected. His lip bled. He had to be patched up and they did it again.

'Oh, for God's sake,' said the director in agony. 'Any minute now, the afternoon rains are going to start.'

They did. And suddenly, he decided that was exactly what he wanted. The fat explosion of raindrops on leathery leaves evoked all the mood he was after. The shoulders of the Marquis' frock coat darkened. His victim's shirt soaked and clung.

'We can see her bra. They didn't wear bras then, did they? Get it off. Get it off.'

The wardrobe assistant dived in to help. No suggestion now of Cleo going back to the house to change. Everyone knew that the fat pattering stage lasted a few minutes, at most. And then it went into full-scale downpour.

Cleo stripped off her bra, and pulled the soaked shirt back on again. It felt horrible.

'She's shivering,' said the wardrobe assistant. 'Do you think this is wise? She may have a fever.'

But the director was beside himself. 'Get on with it,' he roared.

They just about got through one more take before the rain fell down in a sheet.

'Run,' yelled the director unnecessarily, as everyone gathered up their things and pelted for the house.

For a moment, Cleo just stood there. She felt dazed and more than a little light-headed. The rain seemed to drum on her skin as if someone had emptied a bowl of sweets over her. Her ears rang with it. She felt as if she could hardly move.

But she was getting soaked. The rain was streaming into her eyes, blinding her. She began to run, swaying.

And then – suddenly – out of nowhere – the tall watcher appeared. His cotton shirt was soaked too and she saw the outline of bones and muscles. He called something. But she could not make out what he said. All she could make out was his face. For the first time he had lost that concealing hat and she saw his face. She knew it. She knew it mobile in amusement, tight with disapproval. Contorted in passion.

Passion!

*I'm going mad,* she thought.

He said – she thought he said, 'Tell me the truth.'

But he had said the same thing on that night that she ought to forget and couldn't. She must be going mad indeed. Cleo clutched her head. She began to shake it from side to side.

'No. No. *NO.*'

She began to run.

She heard him call out, sharply. Or she thought she did. She did not stop.

She was running from everything that man had made her feel. Everything he had let her hope, for just one night. Everything that she knew was hopeless. And from the dream of passion that would not let her go.

Blundering, sobbing, she scratched herself on bushes, thrust her way into vegetation that tore at her clothes, grazed herself against rough-barked trees. And still he got closer.

She looked over her shoulder.

'Go away,' she screamed at the dream which she should never have allowed herself to dream. 'Go away.'

And missed her footing.

And fell, not onto the pulsing, sodden jungle floor of the viewing platform, but down the slope beside it. Fell among roots and mud and leathery stalks and sharp-needled plants that stabbed at her. No even ground anywhere. Nothing to grab on to. She felt herself go head-over-heels and suddenly laughed.

*So this is what it's like to die. I'm off the hook, after all. Sometimes you just get lucky!*

Eventually, she came to rest at the bottom, by a fast-flowing river of green-yellow water. But she did not know anything about that. Her head was bleeding and she was unconscious.

So she did not know anything about the man in sodden, mud-encrusted clothes who scrambled down into the valley after her. Who knelt beside her, feeling gently for broken bones. Who tore off his own shirt, ripped a sleeve off, making a pad with the rest of the material, and bound it tightly round the angry graze on her forehead.

Who picked her up and carried her, with meticulous gentleness, along the treacherous river's edge.

Who said her name, over and over again, like a lifeboat, calling to a lost ship.

'Talk to me, my darling. Talk to me. You are breathing and you have no broken bones. You can't be seriously hurt. *Talk* to me, damn you.'

## chapter eight

The rain was drumming on the roof. It made an odd rattling sound, as if it was not rain but stones. Someone was throwing stones, relentlessly, at her sanctuary.

She opened her eyes. At first she could not focus. She had the impression of greyness. A metallic environment. No people.

It seemed to be some sort of hospital room. Or a prison. There were no chairs, no pictures, and no telephone.

'…and what will you do when she comes round?'

She realised that there had been a buzz of low voices all the time. She had been aware of them as background noise, without recognising actual words. Now they sprang sharply into place.

'Hope she makes more sense than she has done so far.'

The second voice was kind, neutral, and faintly weary. But the first? It was a dark, dark voice. Not pleased. Even angry? What had she done to make him angry?

She lifted her head slightly. There were two figures behind some sort of screen. One was restless. He marched up to the screen and back again as if he were pacing the floor. As his image got bigger and bigger, it looked like a huge bird about to swoop on her. Her heart raced. But then he turned. His shadow diminished and her pulse returned to normal.

And then she took in the other one. He was still. Watchful. Like a gunfighter in an old movie, she thought muzzily.

Something very deep in her recognised that stillness. Something very deep and as old as time began to drive every beat of her blood, every breath, like hammers against her shrinking senses. Again and again and again.

*This one! This one! This one!*

The drumming of the rain grew louder until it seemed to shake the whole building. Shake her whole body. It drowned out what the men were saying. It drowned everything but her roaring pulse.

This one. Her inquisitor. Her enemy.

Her Fate.

Dr David Hartley stopped his pacing abruptly. His head came up.

'What was that?'

He ran round the improvised screen.

Rafael followed fast.

The jungle hospital was rough-and-ready at the best of times. Then yesterday's flash flood had turned it into not much more than a dressing station. That was why the woman was in the converted storeroom.

Rafael looked down at the woman. Her cheekbones stood out and he saw that she was milk pale. Somehow, it made the softly parted lips almost shocking. They were crimson and sensuous and vividly alive against all that unnatural pallor. So vividly alive that, for a moment, he had the feeling that if he bent and kissed her she would wake up, like the princess in the fairy-tale. He stepped back sharply.

David did not notice. David was not looking at the mystery woman's mouth. David was taking her pulse. Then he lifted one of her blue-veined eyelids and shook his head.

'I thought I heard her call out.' He straightened, looking down at her with a frown. 'I must have been wrong. She's still deeply unconscious.'

Rafael pursed his lips. 'Really?'

David turned to look at him. He was shocked. 'You sound as if you think she's faking.'

'Do I?'

Their eyes met. David had slept four hours in the last forty-eight and he was out on his feet. But he was no fool and he had a duty to his patient.

'Look, be straight with me, Rafael. You know something about this woman, don't you?'

The dark face was impassive. 'I know nothing about her at all.'

David was exasperated. 'And even that sounds as if you know more than you're telling.'

Rafael gave one those devastating comprehensive shrugs that were his speciality. He did not bother to answer.

'Look, if you know who she is, you must tell me. She might have a medical history that could account for this. I could find out . . .'

'How?'

They both knew that the satellite telephone connection was out during the huge tropical storm they were currently experiencing. Neither phone nor Internet connection would work for hours.

David shifted his shoulders, annoyed. Rafael's relentless logic nearly always annoyed him. It was nearly always unanswerable, too.

He said angrily, 'we should use her name, if you know it. It might call her back.'

'So might playing her the "Star Spangled Banner",' said Rafael dryly. 'Or Muddy Waters. Or Mozart.'

'No. People respond to their name. Even deeply unconscious people will twitch when someone says their name.'

'And you're sure she's deeply unconscious, are you?'

'Look at her,' said David exasperated.

Rafael gestured at the bed. 'It could just be a great performance.'

David stared. 'Why do you think that?'

Rafael shrugged. 'I got her here. She only said one thing all that time – "Who am I?" Just too pat, to my mind.'

David said on a long note of discovery, 'You *do* know her. You couldn't dislike her this much if you didn't know her.'

There was a sharp silence. Rafael's face was an olive-skinned mask.

At last he said in a clipped voice, 'Let's just say, I've known women play dirty before.'

David said earnestly, 'Rafael, you may be right. You may be wrong. But I'm her doctor. Hell, you're a doctor yourself. If you've got a name for her, believe me, I need it.'

There was a pause.

Then Rafael gave another shrug, quick and angry.

'You could try Patti. Or Cleo.' His mouth compressed into a suddenly savage line, 'Or even Cleopatra.'

'*What?*'

'I told you. I don't know anything about her. I met her once, very briefly, very socially. In that time I heard her called all those names. But God knows which is the real woman.'

He looked down at the still figure on the bed. A muscle worked in his cheek.

'If there is a real woman.'

The next time she came round, there was a man bending over her. Not the gunslinger.

'How are you feeling?'

'I'm not sure. What has happened to me?'

'I was kind of hoping you would tell us that,' he said ruefully. 'Rafael isn't much help.'

'Rafael.' She tasted the word.

Did she know the name? She was almost certain that it meant nothing. Yet there was something niggling away at the back of her brain that said, yes, this was important. But it didn't *feel* familiar.

But then – as she was beginning to realise with increasing panic – neither did anything else.

She struggled to sit up. At once, the nurse was beside her. She supported her, murmuring soothingly, kindly, as she pulled a rough pillow into place. She sounded concerned.

The doctor in the cowboy shirt was unmoved. 'Well, that answers another of my questions. You can move. Does it hurt?'

She thought about it. She realised that it didn't. 'N-no.'

'And you can see. And the light doesn't hurt your eyes. So, how do you feel?'

'I feel…' her voice scraped, 'I feel – odd.'

She felt, rather than saw, the nurse and the doctor exchange glances.

He said calmly, 'Odd? Like how?'

She struggled to put it into words. 'Like I've only got about half the blood I ought to have.'

He nodded but he did not say anything.

'What's wrong with me?'

He pursed his lips. 'Could be a number of things. What were you doing out there anyway?'

She still stared at him. She looked as lost as if he had broken into a foreign language, he thought.

Behind him a voice drawled, 'Why bother, David? She's going to tell you she can't remember. Aren't you, honey?'

Everyone spun round.

*It was the other one,* she thought. *The still one. The gunslinger!*

The light from the window began to leap drunkenly, like a desk light in an earthquake. He strolled forward. She stared at him. Her pulse accelerated.

It felt like an old movie all over again. He took up his stance at the end of the bed and looked down at her. His face was impassive. He wanted to be impassive, she knew that somehow. But she also knew he was angry.

Suddenly she thought, *Not a gunslinger. A knight-errant who doesn't know what to do. Frustrated. And very, very angry.*

*Why* she thought bewildered. *What have I done to make him angry?*

Her head was beginning to whirl again. The tall, narrow-eyed figure seemed to be coming and going. She shut her eyes against the sickening effect of optical distortion.

It made his voice seem louder. And angrier. And mocking.

'She's going to throw herself on your mercy.'

The bed seemed to be on a turntable. It went first this way, then that. Her whole body revolted against the turbulence. There was a wordless animal noise of distress. She realised she had moaned.

The gunslinger took no notice. He said, 'Lost lady with no identification. Lost her way. Lost her friends. Of course she's going to throw herself onto the charity of the clinic. What else can she do?' His voice hardened suddenly, all laughter banished. 'What's your name?'

And then she remembered.

He had said it before. She could hear him saying it before. He had been just as angry then. *Talk to me.* And, more insistently, so that she felt buffeted by his intensity, *Tell me something real.*

She had not been able to answer him then. She couldn't answer him now.

*She didn't know.*

Her eyes flew open. The light swung and the bed bucked and the doctor and nurse swam in and out of her vision like aliens caught in a faulty positron beam. The only stable thing in the universe was the man standing at the end of her bed like the State Prosecutor.

'I – don't know.' It was a harsh whisper. She sounded appalled, she thought. But not afraid. Not nearly as afraid as she was.

The gunslinger nodded, as if she had just moved a pawn on a chessboard and he was her opponent.

'Do you have any idea how rare total amnesia is?'

'What?'

'Statistically, almost unheard of, except in the cases of extreme head trauma. Which you don't have. On the other hand, it is very convenient.'

She flinched.

'Tell me something you know. Books, music, languages, anything.'

She stared at him, hardly understanding him.

His eyes were accusing. 'Or don't you read books? Listen to music? Speak languages?'

'I…'

The doctor said, 'That's enough Rafael.'

Rafael? *Rafael?* This was the man who found her? Who might know who she was? She stared and stared at his dark, implacable face and thought, *If he knows me, he hates me.*

She moistened her lips. The room was dancing up and down now.

'Do you – know me?' It was a croak.

The dark eyes bored into hers. 'You just don't care about anyone else, do you? There are people out there, hurt homeless people because there's been a flood up-river. They need this man's attention, and here you are wasting his time with fairy tales.'

*He hates me all right.*

'Rafael,' said the doctor warningly.

The gunslinger ignored him. His voice was cold. 'If you're honest – if you know how to be honest – tell me how you justify taking up a bed in the clinic. Especially at a time like this!'

She said again, gropingly, 'Do you know me?'

'Oh please!' It spat out like gunfire. His eyes were black with fury.

She struggled up onto one elbow, though the room had started to spin like a fairground carousel.

She said panting, 'If you know who I am, tell me!'

'More games?'

'*Tell me!*'

He met her eyes as if they were acknowledged enemies. Had been enemies across the centuries.

'I don't know one thing about you,' he said levelly.

She thought, *Why does that sound like an insult?* Even with the room whirling she knew it was crazy. But she could feel his inexplicable enmity beating at her like a forest fire.

'Please. Tell. Me.'

The doctor said, 'That's enough Rafael.'

Rafael ignored him. He bent over her. 'But I'll find out. Every damned detail.' It was a threat, pure and simple.

The room was going so fast it made her feel sick. She closed her eyes against it.

'*Rafael!*' Even in her nightmare, she heard the doctor shoulder him out of the way. 'Are you mad?'

She forced her eyes open.

The doctor had interposed himself between the man and the bed. Rafael was standing there like a rock, his head thrown back as if he was defying the world.

A thought came out of nowhere. *He looks as if he's the one in pain.*

And then he turned his back on her and walked out, brushing past the doctor and the hovering nurse as if they were pieces of furniture.

She could not keep her eyelids open any longer. She fell back into the blackness.

She did not know how much later it was that she struggled back to consciousness. The room had stabilised. There was soft murmur, a cool hand on her head, and the rustle of a cotton skirt as the nurse who was sitting beside her got up and leaned over.

Her throat was dry. She said so. A glass of water appeared. She was held up to take a few sips.

'Where am I?' she croaked. And thought, *I have said that before*.

The nurse said something in a language she did not understand and lowered her to the bed again before flitting away. In a few seconds – or an hour – the doctor was there again. As she focused on the tired face, she remembered the earlier scene as if someone had suddenly run a video of it.

She said hoarsely, 'Rafael?'

The doctor looked thoughtful. 'You remember Rafael, do you?' He leaned forward, shining a torch into her eyes.

'Why was he so angry with me?'

'I was hoping you could tell me that.'

This time the discovery of the blank memory board was almost instant. So was the flare of panic. So was the curb of will, controlling it.

'I – no!'

The doctor straightened. He snapped off the torch and sat on the edge of her bed.

'Still not remember anything?' he asked chattily.

'Just this room.' She swallowed. 'The rain.'

'And Rafael,' he pointed out dryly.

She did not like being reminded of that. She put up a wavering hand to her head. 'Who is he?'

The doctor looked at her carefully. 'Why don't you ask him?'

She remembered that harsh angry voice. 'Do you think he'd tell me?' she said, dry in her turn.

The doctor looked thoughtful. 'You have certainly made him good and mad.'

'But – why?' Her voice was weaker. It sounded as if she was going to cry. But she never cried.

At least she knew that about herself, she thought with relief. She knew she never cried.

The doctor smiled. 'Ask me when you're well.'

With an attempt at humour, she said, 'Ah, but will I remember when I'm well?'

'Of course you will.' He stood up, pulling the sheet smooth where he had disarranged it. 'In fact, you'll probably remember everything the next time you wake up. So you won't need to ask about Rafael or anything else.'

She stared at him.

'Rafael has a point, you know. Total amnesia really is very rare.'

She turned her head restlessly on the pillow. 'Then why can't I remember *now?*'

'Because your mind is telling you to take one thing at a

time,' he said with perfect calm. 'Blow on the head. Rafael got you back as fast he could, but he had to carry you most of the way. So you were dehydrated too. It's not surprising your memory has taken a holiday. Don't try to force it.'

He turned away as the nurse came back and said something. As she watched, he seemed to get taller and thinner. Even the top of his head got even taller and even thinner, so that he looked like a mountain crowned by a wizard's hat. She felt the cold fear rush over her as if he had opened the sluice gates on it simply by turning away like that.

She managed to make her voice work after all. And it croaked, 'Rafael.'

*I'm hallucinating. He's the last man I would call on when I was afraid. He's my enemy. Even if I don't know why. He makes no bones about it.*

But still, she whispered his name again, as if he could somehow keep back the advancing torrent of terror.

Instinctively her hand went out to the doctor. She was so weak that it wavered and fell. The doctor did not turn. He had not heard her. So he did not see the gesture.

But someone else did. He was stopped in the doorway, his mouth cynical. He stood there silently, watching.

She was unaware of him. She gave a small moan. The doctor did turn at that, but it was too late. Her eyes fluttered shut.

She had not seen the man in the doorway. She was unconscious again.

The two men sat in David's office. Rafael had got back to the main house before launching himself into the rescue operation. He had changed into bush shirt and breeches, to take medicine and blankets into areas that boats and helicopters could not reach.

By now, he had been wearing his bush shirt for three days and it was sweat-stained and torn. David had offered to lend him a replacement but Rafael had brushed the offer aside.

'I've got to get back out there with the rescue team. No point in ruining any more clothes.'

'How long since you had any sleep?'

'I'll sleep when we've got everyone to safety.'

David nodded sombrely and did not try to dissuade him. The flood had abated but loosened soil from the area that had been cleared upstream, was threatening a mudslide. They both knew time was of the essence.

'How many are left, do you think?'

There were two deep furrows from cheekbone to mouth. They intensified at the question.

'Just one family.' He ran his hand through the springy black hair. 'They managed to get themselves up to an outcrop over the river. We can see them, but so far we haven't been able to get to them. No means of communication, of course. When the guys come back with my equipment, I'll go up and see.'

'You're going to try and climb that rock face?'

Rafael shrugged. 'No place for a helicopter to land. These are villagers, not supermen. They aren't going to survive up there for long. No food, no drinkable water, no shelter, except the trees. I need to get them down before nightfall. Well, at least the baby and Affonso.'

'But that rock face. It's one hell of a climb.'

For the first time for hours, the dark face split into the grin that David knew so well.

'I'm one hell of a climber.'

He smiled reluctantly. 'I suppose so. But even so – won't it be dangerous?'

Rafael shrugged again. 'What's the alternative?'

'But – you're tired. Everywhere is slippery with this rain. Can't you wait? Even rest, maybe?'

Rafael looked at the chocolate wrapper on the desk between them. One eyebrow flicked up. 'What do you think I'm doing now?'

David gave up. 'OK. You know your own business best, I guess.'

'I hope so. Me and my crampons are the only hope those poor people have got.'

David nodded soberly. 'And they're the last? You're sure?'

'As far as I know.'

David nodded. 'It was lucky you were in Ruprechago. You haven't been here much these last five years.'

Rafael's face was mask-like. 'Yes.'

'And the film people have all gone?'

'Couldn't get out fast enough when it was clear that the flood could be serious.'

David digested this. 'She couldn't be one of them, could she?'

Rafael stood up. 'She'll get her memory back when is suits her,' he said curtly. 'I'd put money on it. I must be going.'

And off he went on his way back to the rescue effort before David could demand an explanation.

The next time she came round, everything was entirely different. For a moment she thought someone was calling her. She half-turned, eager, recognising a name...

And then it was gone. Her eyes snapped open. They focussed at once. She remembered the room, the iron bed, and the people who had been gathered round it. But the name, whatever it was, was gone.

She struggled into a sitting position. Had they left her? Did the gunslinger despise her so much that he had persuaded the others to abandon her?

A little mewling sound of protest escaped her. It sounded like an animal, horrifying her. She pressed her clenched fist to her lips instinctively.

She must not give way to panic. She *must* not. There was problem here. Fine. She would sort it out. She always sorted out her own problems. Only she *must not* panic.

She shook her head slightly, shaking away the cobwebs of fear and residual dreams. She pushed away the coarse cotton coverlet and swung her feet to the ground. She had to hang on to the head of the bed as she hauled herself to her feet. She was as unsteady as if she had been ill for weeks.

From the doorway, a voice that was becoming all too familiar said dryly, 'Going exploring?'

She gasped, her hands whitening on the cross bar of the simple bed head. But there was no strength in them. That terrible weakness struck again. She began to shake. Shaking, she felt her knees buckle.

The gunslinger watched her without emotion. She fell back, half propped against the edge of the bed, half-hanging from the iron cross bar.

He strode across and hauled her unceremoniously to her feet. His hands were not gentle. Something glinted in the dark eyes. *Anger again*, she thought. *Why is he always so furious with me? What have I done to him?*

'OK,' he said coolly. 'You've lost your memory. Maybe. Tell me how it feels.'

She swallowed. 'I – it's like watching a movie. I keep thinking the house lights will be going up, and everything will be all right.'

His heavily marked brows drew together in a fearsome bar across the bridge of his nose. He looked as if he were in a rage so vast he could hardly contain it.

'A movie?'

She made a helpless gesture. 'I know it must sound silly…'

'On the contrary. It sounds very neat.'

The panic was returning again. She could feel it in her mouth. It tasted like bile. To quell it, she turned on him. Fighting the panic by facing down one of its causes.

'Why are you so angry?' she demanded, aloud at last.

For a moment, he looked almost taken aback. Then his eyes were veiled by long, long lashed lids and his mouth laughed.

'Maybe I'm a little suspicious.'

'But *why*?'

This time the pause was longer. More fraught. Then he said slowly, 'If you've really lost your memory, there's no point

in my telling you. You wouldn't understand. If you haven't…'
He shrugged. 'Well, if this amnesia is the charade I think it
is, I'm not going to make an even bigger fool of myself by
telling you everything you already know only too well.'

She blinked. He could deny it all he liked. It made no
difference. His anger licked out at her, like a forest fire. She
stared at him, her eyes widening.

'You hate me,' she said on a long note of discovery.

The panic – or was it bile? – backed up terminally. She
began to gag.

'Oh please!' He sounded disgusted.

She could not stop. He looked round, saw a small bowl and
thrust it at her. Then he strode to the door and called out something in that language she did not recognise.

Steps ran in response. Strong hands held her. She felt the
moisture on her face. Or was it tears? And then she was falling
into the darkness again.

When she had recovered, the little nurse, Bebel, was full
of apology.

'Dom Rafael shouted,' she said marvelling. 'I have never
heard him shout. He is always so calm. So dignified.'

'*Calm?*' That seething man? 'Dignified?'

'Naturally. He comes from a very distinguished family. A
Dourado came to Brazil with the Dom Pedro Primeiro.'

She shook her head. 'As far as I know, I've never heard of
Dom Pedro Primeiro, whoever he is.' She sighed sharply. 'But
then I've never heard of *me* either.'

The nurse was undismayed. 'Then we will have to find a
name for you to use until you do remember.'

Her patient opened her eyes, startled at this practical
thought. The nurse gave a grin, which made her look more
like a schoolgirl than a professional saver of lives.

'The children will be delighted. They have nicknames for
everyone. Even Dom Rafael.'

In spite of herself, she was intrigued. 'What do they call
him?'

Bebel giggled, '*O bandeleiro*. It is very naughty of them.'

It meant nothing. Bebel was still struggling with a translation when the doctor arrived. She turned to him with a welcoming expression, demanding an explanation for their patient.

'*Bandeleiro?*' he mused, taking one thin bruised wrist and looking at the watch he had pinned to his lapel. 'Oh, it's a sort of bandit. Highwayman, maybe in English terms.' He gave her back her wrist. 'Do you think you're English, American or Australian? Or something else?' he said casually.

'English,' she said without thinking.

'Ah.'

She sat bolt upright, as if she had touched live electricity. 'I know that. I *know* that. I'm English.'

The doctor and the nurse exchanged looks.

'That's what Dom Rafael said…' began the nurse. And was instantly silenced by the doctor's frown.

*That man again!*

'He *does* know me, doesn't he? But why doesn't he tell everyone who I am?'

'I'm not sure he knows. Although he says we should call you Cleopatra,' said Bebel, detecting a compliment and pleased about it. 'Perhaps because you are so beautiful.'

Rafael lounged into the doorway, his arms folded across the stained shirt.

'Or because she was unpredictable,' he said softly. 'And no man ever truly understood her. She took good care that they didn't.'

The woman he called Cleopatra looked at him narrowly. She was not under any illusion that it was a compliment.

'And because she was a temptress?' she flung at him challengingly.

Rafael stretched one booted foot in front of him and smiled lazily.

'*Is* she?' he asked, with apparent interest.

There was a tense little pause.

'I told you. I can't remember a thing about myself.' She sounded irritated.

'You told me,' he agreed. He refrained from saying he believed her.

The patient paled.

'Maybe it will help if we think about this temptress thing.' He was so affable that the falsehood shone out of him. Even kind Bebel saw that. 'No, I would say that just at the moment you're too much of a scarecrow to tempt anyone. So, if you feel like a temptress, maybe it's in your memory somewhere.' He paused, then added ironically, 'Locked away.'

The patient flinched. Bebel felt it and was distressed. She had never seen Dom Rafael be unkind before.

She said with a hint of reproach, 'I don't understand.'

'No you probably don't,' agreed Rafael, his voice suddenly hard. 'What about you, Cleo? You understand, don't you?'

Cleo sat as if she were turned to stone. She thought, *He doesn't believe me.*

Then she looked at his eyes. They were dark and secretive and lingered on her mouth so long that she felt as if he were touching her in front of them all. And she thought, *He knows me.*

Their eyes met. Something arced between them so strong that she almost recoiled. They looked at each other for a timeless moment, not acknowledging and yet knowing it was there. A sort of recognition. As if she did, indeed, understand him.

His eyes bored into her, intense and watchful. But she could not answer him. She did not know what he wanted – or what he knew – or what there was to know. It made her feel helpless. Yet oddly excited – as if this man's disbelief gave her a task, a path to tread, in all the frightening fog.

He said softly, 'Yes, you know.'

And she knew it was a declaration of war.

He did not wait for a reply. He strolled out of the room without a backward look.

She became Cleo.

She recovered quite quickly, except for her memory. The skin around the wound at her temple went black, blue, and green and swelled alarmingly. But Bebel bathed it twice a day and applied some herbal-smelling ointment to it and it healed cleanly.

'Maybe you won't even scar,' said Rafael, passing through with another two sodden waifs.

'We hope not,' said Bebel, taking the remark at face value.

But Cleo knew enough of the man by now to know that you could never take his remarks at face value. 'You don't care if I'm scarred or not,' she challenged him.

'I might not. Others do.'

'What others?' she pressed.

But he shook his head. 'It will come back to you when it suits you.'

'Yes,' said kind Bebel, overhearing. 'Amnesia can work like that. You will recall your life, as soon as you grow strong enough to deal with it.'

Cleo eyed Rafael broodingly. 'That isn't quite what he meant, Bebel.'

He gave her a maddening smile. 'If you say so.'

The nurse looked puzzled. But Cleo knew what he meant. 'You don't trust me an inch, do you?'

'Should I?'

And that was just the trouble. She didn't know. She had little jolts of near memory, most often when Rafael was there. But they were just lights in the fog that went out as soon as she thought she was getting up close.

But she was feeling braver all the time. Nearly brave enough to challenge him. Nearly.

She said carefully, 'Give me one reason why you should not trust me.'

She held her breath, waiting for him to admit it. To tell her who she was.

But he sidestepped it so neatly that he not only avoided it, he took Bebel and the doctor with him.

'I just think it's extraordinary that no one seems to be trying to find you.'

She stared, not understanding him.

'There was a parcel of tourist up-river over towards the border. The tour company had a site on the Net with the names and photographs of all their passengers before the rescue operations had hardly begun. David will tell you.'

The doctor nodded. 'We had a look in case you were one of them. But you weren't. Anyway, they are all accounted for now.'

'People just don't get lost in the twenty-first century,' Rafael said softly. 'Not people from rich countries with literate families and e-mail. Yet you appear out of nowhere. No name. No documents. And nobody is looking for you, apparently. Do you blame me for being suspicious?'

The doctor looked struck. Even Bebel seemed to think it deserved an answer. And the trouble was, Cleo had none.

But she strongly suspected that Rafael had.

'What do you know about me?' she burst out.

In the circumstances, she could not have said anything more damning. It sounded as if she was admitting that she was lying about her memory loss. The other two looked away. Cleo could hear their unspoken, unwilling suspicion, as if a mosquito had invaded the room.

Rafael smiled.

He strolled away, passing behind the doctor's chair and tipping his hat over his eyes as he went. The doctor spluttered and shook his fist at him but everyone laughed. It was a schoolboy trick but it eased the tension. Cleo wondered whether that was why Rafael had done it and concluded that it was.

She had not known him long – in one sense she did not know him at all – but she was positive that he was no schoolboy. And not spontaneous either. The calculating little gesture troubled her.

She watched him stroll off the veranda and out to where his horse waited and thought: *I don't trust him.*

She bit her lip, hardly listening to the desultory conversation between Bebel and the doctor. She stared unseeingly at the huge dripping leaves on the trees at the edge of the clearing. It was crazy. He had saved her life, hadn't her? No matter how irritating or how suspicious of her he was, Dom Rafael had saved her life. Probably, as she was coming to realise, at some risk to his own. Yet she, who was certain of nothing – not even of her own name or nationality – was becoming more and more certain that she mistrusted him.

It made her feel very lonely. The others trusted him. More than trusted him, they obviously held him in affection. To say nothing of respect bordering on awe. To be the only person in the place who doubted him made her feel isolated and vulnerable. She touched her bandaged head.

'Headache?' said Bebel, concerned.

'No. I'm fine.'

*But I'm not. I'm in a deep, deep hole and my only way out is to trust a man who fills me with foreboding. And I don't know why.*

She watched him swing himself up into the saddle. Powerful muscles bunched and relaxed, and he sat astride the big horse as if he were born to ride. He must be exhausted but he was controlling the big animal with the economical precision that she had come to recognise as his trademark. He controlled everything. And he didn't waste energy doing it.

She shivered.

*So why don't I trust him?*

## chapter nine

Nobody else shared her reservations, of course. They did not even notice that she mistrusted their hero. Every time Rafael returned to the hospital in the next three days, they made tactful provision for him to speak to her alone.

Cleo could have screamed. She wanted to yell at them, *He isn't concerned about me. He's interrogating me.*

She didn't, of course. And Rafael continued to ask his questions with that voice of spurious concern. Only Cleo was close enough to see into his eyes as Bebel or the doctor or one of the other staff tactfully evaporated. Here was no mistaking mockery.

In the end, she said exasperated, 'Look, why do you keep asking me, if you think I'm lying?'

'Trying to trip you up,' he said coolly.

She did not bridle. She already knew that that was what he was doing, after all. She sighed wearily. 'You haven't in four days. Doesn't that tell you something?'

'Yes. You're very good. But then, you would be…' He broke off, looking annoyed with himself.

Cleo pounced on it. 'I knew it. You *do* know me.'

This time he did not deny it. But he wasn't telling her anything about herself either. He said, 'You're not going to be able to stay here much longer, you know.'

'What?'

'You're taking up a bed. They're needed.'

'Dr David hasn't said…'

Dr David,' he said softly, 'believes you.'

She flushed, looking away. It was crazy, because she was telling the truth and she knew it. But for some reason, she felt as if Dom Rafael's suspicion was deserved.

She said, 'He can't throw me out. I've got nowhere to go.'

'It would be an interesting experiment,' agreed Rafael. 'But I've told him you can come to Ruprechago.'

'Where?'

*'My home.'*

'*Your*…?' She was incredulous. 'But you don't want me.'

There was a complicated silence. Cleo thought, *That was a mistake*. She held her breath.

His eyes narrowed to menacing slits. But in the end he said curtly, 'We have no other option. You don't need medical care and you're taking up scarce resources here. But David says you can't be on your own. He won't release you unless you come to me.' He flushed faintly. 'Us. At Ruprechago.'

Their eyes met. His eyes were not just menacing. There was something else…

Cleo could not think of anything to say. She did not want to go but she had no option. She was horrified at the prospect. And yet – and yet – it seemed as if, at some deep, deep level that she could hardly hear, let alone articulate, that she had been waiting for this all her life.

'He said you were having flashes.' Rafael sounded as if he were talking at random. He had not taken his eyes off her.

Cleo pulled herself together with an effort. 'I suppose I am.'

'Tell me about it.'

'Why bother?' She was ironic, defending herself from those hidden, uncomprehended levels. They felt powerful. 'You don't believe me.'

'Then convince me. Tell me about these flashes.'

There was coffee in a big vacuum jug on the table. It was very black and came with so much sugar that sometimes it tasted more like caramel than coffee. She did not like it. But just now she needed it. She poured herself one of the thimble-sized cups.

'It's not easy to explain.'

He refrained from comment but she saw the mockery

in his face.

'You said you wanted to know,' she snapped.

His mouth tightened. 'I do. I do. So, it's not easy to explain. Describe an episode.'

Cleo thought. 'It's as if I know there's something there, just out of sight. I could take you to it but I couldn't describe it. But when I try to go there...' She spread her hands, fighting to keep the panic out of her voice as the reality of her situation hit her yet again, 'it disappears. And then I wonder if there was anything there really. Or if it was all my imagination.'

He looked taken aback. He leaned forward and took coffee for himself, without comment. 'On the brink of recognition...'

'Yes,' she muttered. For a man who did not believe her, he had described the feeling exactly.

He was not looking at her. 'It's well documented, of course.'

'*Oh!*' The momentary sense of sympathy exploded. 'I should have known you'd say something nasty.'

Rafael ignored that. 'How often does it happen?' he said, watching her like a trained interrogator. 'Every hour? Several times an hour?'

Cleo bit her lip. 'Sometimes it seems as if it's there all the time.' *Especially when you're around.* No, she wasn't going to say that.

'So when does it go away? When you're awake? Sleepy? Cold? Hot?'

Cleo grinned suddenly. 'I haven't been cold since I woke up.'

Rafael laughed. It was a nice laugh, full throated and spontaneous. She found herself smiling at him, hugely pleased to have made him laugh.

'No, it's not normally one of our problems,' he agreed. But the laughter died, inevitably, and he went back to his third degree. 'So when?'

Her hand went to her hair. Bebel had plaited it, and the plait fell over her shoulder, just begging to be fiddled with when she was concentrating.

'Not when I'm sleepy,' she pronounced at last. 'In fact, that's when I seem to be closest to remembering.'

'*Ah.*'

She stopped fiddling with her hair, recalled to their duel.

'Ah what?' she said belligerently.

He opened his eyes wide. 'Ah, that could be useful.'

Cleo felt rage rise inside her. He *knew* who she was. She was almost sure of it. And he was making her go through all this!

She said intensely, 'Oh, it could be useful, could it? Shall I tell you something? I'm not sure I'm ever going to remember.'

She was shaking. Now that he had made her think about those moments just before she fell asleep, she was recalling her feelings a little too clearly. The fog, the fog thinning – then the swathe of black panic that swept up out of it, like a drowning tide.

Rafael said nothing. She hardly noticed. The panic was there again now. Just lapping quietly at the moment. Reminding her that it could build into a tsunami if she let it.

Most of the time, these last four days, she had rested on doctor's serene assurance that most amnesia was temporary. That it was not uncommon after a head wound. That she was neither a freak nor a cheat and all would be well.

*Cheat.* As the word floated into her mind, she started and exclaimed aloud.

Rafael's eyes narrowed. Cleo did not notice.

'Sometimes I think I have done something I can't bear to remember,' she said, not much above a whisper.

'Sometimes? When?'

She swallowed. 'When I'm with you,' she said, as if she was dragging a snake out of her heart. She looked at him in sudden horror.

His eyes flickered. But all he said was, 'Interesting.'

'No, it's not,' she said, shaken into naked honesty. 'It's horrible.'

He was unmoved. 'But useful. We must see more of each other.' He smiled across the coffee cups, as if he was a pleasant social visitor suggesting a trip to the movies. 'See if my baleful presence can bring whatever is in the back of your mind out into the open.'

She recoiled from the very idea. She did not have to say so. It showed in her face.

His smile died. 'That's the way we're going to play it, anyway.'

'What?'

He stood up. 'I'll take you back to Ruprechago' he said curtly. 'I'll stay here overnight, then we can leave early.'

'I'd rather…'

'I'm sure you would,' he said his eyes glinting. 'But I want to see how your memory responds to me being around all the time.'

Cleo's heart lurched. 'You can't…'

The anger licked through, sudden and unequivocal. 'Oh, but I can, my beauty.' It was shocking in its blazing intensity.

Then it was gone, as if it had never been. Rafael was laughing again. Cleo drew a shaken breath.

He touched her cheek, a brief flicker of the tips of his fingers, and then his hand fell. But it electrified her, it was so possessive. As if he had the right to touch her and she ought to know it.

'I'm going to stick to you like glue,' he said softly, 'And we'll see what happens.'

She believed him. She didn't understand him but she believed him. But she wished she didn't.

He went, without a word to the others. So it was left to Cleo to tell them his plans. The doctor nodded, approving, but Bebel went very quiet. *Oh dear,* thought Cleo. *Doesn't she know that Rafael is out of her league?*

There were no new patients injured in the floods that day.

'The system is working now. Dom Rafael has established an emergency shelter close to the flood site. There is a proper First Aid centre there and the seriously injured are being taken by helicopter to a proper hospital,' Bebel explained. 'Dom Rafael says that we can come off red alert here.' She did not sound happy about it.

But that night, everyone who had left the small encampment came back. They all ate together, a protracted meal in the torch-lit jungle night. It almost had a holiday atmosphere, Cleo thought. Time suddenly did not matter. Whatever was not done today would be done tomorrow. Alternatively, it could be postponed forever. Nobody worried any more.

The only person who did not fit into this easy pace was Rafael. And maybe herself. He had been in and out all day, not speaking to her. But it did not make any difference. They were two of a kind, among all these uncomplicated, generous, unsuspicious people.

*It's as if Rafael and I are the only two who know what's really going on.*

Cleo did not like that. But she could not disguise from herself, either, that she watched for him. Even when other people did not notice his silent-footed arrival, even when she was looking the other way, a prickling sensation at the back of her neck would tell her that he was imminent.

An invisible force field seemed to keep them locked. So that wherever she was, he was at the opposite pole, Cleo thought. It was as if there was an extra dimension to the little jungle hospital, and they were the only two who inhabited it.

She tried to tell herself that she was being fanciful. That her loss of memory had made her jumpy. But every time she met Rafael's eyes, she knew, deep in her bones, that it was not just her imagination. He felt it too.

There was never any kindness in those watchful eyes. Nor much compassion either. But knowledge – oh, yes, there was knowledge.

She tried not to meet his eyes.

It was fully dark by the time he came back that night. The others had finished their meal and were sitting on the veranda listening to one of the staff play a battered guitar. Cleo was the only person who heard the sound of a horse's harness, it seemed. She stiffened.

Then the creak of leather got louder, followed by the soft clop of weary hooves. He came into the pool of light cast by the kerosene lamps along the veranda and swung himself off his horse. His face and clothes were streaked with dust.

*More like a gunslinger than ever*, thought Cleo. She did not say it aloud. She pulled her cane chair as far into the shadows as she could.

Bebel was tired. She had had a heavy day, helping David operate on the badly broken leg of a young woodsman. But she still jumped to her feet, calling a welcome, offering food, a chair, some measure of comfort.

*She's got it bad*, thought Cleo sourly.

Rafael tossed the reins so that they looped round the bamboo shaft outside the shack and came up the shallow steps. He bent his tall head and kissed Bebel on both cheeks. Cleo jerked back, the legs of her chair scraping loudly on the wooden floor. He looked round.

'Good evening, Cleopatra.'

Bebel continued to hover. 'You look so tired,' she said in a worried voice.

'It's been a tough few days.' He sank onto one of the rattan chairs. 'Don't look so worried, little one. A little hard work won't kill me. Now the Red Cross are here in force, I can let up, anyway.'

But Bebel knelt in front of him and began to pull off his boots. It was an intimate little service. The affectionate scolding she kept up all the time only heightened the impression. Cleo did not like it. She did not like it at all.

'You take no care of yourself. You go away for years, and then think you can come back here and take up again where you have left off. It is stupid. How long is it since you stayed in the saddle all day? You are just asking to get hurt. And then what will we do?'

He stretched out a lazy hand and ruffled her smooth hair.

'Agreed, agreed,' he said in mock surrender.

She pulled off his second boot and smacked his ankle, only half-pretending anger.

'You should be more careful of yourself. Who is there to take care of you if you are hurt?'

Cleo shifted uncomfortably. She did not like seeing Bebel expose her emotions like this, she told herself. Bebel was too kind, too vulnerable, for that worldly gunslinger. Besides, he lived in that different dimension. And there was no woman there but his polar opposite, Cleo herself.

*I'm jealous,* she thought. It shocked her to the core. She sat very still, fighting the realisation with every instinct she had.

Something about her stillness must have attracted Rafael's attention again. His eyes found her in her dark corner and all the lazy friendliness went out of them. They were as they always were when they looked at her – hard, assessing, speculative.

'Why are you lurking in the shadows? Have you too had a bad day, like Bebel?' The mockery was like a whiplash. He made no secret of the fact that he thought she was a parasite in this settlement of good, hard-working people.

Cleo said in a suffocated voice, 'My day was fine.'

'Then you won't be too tired to get me some supper,' he told her dulcetly.

His eyes challenged her. Nobody else but them, again.

In that other world, Bebel protested. Of course, *she* would fetch Dom Rafael some dinner. Nobody had ridden as far or rescued as many people as he had today.

Someone needed to get Bebel out of the gunslinger's clutches thought Cleo, wincing. She stood up, holding his eyes with her own, ignoring Bebel.

'Of course, I'll get you some food if you want.'

'I'll come with you,' he said abruptly.

Bebel fell back, still clutching one discarded boot. Her gentle face was disappointed. Cleo did not look at her as Rafael left the nurse behind without a look. He crossed the veranda to Cleo's side, silent in his stocking feet, intent as a jungle predator.

She felt a little shiver of trepidation creep up her spine. She quelled it. She could deal with this dangerous jungle animal. Gentle Bebel couldn't.

The nurse accepted defeat graciously. 'There is plenty of *feijoada* left but you will need to cook more rice, Cleo,' she said, without a trace of resentment.

Rafael had slipped an arm around Cleo's waist in a courteous gesture, worthy of the ballrooms of a more elegant age. Except it wasn't elegant and it wasn't courteous. She could feel his fingers burning through the light cotton shirt that she had borrowed.

Cleo was glad that she was removing the danger from kind, unaware Bebel. 'Right,' she said lightly over her shoulder. 'Warmed over stew and fresh rice. What more could a man ask for?'

They went through the door at the end of the veranda into the rough kitchen area. Inside, it was airless and suffocatingly hot.

Rafael slipped the hand at her waist further round her body. He then brought her to an abrupt stop in the dusty stillness.

'A man could ask for a lot more,' he said huskily. And kissed her hard.

Panic rose in her throat. But it was not the only thing she felt, not even the most powerful. Her whole body thrummed with awareness of him, like a base drum that had been set reverberating and could now not stop. Her mouth softened under his and her body adjusted itself to his, as if there was no alternative. Opposing poles falling into place, without either of them having much control, she thought.

She still heard voices faintly. Anyone getting up to follow

them would bump into them, locked together in this stifling little room. The thought only increased the urgency.

His body was harsh, alien under her fingers. In spite of his evident weariness, he held her in a grip of iron. Her flesh felt impossibly soft, bruising itself on the buckle and studs of his belt, even on the metal buttons of his linen shirt. She did not care. He smelt of leather and dust and sweat and the tang of the forest, where plants smelled like animals. She knew that smell. She knew *him*. Somewhere deep and dark, beyond amnesia or convention, Cleo knew that she had never known anyone so totally.

The arm around her was sinewy, as strong as one of the unbreakable plaited ropes he had used in the jungle. And he was giving no quarter. His body burned. She felt the heat beneath his shirt under her fingers. And when his hips moved, she gasped at the unequivocal evidence of his need.

*Not so tired after all then*, she thought exultant.

She wanted her hands on his naked skin. She plucked feverishly at the linen shirt, pulling it out of his waistband, eyes shut, mouth seeking, mindless.

To her amazement, he released her at once. Well, he did not exactly release her. He put his hands like a vice on her shoulders and held her away from him.

'Ask and you shall receive,' he said under his breath. 'Tell me the truth, my Cleopatra. Tell me *now*.'

But she just stared at him in the darkness, the hunger shot out of her at the challenge. Her body took some time to catch up. But her brain was ice-cool and flinching the moment he spoke. Now her pulses steadied slowly.

When her breathing came back under her own control, she said at last in a thin little voice, 'You had no right to do that.'

'Right?' His voice was not much more than a whisper but it was fierce enough to make her jump. 'What have rights got to do with it? I want you. You wanted me too for a moment.'

'No.' She was appalled at the thought.

Rafael laughed, but wearily. 'Fine. Lie about that too, if

you want to. It doesn't matter. I know you wanted me just
now. And so do you.'

She sought for excuses. 'I owe you my life.'

'Sure. You're a real virgin sacrifice on the altar of gratitude,'
he said bitingly. He flung away from her. 'Oh, forget it.'

Instinctively, she rubbed her hands over her bare arms
where she had pushed up the sleeves of Bebel's shirt to the
elbows.

'Why are you so bitter? What have I ever done to you?'

He ignored that. 'Here's the rice.' He threw a handful into
a wide pan. 'Want to take over?'

Cleo took the pan away from him and measured boiled
water from the canister carefully onto the grains. Water was
precious here.

She had already learned how the crude, log-fired stove
worked. There was a hot cupboard in which bread and the
ubiquitous stew were cooked, and a single big hot plate above
it. Now she turned the knob that controlled the plate up to
maximum. It would make the corrugated iron kitchen unbear-
ably hot but it would get his food heated faster. She gestured
to the doorway.

'Do you want to sit outside?'

'In a moment.'

He had found candles and lit them from the one left in the
window, more as a discouragement to flies than anything else.
They had a pungent smell, not unpleasant, like liquorice or
aniseed. Outside, the guitar started again.

Rafael strolled to the big American fridge. In this outpost,
it was run on bottled gas.

'A drink while you're cooking?'

Cleo shook her head.

'You'll boil along with the rice.' He didn't sound as if he
cared. But when he had extracted his beer, he didn't go
outside with the others either.

The water had begun to boil. Cleo turned down the heat
and stirred it.

Rafael leaned back, hooking one foot behind him round the crossbar of the bench beside the kitchen table. He watched her over his beer can.

'So you remember how to cook.'

Cleo shook her head. 'Bebel showed me.'

'She'll have to bill you for cookery lessons as well as nursing care then.'

Cleo stirred the rice with concentration. 'That's just so pointless. You know as well as I do that I have no money. You found me, for God's sake. You know exactly what I had on me at the time.'

Out of the corner of her eye, she saw his smile. His teeth were very white. A jungle predator again. He took his time, tipping beer down his throat.

Then he drawled, 'I do indeed.'

Cleo tensed but she was not quite sure why. 'What does that mean?'

'It was very – alluring.'

She forgot to stir. 'What?'

'A few artistic rags and a kilo or two of mud. Wasted on me, really. Now, if you had got David – he's a romantic. Always very chivalrous to ladies whose clothes fall off them.'

She swung round, the rice forgotten. '*What?*'

He grinned. 'Don't tell me you've forgotten that too?'

Her tongue was tying itself in knots. 'Are you saying that I – do you – I mean…'

He straightened suddenly. The bench shot away under the table as if it had been kicked furiously.

But his voice was cool. More than cool, dispassionate. 'I mean that I think you had dressed the part of damsel-in-distress, long before you got that knock on the head. No, make that "undressed the part".'

This was a nightmare. Cleo felt all the blood drain out of her face. It felt stiff and cold.

'What part? What are you talking about?' Her voice rose out-of-control, alarmed. 'I don't understand.'

'That rice is going to boil over,' he pointed out helpfully.

She whipped back to the pan. He was right. She pulled it off the heat, stirring frantically.

Behind her, the hateful drawl said softly, 'Then let me explain. If you get lost in the forest, there are certain things that tend to stay intact. Even if you blunder around for hours tearing your clothes.'

Cleo's neck felt stiff. 'Like what?' she said, not taking her eyes off her task.

'Like your underwear.'

'*What?*'

'You see,' he explained, still soft and rational and horribly, horribly unconcerned. 'Branches tend to tear the top layer. In your case, that was all there was.'

Cleo closed her eyes. She was trembling so much she could hardly stand. She wanted to shout that she didn't believe him. But she *did*. It was awful, hateful, embarrassing…and worse. But she did.

She could not explain it. But it seemed that this was one of those dim scenes which she hardly remembered. Herself dishevelled and half-clad. And distressed. And Rafael was in there somewhere.

Had she tried to seduce him? Deliberately dressed for it, as he said? Surely, she could not have done so. He didn't feel like the sort of man you tried to seduce. He didn't feel like the sort of man you could talk into doing anything except exactly what he wanted.

But maybe he had wanted to…

'And so,' he went on in that deadly, meditative tone, 'I concluded that you had set out without any in the first place.'

'Oh God,' said Cleo.

'No, I didn't think it was very subtle either,' Rafael said, as if he was agreeing with a comment she had made. 'Effective though. I'll give you that. Very effective.'

She stared blindly at the rice. It was bubbling like an underwater volcano. 'But why?' she said numbly.

'I was wondering that myself. Don't you remember that either?'

She shook her head.

'Then I can't enlighten you.'

'But you know,' she said despairing, 'You won't tell me anything about who I am. But you know.'

He leaned past her and took the pan off the heat. 'That rice is done.'

She turned off the power automatically, and then turned her back on the stove. 'Why are you doing this?'

He raised his eyebrows. 'David tells me that amnesiacs recover best if they are allowed to explore their own memories unassisted. I thought I was being helpful.'

She searched that clever, shuttered face. 'No, you didn't,' she said with certainty. 'You thought you'd force me into…' She broke off.

'Into what?' he said softly.

She shook her head.

'Go on. Say it. You thought I'd force you into admitting the truth?'

Cleo stared at him with hot eyes. 'Why are you so certain that I'm a liar?'

There was a pause. Rafael looked at her broodingly, as if he was seeing not her but someone, or something else. Whatever it was, it clearly filled him with disgust. Something in his past? Something – she shrank from the implications – in *her* past?

His lips did not move. But, as if he was speaking aloud, she heard him say, *Tell me something true.*

Shocked to the core, she said abruptly, 'How *well* do you know me?'

He brought himself to the present with a jerk. His eyes locked on hers. 'You either know the answer to that. Or you don't. And if you don't, then I don't know you at all.'

He found a plate, tipped the rice onto it and held it out to her with a bland smile. 'Stew please?'

She sighed and got the pot of *feijoada* out of the oven. She half-thought he would sit at the kitchen table, but he took his plate of stew and rice and a fork and went back out onto the veranda among the warmth and music.

'Success,' he announced. 'Cleopatra can cook.'

Dr David looked interested. 'Loss of memory can be like that. You remember acquired skills, but lose anything personal. I wonder if you can ride a bike, Cleo?'

Rafael gave a crack of laughter.

Bebel looked reproving. 'It is a step forward.'

He looked sceptical. 'If you say so.'

He flung himself back into a cane chair and applied himself to the food.

'Did anything else occur to you?' said David. 'What you cooked. Who you cooked for. That sort of thing.'

'No,' said Cleo. She felt stifled.

'Oh well, not to worry,' he said easily. 'It will come back in its own good time.' He laughed. 'And if you have a husband waiting for you to cook for him, he'll probably find you before you find him.'

'A husband?' She gaped. The possibility of a husband had truly not occurred to her.

And then she looked at Rafael. He was still eating, calmly enough. But he was jabbing the fork into the stew as if he was killing something. And his face was a mask.

She thought, *Why doesn't anyone but me notice that?*

But the others were all laughing, teasing her about her imaginary husband.

'He has employed James Bond to look for you already.'

'He is consulting a shaman.'

'No, no, he has offered a huge reward on global satellite television. The whole country is probably looking for you by now.'

Rafael put his plate down with a bang. 'There hasn't even been a radio report of a woman going missing,' he said flatly.

Their laughter died in unease.

Bebel said uncomfortably, 'I am sure there's an explanation.'

'So am I,' said Rafael, never taking his eyes from Cleo. 'So am I.'

He did not have to say that he thought she was pretending. It stuck out all over him. The others looked away, embarrassed, but he held her eyes levelly. He thought she knew very well who she was, and had some deep personal reason for denying it.

But she knew different, thought Cleo. And she was the only one who did. The only who *knew* she wasn't lying. The fog swirled, terrifyingly, all of a sudden.

She had to be careful. She had to stay in control, or hysteria could rise up and take her over. She knew that.

She said intensely, 'I don't know why no one is looking for me. Maybe somebody wanted me dead.' She was starting to shake. 'Maybe somebody tipped me out of a boat or a jeep and left me to die.'

He looked contemptuous.

And she thought, *Oh God, he knows that too. He knows what caused the accident that knocked me out. If it was an accident.*

'Fascinating theories,' Rafael said softly.

*He doesn't just know who I am. He knows what happened to me to make me like this.*

He was looking at her as if she were an enemy. The panic was a bitter taste in her mouth now. Her skin felt cold and shivery. She knew there was sweat at her temples.

She put a hand up to ward him off, though he had not stirred from his cane chair.

'No,' she said on a thin, breathless note. 'No. Someone hit me. I'm sure. I can feel – anger. I was afraid. I wanted to run – anywhere. I wanted to run into the jungle and never come back. Somebody was pushing me…'

His eyes narrowed to slits. 'Don't be ridiculous,' he rapped out.

*It was you. It had to be you.*

He stood up. His shadow was huge and black. It wavered in the guttering candlelight. Cleo felt engulfed by it. She made a futile little gesture as if her hands were trying to unwind the shadow's embrace from her body. His foot kicked the plate and fork with a noise that sounded like thunder to her heightened senses.

She gave a sigh and dropped like a stone where she stood.

## chapter ten

This time, the darkness was full of people. Cleo was on a roundabout. The fairground horses went up and down, sometimes fast, sometimes slow. There were people she knew on the other horses but they were all out of sync. She called out to them but they waved back, enjoying themselves. They did not know she was frightened.

Except for the masked cowboy. He sat on his horse as easily as if it were a real animal. One gloved hand rested lightly on its wooden mane. The other was ready to seize the gun out of the holster at his hip. His horse kept exact time with hers. She was very frightened of him. And he knew it.

He leaned towards her. She turned her head away from him, but it was no use. He just leaned closer. Recklessly, she leaned out even further.

She heard him say, 'I am your knight-errant. I am your husband.'

That was when her whole body finally leaned too far. She began to slip over the precipitous edge of the high roundabout. She felt herself tumble into the peopled darkness, while the word bounced mockingly off the glass column and painted horses above her.

*Husband. Husband. Husband.*

Her ears rang until she cried out in protest. And then, the ringing stopped slowly. She began to make out words that did not echo.

'We shouldn't have teased her. She is very upset.' She knew who that was – Bebel, concerned as always.

'But she's been so sensible about it.' Dr David, slightly put out. 'I think Rafael is right. He ought to take her to Ruprechago. At least there, he can start a few enquiries into who she is.'

*Rafael*. The name was familiar. She knew it was familiar. She heard someone saying harshly, 'Tell me something real.' She was almost sure that was Rafael. She put a wavering hand to her head. She still had that dancing roundabout sensation and it was an effort to open her eyes. But she had to know.

Her lids lifted. The world lurched sickeningly. She held on to a rock, gripping hard.

'Rafael…' she said on a wincing breath.

'I'm here.'

He was. Taller than she remembered. Dark as the devil. She didn't recognise him. And yet…

She whispered, 'Tell me something real.'

His eyes flared.

She said, 'Are you…?'

But the roundabout was going faster, the noise it made was getting louder, and she couldn't remember what she wanted to ask him. She fell back.

'That's some effect you have on the woman,' Dr David said dryly. He lowered Cleo slowly back onto the cushion Bebel had fetched for her head.

Rafael did not answer for a moment. He flexed the hand she had been holding. There were little red arcs where her nails had gouged into his palm.

'She certainly seems very disoriented.'

'Seems? You're crazy. The woman is completely out of it,' said David curtly. 'I've tried to keep it low key because I didn't want to worry her. And I can't do anything about it here. I can't even give her a decent X-ray. But I don't understand this amnesia.'

'You don't think it's contrived then?' Rafael looked at him searchingly.

'No. She's too scared. Oh, she's trying to hide it. But she doesn't trust anything. She keeps testing everyone to see if they know her. I've seen that before.'

'But you said the wound to her head was not very severe.'

'I don't think it is. And she's laying down subsequent memory fine.

'What?'

'She remembers everything that's happened since. That's a very good sign, from what I can learn off the Net. But there could be a pre-existing condition. Or some psychological reason for her wanting to block stuff out. I'm no expert but I've heard that it happens. Say a motorist kills someone – they can effectively block out everything to do with the accident. Refuse to believe it ever happened.' He looked down at her broodingly. 'It would help if we knew what she was doing before she fell down that mountain.'

Rafael flexed his fingers restlessly. 'I'll ask her when we get back to Ruprechago.'

'Don't go bullying her,' the doctor warned. 'She's not going to respond well to being told to pull herself together. That's one worried lady you've got there.'

Bebel said practically, 'If you will carry her to her to bed now, Dom Rafael, I will sit with her until I am sure she is sleeping properly.'

Rafael looked down at Cleo. His face was unreadable.

'And you're sure she's not faking?'

Dr David shook his head. 'She'd have to be an Oscar-winning actress to give a performance like that.'

Rafael's expression closed. 'Ah.'

He bent from the knee and raised her easily in his arms. She murmured a little, burrowing her head against his shoulder, as if she was used to being there. He found the others were looking at him speculatively.

Dr David said, 'And you're sure you don't know her?'

Bebel looked up, shocked. 'What are you saying? Dom Rafael brought her here, through the forest, didn't he? Of course she's used to him carrying her. He is her guardian angel.'

She said it again to Cleo the next morning. 'You are so lucky,' she concluded.

'Yes,' said Cleo without enthusiasm.

'Dom Rafael is a wonderful person.'

'Oh?'

Bebel detected coolness. 'He must seem very dictatorial to someone like you,' she said accusingly. 'And he has so many responsibilities. But Dom Rafael is a very caring person…'

'Why do you call him that?' interrupted Cleo, not wanting to hear about Rafael's caring qualities. '*Dom* Rafael. Why not just Rafael? You call David by his Christian name, after all. And you work for him, for goodness sake. What's so special about Rafael?'

Bebel smiled. 'David is not the *patrão*,' she said simply.

Cleo blinked. 'This sounds like "Gone With the Wind", Brazilian style. The *patrão?* This is the twenty-first century, for heaven's sake.'

'Not in Reprechago,' said the nurse with a twinkle. 'Who do you think keeps the hospital going? Sees that the village houses have their roofs repaired? Provides education for the children? This is a poor state and Ruprechago is very remote. If the estate didn't provide basic services, we wouldn't have anything.'

Cleo tried hard not to be impressed. 'Sounds feudal.'

'Maybe. But it works.'

'And Rafael lives here in the middle of the rain forest and runs his kingdom? No wonder he comes on like the king of the castle.'

Bebel looked at her thoughtfully. 'You don't like him,' she deduced.

Cleo did not answer that. Largely because she did not know how to.

Bebel was troubled. 'Will you find it difficult to stay in his house? He does not live there most of the time but at the moment…'

'Oh, an absentee landlord!' said Cleo scornfully.

'At the moment,' Bebel went on steadily, as if she had not

spoken. 'He is putting the estate to rights. So he will stay around. If you are uncomfortable with that…'

Cleo stuck her chin in the air. 'I can handle it.'

'Well, it would be better.' Bebel was still doubtful. 'You need to find out who you are, where your friends are. There is a limit to what we can do from here.'

Cleo softened. 'You've been an angel. Everyone has. I know I've taking up resources you need for other people.' And, as Bebel's expression did not lighten, she added reassuringly, 'Don't worry about me. I can handle men like Rafael with one hand tied behind my back.'

'Another bit of your memory returned then?' said a voice behind them.

Bebel jumped up, blushing. She was as confused as if she were the one he had caught out. Cleo, on the other hand, pursed her lips and tilted her head to look up at him. She smiled, slowly and deliberately.

'Don't need my memory for that,' she assured him. 'I feel it in my bones.'

He looked down at her. Her chin lifted a fraction higher. It was as if there was no one but the two of them in the whole busy place.

'I just bet you do.' He sounded almost admiring. 'But you'd better say your goodbyes. The chopper just radioed in.'

Cleo stood up without haste. 'I'm ready.'

She sounded it too. Just as well neither of them could see inside her head. The mere thought of leaving the little hospital complex terrified her. This was the only life she knew, the only Cleo she knew. Who could tell what was waiting for her out there?

But she was damned if she was going to let them see she was afraid, particularly Rafael. So she strolled round the place, saying goodbye, as composed as a visiting celebrity. She did not let herself start to shake until she was belted into the helicopter seat. And then, thankfully, the vibration was so great there was some excuse. And – a real gift from Heaven – the noise was far too loud to allow for conversation.

So she got back to Rafael's family house without having to exchange a single word with him. Not on the silent battle between them, not on anything.

It was an extraordinary enough journey. The helicopter followed the course of the river back and up clearly going towards its source. The river got narrower and faster the further they went. Pressing her forehead against the curved glass wall, Cleo could make out white-topped waves. They turned to turbulence, then a swirling, rolling whirlpool. And then – the helicopter chugged round an acute bend and Cleo gasped.

It was a waterfall – a full-scale roaring waterfall. Even in the helicopter, she picked up the tympani of the water. It did not look like water. It looked like a white wall, seen through fog and hail. It was frightening in its power.

And she knew it.

She knew what it felt like, the stinging spray on your face, the air full of electric ions.

She thought, *I've been here before.*

She looked quickly at Rafael. But he was talking to the pilot, using hand signals. The helicopter banked and then rose dizzyingly. For minutes, it seemed there was nothing on her side of the helicopter but that great wall of water. And then, as if a giant had released them into the free air, the helicopter slewed sideways and they were out, flying in a blue sky.

Cleo looked down at the vegetation. She had got used to huge trees with their dark umbrella leaves. But the landscape below her was almost gentle. There were more bushes than trees and then – startlingly – a great sweep of lawn, like some European parkland.

*Lawn?*

There were formal beds, planted with bushes sprouting huge flowers, as bright as neon. But there was no doubt, this was a designed and cultivated garden. She knew this place too! She knew that behind there were mango trees, then a bank of fan like palms. Then a house, half-overgrown with creeper.

She did not think she liked the house. She felt a clutch at her stomach that told her this was familiar too. And not friendly.

And it was Rafael's house. She glanced at him. He must have brought her here before. Could she trust her head? *I am your knight-errant. I am your husband.*

But if he was her husband, why didn't he tell her so? And why didn't Bebel, who loved him and knew him well enough to remember that his family arrived with Dom Pedro Primeiro, know that she was his wife?

It had to be just a dream. It *had* to be.

The helicopter cleared the mangoes. And the house was there, just as she had known it would be. She saw the terrace, with its graceful columns, and knew that it was shady even in the heat of midday. She remembered the great floor-to-ceiling windows. She remembered the way they opened out onto the sensuous smells of the flowering vines.

Cleo licked dry lips. No point in worrying about it. There was only one person who knew the answer. She had to challenge it out of him.

With a heavy heart she said, 'I've been here, haven't I?'

This time, Rafael saw her lips move. But he shook his head. And he was right, the noise was too great.

The helicopter settled down like an oversized bumblebee. It came to rest on a patch of deep green at the back of the house. The blades stopped at last.

Cleo just sat there. She felt winded. How could she know this place? Why had he not told her she knew it?

Rafael climbed out of the helicopter, then turned and reached a hand out to help her. She hesitated.

'Why am I here?' she said slowly.

'It's a start.' He shook his hand impatiently. 'Come on. Federico can't leave the chopper until all his passengers are out. And he needs to eat before he goes on.'

Reluctantly, she took his hand. All the bruises that she had been forgetting about for the last three days seemed to join together and scream. Outside the helicopter she straightened, wincing.

'Stiff?' said Rafael, not without sympathy.

'Yes.'

'A hot bath will fix that.'

She was limping towards the house but at that she stopped and looked at him incredulously.

'A hot bath here? But I thought during floods you had to save every egg cup full of water in the middle of the jungle?'

He smiled. 'This is not jungle. This is a clearing in the cloud forest. And certainly you can have a hot bath.'

She forgot her suspicion of him in the simple prospect of bliss. 'I'm not even going to ask how.'

'The river gives us water. Our own waterfall gives us power. We're very ergonomic here.'

She began to walk towards the house. She was getting her second wind, fighting back.

'I don't care if you run on full-blown magic. If there's a bath, lead me to it.'

He took her across an area paved with uneven stones, the colour of the rocks they had seen below the waterfall. Then into a dark corridor. She stopped dead, blinking at the sudden loss of light.

A small woman in a dark dress came out of a doorway. She gave a gasp and Rafael turned his head. He said something short and savage in Portuguese.

Cleo's eyes adjusted. Just in time to see the woman throw up her hands as if disclaiming all responsibility. He spoke again more gently. But the woman looked appalled. At once, all Cleo's suspicions flooded back.

But Rafael was saying easily, 'Maria will take you to your room. I've told her to show you how to work the taps. They are still the originals. Circa 1910, according to my Great Aunt.

You've probably never seen anything like them.'

Again that little wasp sting of memory made Cleo stiffen. He did not appear to notice though. And the woman, Maria, refused to even meet her eyes.

Yet it was there, stronger and stronger, as she went up the heavy staircase, all dark polished wood and intricate carving. There, too, as she looked at the portraits of men in dark suits seated behind desks with tall flags at their sides. Then she paused in front of a portrait of a beautiful woman in full Edwardian evening dress, with a cloud of dark hair and a wickedly sensual mouth. She knew that mouth.

She said, 'Who was she?'

And Maria said in guttural English, 'The grandmother of Dom Rafael.'

There was a sudden, shocking, silence.

Cleo thought, *We've both said that before.*

She turned to the woman. Maria had clapped a hand over her mouth. Her horror was unmistakeable. She could not have looked more conscience-stricken if she had just sworn like a trooper.

Cleo's eyes widened and widened. She could not tear her eyes away from the woman's shocked expression. Inevitably, she missed her footing on the polished tread. She stumbled.

'Cleo…' His voice ripped out from the hallway below.

He ran up the shallow stairs three at a time and seized her. Cleo turned to him blindly. Shaken to the core, she buried her face in his shirt.

His arms went round her. He felt like a rock.

He said, 'It's OK. I've got you. It's OK.'

Cleo said, 'I can't *remember*…'

'I know,' he said.

Her head felt as light as air. She pulled away from him, staring up into that gunslinger's face that she mistrusted so deeply.

'You believe me?' she said doubtfully.

'I think I have to.'

The faintness swirled round her again. She staggered, putting a hand out blindly for the banister.

He said something under his breath.

At once Cleo was suspicious. 'What?'

In the shadows, his teeth glinted in a rueful smile. 'I said, this is getting to be a habit.'

And he swung her off her feet and ran lightly with her to the top of the stairs.

She made a small sound of protest, then clung. As she was almost certain she had clung before. But then, she knew she had. Rafael had carried her to bed at the jungle hospital. And yet it felt different – more intimate. More…personal.

Or was that the fantasy of a woman without a past, clinging on to the only person she recognised in the world?

She *hated* the thought. She was never, ever going to cling to anyone. Even if she never got her memory back and had to build her life starting from the day she woke in the hospital. She was certainly not going to lean on Dom Rafael.

The moment he got to the gracious bedroom, with its high ceiling and four-poster bed, she drew a shaky breath.

'I'm all right now, thank you. I can walk.'

'I'll just…'

'Put me down,' she said, more sharply than she meant.

He did.

Cleo was hard put not to hang onto one of the posts. But pride came to her aid. Pride and the horrible sensation that if she broke down now, in her first move out of the safety of the hospital, she was going to lose any chance of standing on her own two feet.

She said, 'I really am fine. And that bath sounds wonderful.'

Rafael looked serious. 'Is that wise? Hadn't you better rest first?'

'Baths are very restful.' She let go of her supporting post and went to the chest of drawers. She extracted underwear

and a cotton shirt, still talking over her shoulder. 'A long hot
bath scented with jasmine. Just what you need after a noisy
flight through the jungle.'

There was an old-fashioned mahogany towel horse behind
a Louis quinze brocade chair. She kneed the chair out of the
way, proud of her balance, and flipped a huge fluffy towel off
it and over her shoulder. He watched her thoughtfully.

'I really will be all right,' she assured him earnestly. 'I'm
not going to collapse and drown or anything.'

'I'm sure you're not.'

'Well, then…'

'Don't you want some jeans?' he said idly. 'Or a skirt?'

Cleo jumped. 'Yes, of course.'

She went over to the enormous wardrobe that smelled of
lavender bags and dwarfed her simple clothes. She was
pulling out a soft cotton wrap when her hand froze on the
door.

She started to shake.

Rafael did not notice. He said, still in that idle tone, though
his eyes were watchful, 'What have you got to do today?'

She shook so hard that she could hardly stand upright. Her
palm was suddenly wet. It began to slide down the old-
fashioned wardrobe door, though her fingers tightened
convulsively as she tried to keep her balance.

She said in a voice she did not recognise, 'What am I doing
here?'

Rafael came round the bed. 'Sorry?'

She whipped round, letting the door swing wide. The floor
must be uneven. Either that, or suddenly she had one leg
shorter than the other. Cleo felt the floorboards give and staggered again.

Rafael took a hasty step towards her, arm out, but she
recoiled. He stopped cold, as abruptly as if she had pushed
him away.

'It's a trap,' she said panting. 'I belong here, don't I?'

He watched her. 'Possibly,' he said at last.

'Don't play word games with me,' she said furiously. 'Are those my clothes in the drawer or aren't they?'

'They are.'

'And this is the master bedroom.'

'I…' He stopped. 'Yes,' he said at last, without expression.

'*My* bedroom?'

'Yes.'

She swallowed. 'So what does that make me?'

He looked startled. For a long moment they looked at each other. He did not seem to know what to say.

She shut her eyes. 'Oh God. Oh God. Oh God.'

'I don't see what's so terrible. David said that your memory might come back in bits and pieces,' he said at last.

She opened her eyes. 'And you didn't believe him.'

'That was when I didn't believe it had gone at all,' he said swiftly.

'Then why did you get me here?' Cleo's heart lurched. 'Oh, you were going to shake it out of me? Is that it? Follow me round and bully me until I admitted that I knew this place?'

Rafael interrupted. 'I see I was wrong. I saw it the moment we got here. You looked so – confused. I'm sorry I ever doubted you.'

'Great,' said Cleo, bitterly. 'Just great. So where does that leave me? You know who I am and I don't. And I'm living in your house. Brilliant.'

Rafael shook his head, irritated. 'Do you want me to apologise for giving you a roof over your head?'

She glared at him. 'I want you to tell me who I *am*.'

He hesitated. Then he said in a reasonable tone, 'Look, I'll make a bargain with you.'

Cleo clutched her pile of clothes and the fluffy towel to her breast. 'What have I got to bargain with?'

He winced theatrically. 'And would you trust anything I told you?' he countered with justification. 'Let's give it a try.'

She sat down suddenly on the edge of the great bed. 'Try what?'

'You stay here. Explore whatever you want. See what is familiar. Get on the Net. Call any phone number you remember. Anything. Try and piece together what you know. At the end of the week, if you there are still blanks, I'll tell you what you want to know.'

She digested that. 'Like I have a choice.'

Rafael bit his lip. 'You have a choice,' he said at last. 'If you want, I'll fly you out today. You can go to a clinic somewhere. Manaus. The States. Switzerland. Choose.'

She said slowly, 'And why don't you think I should do just that?'

'Because if you go to a clinic, they'll slap you in a private room and do tests on you. There won't be anything familiar around to jog your memory. You'll be passive, no chance of exploring anything for yourself. Personally, I think it would make things harder. But it's your choice.'

'Anything familiar? Or anyone?'

His eyes narrowed. 'What do you mean?'

'You're the only person in the world who knows who I am, aren't you?' she said slowly.

His mouth tightened. 'Of course not.'

'So why do I feel as if I'm in your power?'

'Because you're tired and not thinking straight,' he said fluently. But his face had darkened. 'Look, have your bath. Then if you want to go to a clinic, I'll arrange it. You can ship out as soon as it's set up. That's a promise.'

Cleo scanned his face. She thought, *He means that.*

A great wave of tiredness washed over her. The muscles in her legs felt as if they had turned to frogspawn. They were shaking as if they were never going to carry her weight again. But they had to.

She struggled to her feet, pushing her free hand into her hair. Her temples felt tight and her scalp was gritty. He was right. She really needed that bath.

'OK,' she said, 'I'll think about it.'

She went to the door that she knew – oh, that selective

memory of hers! – led to an *en suite* bathroom.

'Good.' Rafael watched but he did not touch her. 'Don't lock the door.'

Her eyes flew to his, wary.

He sighed. 'No, I was not thinking of coming and jumping on you. It's just a reasonable precaution. You're not well yet and you've had a tough day. If you faint in the bath, I want to be able to get in without breaking the door down. They're the originals, hand-carved locally.'

To her astonishment, Cleo gave a choke of laughter. 'You're all heart.'

He searched her face. 'I try to be sensible.'

The remark fell between them like a stone. She searched his face. She could not read his expression but there was *something*. A muscle throbbed in his cheek. He did not look like a man who had just won a battle. Her fragile laughter died.

Rafael turned away sharply. 'Don't stay in there too long. I'll send Maria up to check on you in ten minutes.'

Cleo tried to pull herself together. 'Yes sir,' she teased, albeit shakily.

He made an odd, angry gesture, quickly stilled. 'You are – not – in – my – power,' he said between his teeth.

'No?'

His eyes bored into hers. 'In my care, maybe.' He said it as if it were wrenched out of him. 'For my sins.'

She thought, *He doesn't want me.* She was shaken to the heart.

## chapter eleven

The bath was another disturbing experience.

Cleo found that it had the same dreamlike familiarity as the bedroom. She knew which of the old-fashioned unmarked taps delivered hot water, without having to experiment. And she knew exactly which of the collection of decorative bottles on the mahogany washstand held her jasmine-scented bath oil. She even knew that there was not very much left.

And yet – it didn't feel as if she belonged here.

She did not lie soaking for very long. It was too unsettling. She washed her hair – and found a comb as easily as if she had only just that moment put it down. She shivered.

*Maybe I don't want to remember.*

She stared at herself in the spotted mirror. The face that looked back was pale, sea-green eyes huge in the afternoon shadows. It seemed that she had done this before. Only the mirror was bigger, brighter, and she was not alone.

She thought, *There ought to be better lighting. How are they going to check my make-up in light like this?*

The comb fell from her fingers. They? Check her make-up? For some reason, her heart felt as if it had gone into freefall. She looked at the pale reflection in the mirror and heard someone say out of her memory, *This is no time to be temperamental.*

And she had answered. She had been angry. More than angry. Almost afraid. But she had hidden it. What had she said? 'Go away and stop giving me the heebie-jeebies.'

And the other – a woman. She was certain it was a woman. The woman had been angry, in a panic herself, absolutely determined to make Cleo do something. Do what?

*How many other offers do you think you've had?*

Offer? What offer? From whom? From Rafael?

Her heart clenched at the thought. She knew that whatever the offer had been, she had not wanted to do it. She had not wanted to do it so hard that her muscles locked at the thought. She felt sick with misery just recalling that conversation, even though she did not know what it was about. Even though she did not know who was speaking.

She left her hair damp on her shoulders and ran down the ornate staircase. The small housekeeper was standing in the hall and looked at Cleo uneasily as she passed. But Cleo did not need help to find her way. She went through the doors as if she had done it a thousand times. Big salon, huge windows, columned terrace.

And at the end of the terrace, with trumpet vines, making it feel as if the house was growing back into the jungle again, there were old rattan chairs and a coffee table. And a man was sitting there, while a twist of vine sent a wavering shadow across his face and he stared out across the lawns.

She ran to him.

'Is there a woman here?'

Rafael stood up, startled. 'Are you all right?'

'I'm fine.' Cleo was impatient. Full of trepidation but eager to know. 'A woman. Older than me. A lot older.'

'Of course.' He was slightly offended. 'You've seen Maria and there are other servants. But I assure you, you don't need a chaperone.'

'No, you don't understand. A woman who doesn't belong here. North American. Or no...' She could hear that voice again suddenly. Not just the savage pressure from the panicking woman but the odd, distorted syllables. 'Nearly English. Someone who's grafted one accent onto the other and they haven't gelled yet.'

His eyes narrowed to slits. 'What are you talking about?'

'I remembered...'

But, of course, she had not remembered enough. She described everything she could think of about the little scene she had stumbled over. And it told them precisely nothing.

At last, he shook his head regretfully. 'I don't know anything about it. If it happened, I wasn't there.'

'If?'

Suddenly she faced another nightmare. Were the memories not just fragmented but shot through with fiction?

Rafael frowned. 'Maybe you should go to a clinic anyway. I don't know enough about amnesia to help you.'

But suddenly it was Cleo who wanted to stay.

She said positively, 'No. I'm sure the answer is here. I can feel it, somehow.'

He hesitated. 'Are you sure?'

'Yes. Let me stay. We can stick to our bargain. If I'm still Mrs Nobody from Nowhere at the end of the week, I can go looking for professional help.'

He took her hand unexpectedly. 'You're a brave woman.'

Cleo was surprised how much that warmed her. 'Just trying to be sensible,' she said gruffly.

'And *we* go looking for professional help,' he corrected gently. 'You're not on your own in this.'

She took her hand away, confused. Her eyes fell. When he looked at her like that, she felt as if she had known him forever. As if she would trust him with her life. As if…

*Hang on there, Cleo. You can't unload on him. You're an independent woman. You sort out your own mess. You have to. You always do.*

Somehow, she knew that was true. She did not rely on other people. Not even Rafael.

She moved her chair, so she was just out of touching range. 'So what do we do next?' she said with an effort.

Rafael looked at her under frowning brows. But he did not try to take her hand again. 'Play it by ear, I guess. No pressure. Just go with the flow.'

And they did.

It was a relief, Cleo told herself. The dark undercurrents,

which had been there when he mistrusted her, had all dissolved. Rafael no longer watched her covertly, as if he alone knew her innermost secrets and despised her.

For her own part, she was no longer constantly aware of him. Or so she told herself. Certainly, he did not prowl about at the edge of her consciousness like some demon inquisitor refusing to be banished. They talked calmly and openly. They had reached a state of disinterested good will.

At least, they had as long as she did not let him touch her. That sent all her calm good sense out of the window and replaced it with something like panic. Cleo took care that she stood out of touching range.

But she did ask him about himself. She could not resist that.

'Were you born here?' she asked, as they sat on the terrace the second night after he had brought here there.

He was smoking a cigar. He said it kept the mosquitoes away.

'No. My mother would have been horrified at the thought. She was attended to by the best gynaecologist in New York.'

'You must be very rich,' said Cleo involuntarily. She thought of what Bebel had said. 'This is your kingdom, isn't it?'

He sighed. 'Less of a kingdom than it once was. Satellites have brought us phones and the Internet. We can't keep the outside world out anymore, even if we wanted to.'

'Do you want to?' she said curiously.

'Sometimes. When you see the effects of twenty-first century development.'

'Like?'

He shrugged powerful shoulders. 'Well, logging for example. A lot of the people who were injured in the flood were loggers. Yet they probably helped cause it, in some ways. They destroy the shoreline and the earth just erodes into the river. Do you know that if you compare satellite pictures of earth, even over a period of ten years, the brown silt at the mouth of the Amazon gets deeper and deeper out into the Atlantic? Astronauts can see it from space. But we can't wake up to it here, where it's actually happening.'

'Are you a green activist then?' Cleo was surprised.

'No. But one of my great aunts is. Has been for fifty years.'

She was startled. 'You have aunts? Do they live around here somewhere?'

'Here in the house,' he said coolly. 'Just at the moment, they're on an extended trip to Europe.'

Her skin prickled. 'Did you send them away? Because of me?'

He laughed aloud. 'If they knew about you, I wouldn't get them out with a dockyard hoist,' he said frankly. 'I've never met such a nosy bunch in my life. It's the last hangover of colonial society, I suppose, this determination to know everything that your family and neighbours are doing.'

'Colonial?' Cleo was puzzled and faintly disapproving.

He stood up and went back through the open window into the salon. When he came back, it was with a battered paperback. He threw it down on the coffee table.

She leaned forward. 'Cloud Orchid', she read aloud. She looked up. 'Did you write this?'

He grimaced. 'Hardly. It's a twentieth-century, Latin-American classic. But I recognise some of the attitudes.'

She picked it up, turning it over. 'A sweeping saga of passion and betrayal over one-hundred-and-fifty years. A middle-class Spanish family tries to tame the wilderness. And the wilderness assimilates the family,' she read.

He smiled. 'I recognise those people in "Cloud Orchid". God help me, some of them are in my family.'

'I'd never have had you down as a man who lived with his Great Aunt.'

He stared at her. At once, she blushed, her hands flying to her cheeks.

'Oh what a *stupid* thing to say. I'm so sorry. I had no right. Forgive me.'

'Not at all,' said Rafael, unholy laughter in the deep voice. 'I'm relieved.'

Cleo groaned.

'And you're right. I don't live with them.'

She remembered Bebel saying something about it – and herself replying scornfully, 'Oh, an absentee landlord.'

She could have kicked herself. 'I even knew that, if I'd bothered to think about it. Now I can't even remember what I *can* remember,' she said, not very coherently.

He flung back his head and laughed until he choked.

'I'm glad to amuse you,' she said stiffly.

'No, you're not.' He stopped laughing but his eyes were still alight with it. 'But it gives me hope.'

She looked at him doubtfully. 'It does?'

His eyes danced. 'It shows that you know me better than you realise,' he said solemnly.

Cleo shook her head. 'It would be a great deal more use if I knew *me*,' she pointed out with asperity. But she stopped blushing and gave him a wry smile.

His eyes darkened. 'That's my girl,' he said softly.

Or she thought that was what he said. She was so startled that she did not know what to say. She just held her breath, astonished at the confused feelings that flooded her. Feelings of pride and humility and shyness and…well, if she were honest, a strong desire to go to him and put his arms round her and say, 'Am I your girl? Really?'

Only she had held her breath too long. It was too late. Rafael was already talking about the estate and the next day and what he had to do. And the moment was gone.

But when she went upstairs to bed that night, she paused in front of the Edwardian beauty with the sumptuous sleeves and Rafael's mouth. They were both so familiar. She could almost feel the long skirts weighing her down in the heat of an equatorial afternoon. Feel his mouth on hers.

Cleo put a hand to her head.

Did she belong here then? Was Rafael not telling her

because he wanted her to remember for herself? But had he brought her here before as his lover?

Not his wife, surely! There was no sign of his presence in that great bedroom. In spite of the huge bed, she did not think he had ever slept with her there. And – she checked again – there was no mark of a wedding ring on her finger. Besides, if they had been married, surely she would feel it in her bones, even if she could not quite remember her history?

Or did she?

*Am I your girl?*

Oh, she wanted to be. She really, really wanted to be, didn't she?

*Face it, Cleo. You may not trust him. But that doesn't make any difference. You're still in love with him.*

'Damn you,' Cleo told the Edwardian beauty with concentrated hatred. 'You've fogged me up even more than I was before.'

She stamped off to bed in such a temper that, for the first time in days, she fell asleep at once.

She slept so well that the next morning Rafael congratulated her. 'You're looking much more rested. You must be beginning to sort things out.'

*Oh sure. Like I can feel your mouth on mine and spend half my waking hours wondering whether we slept together in that great bed.*

'Yes,' she said in a strangled voice.

'Feel up to a trip?'

At once she tensed. 'Delegating me to the clinic?' she said, trying to keep it light.

He frowned blackly at once. 'Not unless you want to.'

She shook her head.

She thought he looked relieved. Or was that just because she wanted him to look relieved?

'I've got to go up to my grandfather's observatory. I wondered if you'd like to come along for the ride.'

She hesitated.

'Forget it,' he said at once. 'It's only sightseeing. I told you, no pressure.'

Cleo made a decision. It might be reckless, to go off completely alone with him. Up to now there had always been the restraining presence of others in the background – the doctor and Bebel at the hospital, the servants here. But she felt in her bones that it was time.

'No. I'd like to come.'

'Good.' He was clearly pleased. 'You'll need sun block and a hat. If you haven't got them, I'll ask Maria.'

But, she found, she had got them.

'I was pretty well-prepared for this place, wasn't I?' she said, strolling out the back door to join him. 'Did you tell me what to bring?'

'No.' He led the way to an open buggy. 'I hope you don't mind being blown about.'

This morning, she had put her hair up in a loose knot at the back of her neck. He was looking at some of the escaping fronds as if they fascinated him. Cleo felt hot all of a sudden. She crammed the hat on her head like a schoolgirl.

'I'll be fine.'

But she did not take his hand when he offered to help her into the buggy and she sat as far away from him as she could, so that their shoulders did not touch when the thing bounced over the ruts in the grass. Well, they did not touch often.

They zipped over the sward and then onto a deeply-rutted unmade track. It climbed dizzying. Little pebbles scattered down the track in their wake. But Cleo was not scared. Rafaél drove with a cool expertise which, she was certain, was absolutely typical. If he bothered to do anything, he would do it to perfection. She wondered when she had worked that out. She was sure she was right.

When they stopped, she came out of her brown study with a jump. He hauled on the handbrake and turned to look at her.

'You OK? We walk from here. But, if the ride has shaken you up, I can easily go on alone. I'll only be twenty minutes or so and you're in the shade here.'

Cleo shook her head, dislodging her straw crown. 'No. I'd love a walk.'

He nodded. 'Then keep your hat on. It's very hot and the air is thin up here. You might not notice that you are getting burned. Sunstroke is the last thing you need now.'

She smiled. 'In your care,' she teased gently.

Rafael sat very still for a moment. Then, to her astonishment, he leaned towards her and drew a careful thumb along her lower lip. As if he could not help himself. But as if he was determined not to crowd her either.

'You'd better believe it,' he said softly.

Her whole body responded. Not just to the caress. To his words.

This time, she gave him her hand to help her out of the buggy.

There was a breeze. It was warm, full of the scent of lush vegetation and pollen that drifted in the sun. Cleo gave a small sigh, closing her eyes.

'Oh, it's perfect.'

Rafael held onto her hand. ' It was my favourite place when I was a child. I used to come here and pretend I was a pirate.'

He helped her up the steep path. She could see the tower ahead of them, in a clearing, outlined against a brilliant sapphire sky.

'Did you tell yourself stories?' she said amused, toiling steadily.

'When my grandfather ran out of his, yes.'

'I was always telling myself stories when I was a child,' Cleo told him. 'I suppose it comes of being an only child. My mother used to worry about it. That was why she took me to stage school on Saturday mornings originally. So that I could play in scenes that somebody else had written.'

Rafael's hand tightened on hers but he continued to walk steadily.

'Did it work?' he asked casually, scanning the horizon.

She gave a choke of laughter. 'No. I made the other kids play in my stories.'

'How old were you?'

'Oh, five or six,' she said absently, watching a bird labour out of the treetops. 'What's that?'

'A parrot,' he said at once. 'Body like an old bomber, slow flight. Terrible cawing noise before it takes off. Definitely a parrot.'

'I've never seen a parrot in the wild before.'

'We've got a couple of rare species up here. My Great Aunt Violetta wants to start some wildlife tourism. On a very limited scale, of course, or it defeats the object. I'm beginning to think she's right.'

'Well, that's big of you,' said Cleo, torn between amusement and annoyance. 'If you don't live here and she does. Male chauvinist.'

He laughed down at her. 'Ah, but I pay the bills.'

'Capitalist male chauvinist,' she retorted.

'You're laughing at me,' he accused.

But he was smiling. And when she looked into his eyes, she saw that there was a lot more than a smile in the dark depths. Her heart began to race.

'Am I not allowed to laugh at you?' she said breathlessly.

He considered her for a minute, then said, 'You're allowed to do anything you want,' with great deliberation.

She shivered. Which was crazy, as she felt warm all over. His fingers tightened so hard that she could have cried out. *I'm melting,* she thought. They walked faster.

The path turned and suddenly the tower was no longer in the distance. It was there in front of them, a needle of grey stone with an old wooden door, barred and braced with metal. Cleo blinked.

'The tower was the first thing anyone built here,' he told her. 'At the very end of the eighteenth century, as far as we can tell. A bunch of pirates managed to push their way up the tributary of the Amazon until they got to the waterfall. They seem to have thought that if they built it high enough, they would see the sea.'

'And can they?'

He laughed. 'Just the forest. But it's very good for watching the stars, as long as you keep the area cleared. That's what my grandfather used it for.' He strode forward and wrenched up the bar. 'Come up and see my telescope.'

Inside, it was blessedly cool. It was a perfectly circular building with a spiral staircase going up the central column. On the ground floor, there were a couple of chairs, much battered, and a rough couch with a pillow and some sheets folded at one end. It looked as if someone had clearly been sleeping there.

He mounted the stairs. 'Coming?'

Cleo hesitated just for a second. There was no rail to the spiral and the wooden steps were worn. Then she shook herself. Rafael was there, after all. And she was in his care. He would take care of her with the same easy mastery he did everything else. She *wanted* him to take care of her. She followed him.

There were four floors in all, each with window slits. She could imagine it being a perfect children's hideout. There were even old books and board games at the third level, where a paint-stained table was set under a window slit. Incongruous among the well-used furniture and toys, there was also a state-of-the-art laptop computer.

'There's electricity up here?'

'Battery-powered,' he said curtly.

But she had the impression that he was annoyed. That he wished he had put the laptop out of sight before bringing her here.

'Only one more flight to go and then the look-out gallery,' Rafael said. He reached out a hand to draw her up the stairs. Or away from the laptop, she was not sure which. 'Can you make it?'

'Of course.' But some of the warmth had cooled, and the

excitement had dimmed. He was not trusting her again and she did not know why.

He was less solicitous now. More challenging. She lifted her chin to meet the challenge and climbed the last spiral unaided.

The telescope was bigger than she expected. It was mounted on something that looked more like major scaffolding than a traditional tripod. He touched it and she saw that the telescope rotated freely. He pulled a lever and the roof caved in, scattering leaves and dust and feathers.

Cleo coughed uncontrollably for a bit. 'Hasn't been opened for a while, huh?'

'No, I didn't bother to come up here…' He broke off.

'So, you're the one who's been sleeping here,' Cleo deduced. She shook her head, confused. 'Why on earth? You clearly haven't been star gazing.'

'The house was full,' he said curtly. 'Don't you want to see the view now you've climbed all this way?'

He pushed open some wooden shutters and stepped out onto a tiny ledge. It was encircled by a parapet but, even so, it looked dizzyingly precipitous. Cleo stepped out gingerly.

She wanted to say, 'How could your own house be too full for you to stay there?' But she was too intent in hanging on.

The breeze was much stronger up here, almost a wind. It had her hat off in a second, then set about whipping her hair out of its loose confinement. Rafael fielded the hat easily but there was not much he could do about the red hair. It blew freely into her eyes, into his. Cleo tried to calm the wafting fronds by dint of clamping her hands over them. When that didn't work, she turned away from him, wedging herself into the corner of the parapet, up against the tower wall.

'No,' said Rafael very quietly. He turned her back to face him. 'Never turn away from me.'

She stared at him, arrested. Her hands forgot to clutch the flying hair. It flew around them. His own dark hair was wildly disarranged but she was not looking at his hair. His eyes were so dark, they looked almost black. She had never seen eyes so intense.

He bent his head and brushed her lips with his. It was the lightest of kisses but Cleo jumped as if he had burned her. She placed her palms against his chest as if she wanted to push him away. But she did not. She felt as if all the strength had drained out of her but she did not want to push him away. She saw him watching her mouth and wanted to be closer. Saw his eyes glint and knew that he saw her desire.

Confused, half-angry, and vulnerable, she said, 'You've done this before, haven't you?'

He went very still.

She thought, *I've said that before.*

Confusion and anger fell away, which left her just as vulnerable.

The discovery alarmed her. She drew back, as far as she could on the little ledge. She dipped her head, so that the flying hair hid her expression.

Rafael said, 'Don't hide from me.'

She strained against his encircling arms, refusing to look at him. She was breathless and it was not just the sense of vertigo or the wind. It was him.

She wanted him…and he knew it. She did not trust her feelings. He probably knew that too. Oh, he had stopped needling her, maybe even abandoned his suspicions altogether. And replaced them with naked challenge.

*I'm not ready*, she thought, trembling.

His fingers moved in her hair. Was it her imagination – or the buffeting of the wind – or were they not entirely steady?

'Look at me, Cleo.'

She shook her head. She knew that she was desperate to get away from him, run from that terrifying challenge, *escape…* But, somehow, she could not move when he held her like this. And not because she was afraid.

'Look at me,' he insisted.

When she did not, he put a hand under her chin. She fought

him, silently. But with inexorable strength, he tipped her face up to his. He did not like what he saw there.

'What *is* it?'

She closed her eyes. 'How can you ask?'

'How can I know if you don't tell me?' He sounded exasperated.

Her eyes flew open. 'Well, let me explain.' She strove to keep her voice level but her breath was coming fast and her whole body was shaking. She was, she thought, pretty close to falling apart! 'Look at it this way. You call me Cleo. But I don't know if that is my name. You tell me not to hide. How can I hide from you? You know who I am and I don't.' In spite of her effort, her voice rose until it was almost a scream.

'Ah, don't,' he said involuntarily. 'Don't look like that, my darling.'

The arms round her tightened savagely. He rocked her against him, as if he would protect her from the world.

Cleo was stunned.

It had never occurred to her that he could be moved like this. Well, not by her anyway. He was almost anguished in his concern. He held her away from him, pushing the hair off her face with a movement that was almost clumsy.

'I'll do anything you want,' his voice rasped. 'Tell you everything I can. Just don't look at me like that. What do you want to know?'

Suddenly, she did not want to know anything except how he felt. Really felt, now that he had stopped playing games. She put up her hands and pulled his face down to hers.

It was not a gentle kiss.

He backed her against the wall of the tower. His body ground into hers, aroused. She thought, *He's hanging on to control by a whisker.* Which made him stronger than she was. She was losing control completely and she knew it.

The wind whipped her hair about them as if they were one person. Neither noticed. Cleo was trembling so hard that she would have fallen if Rafael hadn't had her clamped in place.

Her eyes shut tight. Her whole being concentrated in sensation – her hungry mouth, her body thrust wildly against his, ignoring the impediments of clothes and wind, her racing blood. His palpable need. Hers.

She began to scrabble at his belt, hands shaking.

'Not here.' His laugh was a half-groan.

He got them back into the turret room without breaking the kiss. Cleo got his buckle open. She felt a fingernail break and didn't care. A surge of dark response was building, building . . .

They crashed into the telescope.

'Downstairs,' he said, breathless. 'There's a bed…'

'I remember.'

They half-ran, half-tumbled down the spiral staircase. Cleo got rid of his chinos, then his shirt, tossing them away without looking where they fell.

'Yes, darling,' he murmured into her mouth. 'You know this is crazy?'

But Cleo was not taking time out for conversation.

'Don't talk.' They had hit the ground floor and she was urgent. 'Don't think. Make love to me.'

Rafael drew in his breath sharply.

Cleo flung herself onto the bed, dragging him with her. She was no longer coherent. It was as if some unseen hand had thrown a switch. Suddenly, she and Rafael were travelling fast, accelerating towards some precipice that terrified her but that she could only throw herself towards. She felt as light as air, cool as a waterfall! – and as focused as an arrow in flight.

His kiss was savage. But so was hers.

'I want you,' she said harshly.

The room was baking after their windblown eyrie but it didn't matter. It could have been as hot as Hades or polar-icecap cold. It would have made no difference. The bed rocked. Pillows fell squashily. Cleo did not notice.

He kissed her everywhere. She arched to him, every bone shaking with tension, every muscle – well, nearly every muscle – clenched fiercely. He took one lifting nipple in his mouth and she bit down so hard on her lower lip that she yelped.

His head came up at once. 'I'm hurting you?'

'No.' She could hardly breathe. 'But no more teasing.' She reached for him to guide him into her.

He stilled her. 'Careful.'

'Who wants to be careful?' She rocked against him.

Rafael closed his eyes as if he were in agony. 'I've said it before. The lowest flashpoint in the universe.'

Cleo took it as a compliment. She wriggled. 'Then what are you waiting for?'

Rafael breathed hard. 'Strength.' He hauled himself up on one elbow. 'Give me a minute and I'll…'

She thought he was going to leave her and cried out, clutching him to her with hands suddenly as strong as steel.

'Ouch,' said Rafael, laughing. His eyes glinted. 'I'm going to protect you if it kills me.'

'I don't want protecting.'

'Yes you do. And I…' Suddenly he bent his head and brushed her taut breast with his inner lip, so that she trembled with sensation. '…need to get some responsibility going here.'

She did not make it easy for him, twining and murmuring and running her fingers round him sensuously. But he set his jaw and reached out to the drawer in the desk beside the little bed and got what he wanted. He held her off, muttering horribly, while he dealt with the condom. All the while, Cleo amused herself by experimenting with the degrees of friction he could sustain. In the end, she drove him to break off, screwing his eyes shut as he fought for control.

'Not fair,' he said.

'Who wants fair?'

But now the condom was on and it was Rafael who had no time for conversation. He held her hands above her head while she protested, laughing, and began to ease himself inside her.

At once, exquisite heat rippled through her. Cleo stopped laughing. Her head went back in the approach to ecstasy.

She heard his breathing. Her own. Her head was spinning. But her body clenched hard. He filled her, sustained her climb through frenzy to the edge of bliss. And then, deliberately, took her over the edge and into pure sensation.

Cleo didn't recognise the sound she made. It hurt her throat. But that didn't matter – she was flying.

And so was he.

## chapter twelve

She fell asleep in his arms almost instantly. Carefully, Rafael rescued the abandoned cushions and slid them behind his head. Then he shifted Cleo, so she lay softly against his shoulder.

She murmured a little. He cupped her cheek and she quietened, smiling in her sleep.

It was as if they belonged. As if she knew it, even in her dreams.

Rafael looked down at her. Her mouth was swollen. Even more voluptuous than normal, he thought, smiling. He ran a possessive finger between her parted lips and she winced. Ah, he saw now. She had bitten her lower lip. He kissed the air above it.

He felt emptied, and yet the king of the world.

How could he have doubted her? Of course she would not think of spying on him. Nor could she have ever set out to seduce him. Not with a flashpoint like that, he thought, grinning. She was not in control of herself sufficiently to seduce anyone!

He had always known that, instinctively. Even in LA when she had lied and tried to mislead him, he had seen through her. His arm tightened. He should have remembered that when he had taken her to the hospital. He should never have believed for a minute that her amnesia was a trick. He should have trusted his instincts.

How could he have been so unkind to her? Would she ever forgive him?

He looked down at the woman sleeping trustfully in his arms. It looked as if she already had.

I don't deserve that, he thought shaken. But I will. I will.

He held safe, watching her dream.

Cleo woke slowly. She had never felt so warm in her life. She gave a long, luxurious sigh and let her eyes drift open.

Rafael was propped on one elbow, looking down at her quizzically. He smoothed a strand of hair away from her eyes.

'You look as if you've just completed an assault course,' he told her with soft amusement.

She was oddly embarrassed. She shifted under that worldly gaze and found her body ached amazingly. Not just her body, her throat felt abraded. She remembered that feral cry and blushed.

'What?' she croaked.

'Dust in your hair. Bruises on your arms.' He bent and kissed a reddened mark on her shoulder where she had hit the telescope a lifetime ago and smiled against her skin as she trembled. 'Splinters in your bottom, I wouldn't be surprised.'

'*What*?'

'Well, those steps are wooden and we came down them pretty hard.'

She struggled to sit upright, wincing. He kissed her back down again.

'No, don't move. We must talk.'

His hand stroked down her body. Lingered…

'Talk?' said Cleo. She was dazed by the memory of sensational lust. And the apparent promise of more.

He grinned lazily. 'Why not?'

She tried to unscramble her thoughts from what he was doing to her nerve-endings.

'Not sure I'm together enough to talk,' she said candidly.

His eyes danced. 'I'm good,' he agreed.

Something sparked in her brain. His voice saying gently, *Hey, I'm good. But not that good.* She went very still.

He sensed the change at once. 'What is it?'

And there was something else he had said, as they were writhing on the bed earlier. She had been too preoccupied to challenge him. Hell, she had hardly noticed at the time. But now it was coming back a little too clearly. *I've said it before. The lowest flashpoint in the universe.*

She said slowly, 'This isn't the first time we've done this, is it?'

Rafael hardly hesitated. 'I've never fallen down four flights into bed before,' he said lightly. Falsely.

The falseness sobered her as nothing else would have done. Cleo sat up. This time she brushed his caressing hand aside, frowning.

'Why won't you admit it? What happened before I lost my memory? Did we have a fight?'

His hand was warm on her hip. 'Does it feel as if we had a fight?'

She closed her eyes briefly. 'Don't do that. I can't think straight when you do that.'

'Good.' There was a smile in his voice.

'You said you'd do anything I wanted.'

'Are you telling me I left something out?' he said, injured.

But she didn't laugh. '*And* tell me everything you knew.'

There was a small silence.

'Yes, I did, didn't I?' he said at last, heavily.

'Well?'

'We'd better get dressed,' he said, giving up. 'You'll only distract me otherwise.'

Cleo was indignant. 'I distract *you?*'

'Completely. Don't try to deny it.' He swung his legs off the bed and stood up. 'Where did you throw my clothes, you serpent woman?'

She waved a lofty hand. 'Oh, around. I wasn't looking.'

He sighed theatrically and padded up the spiral staircase.

Her smile died as he disappeared. Oh, it was lovely to tease each other. Just as it was lovely to make love and then sleep in each other's arms. It felt as if they belonged together. But that was not what he had said in the little jungle hospital.

There, he had been hostile. More than hostile. Contemptuous. He had virtually accused her of trying to seduce him!

'Not that it took much seducing,' she muttered, getting out of bed in her turn.

Whatever it was he thought she was doing, he had certainly not trusted her. He implied that she was faking amnesia, embarrassing everyone, and making her feel as if he hated her.

Her body told her that they were lovers. That they knew each other's bodies as only lovers do. Yet, why would he hate her if they were lovers?

She bit her lip, pulling on the clothes he had not scattered as widely as she had. Then she straightened the pillows and the discarded covers. In passing, not really sure why, she buried her nose in the cotton coverlet.

And knew the answer at once. It was unmistakeable. She knew the smell of his skin as well as she knew her own now. Rafael was the one inhabiting this ramshackle tower. Now she came to think of it, Rafael had actually admitted to sleeping here.

*Why?*

Cleo moved round the circular room, frowning. Why would he need to sleep here? He owned a great colonial mansion! He had said that the house was full but she saw no sign of it. There was only her and the servants.

And then it struck her – he did not want to sleep in the same house as she did! Her instincts were right, after all. They must have had some truly terrible row to cause this self-banishment.

*What did I do?*

Her head was thumping. She pressed her fingertips to her temple and sank bonelessly into the chair in front of the little laptop. The movement dislodged a scatter of diskettes.

She was bending to pick them up, when Rafael came thumping down the spiral staircase again, saying cheerfully, 'I've found everything except...'

And stopped dead. His eyes went completely opaque. Suddenly, he was not cheerful any more. Or even her lover of so few minutes ago. He was a dangerous stranger.

Cleo stared at him, stilled halfway up from the floor.

He looked wonderful, long feet still bare and open shirt flying back to reveal a chest of even tan with its dusting of hair and its classically beautiful structure of bone and compact muscle.

A bit of her brain thought, *He's gorgeous. It had to be a mistake. A man like that would never want me for real.*

And another bit thought, *He's hostile again. Why?*

She straightened at last. Her head was beginning to pound. She put the diskettes back on the desk and pressed her palm to her temple.

He made a movement, quickly stilled. But something told her that this was important. She followed his eyes.

He looked away almost immediately but she saw what he was looking at. The diskettes! Then his eyes flickered and he looked her straight in the eye, limpid and honest and utterly, utterly deceptive.

Memory came back, strong and fast as a striking shark.

'What's that?'

'My insurance policy.'

The pain in her head was blinding.

She said, 'You had it – taped to your side.'

She looked at the tanned torso, with the creased shirt pushed back. She could see it so clearly. He had not been wearing a shirt at all. He had been carrying her. He had lifted her up...she had been momentarily alarmed...grabbed at him...and the thing had been taped half under his arm...

There was a roaring in her ears.

Through it, she said, 'Is that why? This diskette? Is that why you moved out on me? Wouldn't sleep in the same room as me anymore?'

Rafael's brows twitched together. He did not say anything. But his face was closed and suspicious again, as it had been at the hospital.

'You made love to me like a dream,' she said gropingly.

'And you don't trust me an inch.' Her little laugh broke in the middle. 'What am I? Your wife?'

The moment she said it, she thought, *Yes. That's it!*

She stood up. The sound in her ears was like the waterfall, drowning out everything. She put a hand on the desk to steady herself.

That big empty bed in her room, the unacknowledged feelings simmering between them all the time, that wild sexual compatibility. They all added up to the same story. Oh, he knew her body all right. And mistrusted everything else.

Her wound hurt, as if it was opening again. Or someone was jabbing a wooden spike onto the scar, rhythmically, over and over again. She leaned forward, both hands on the desk, trying to breathe through the pain.

'Not much of a marriage then,' she said, with the ghost of a smile.

Rafael moved then.

'What's wrong?'

She shook her head. Or she tried to. The pain was so great that she cried out. Her knees sagged. He caught her.

'Cleo. Darling?' His eyes were not unreadable any more. They were hot and anxious. 'What is it?'

She knew then. Without any doubt.

'Cleo,' she gasped. 'My real name. You knew it all along.'

And watched his look change to one of horror. She put both hands to her head, crying out. But nothing could stop it. She felt herself lifted, carried, but she was beyond resisting. The percussion in her head drowned everything. She thought perhaps she cried out.

And then there was nothing.

Rafael got her back to the house somehow. There was no alternative. She was moaning and feverish, clearly in pain in spite of being virtually unconscious. But if she needed treatment, he would have to get her out to Manaus. Getting her to the house was just the first step on the road.

It was a nightmare journey. Another nightmare journey! He told himself that, at least, it was not as bad as the last time. At least she wasn't bleeding. At least he knew she hadn't cracked her skull open.

But it didn't feel much better. Last time had been an accident. This time felt like his fault.

At Ruprechago, he put her to bed carefully, while Maria and the maids hovered, pointing out all the things that he was doing wrong. When Cleo seemed comfortable, he let them take over and went to the study. He raised David at the hospital on short-wave radio eventually.

'What happened?' said David, once Rafael had run through her symptoms. He sounded unsurprised. 'Did she have a fall or something? Some sort of physical trauma that would account for it?'

Rafael winced. *You made love to me like a dream.* 'Not really,' he said with constraint. 'That wasn't why she collapsed anyway.'

'Right. Then she was probably having flashbacks. Right?'
*My real name. You knew it all along.*

'Right,' said Rafael heavily.

'Sounds as if she's into the memory retrieval phase then.'

'But should she have passed out like that?'

'Look,' said David. 'I'm doing the best I can. You know I'm not an expert. Get her to a clinic if you're not satisfied.'

'But I'm not sure how wise it is to move her.'

David curbed impatience with audible effort. 'Rafael, I'm a fever guy. Show me rashes, show me bugs, I know where I am. All the rest, I get out of the manuals. You know that. You're the same with your ninety thousand types of cancers. You know as much about her condition as I do.'

Rafael glared at the portrait of his grandfather in full military uniform over the bookcase. 'But I don't *treat* people.'

'Maybe not. But you're the one with the contacts. If you're worried, get on the Net and talk to the researchers round the world.'

Rafael felt the inevitability of it like a gathering cloud.

'Yes,' he said quietly.

*Keep off the Net. They can trace you through the telephone line. And Toussaint's got the contacts to do it.*

He had been safe since he had stopped using his e-mail. But this was an emergency. This was *Cleo*. He would have to take his chance with Paul-Henri Toussaint.

For a moment, he contemplated using his aunt's e-mail address though. He discarded it almost instantly. Top researchers responded to other top researchers. Not to e-mails from people who claimed a prestige name and used a completely different Net address.

Rafael took a deep breath and dialled the local server. He gave his international code. And, at once, he was into his mailbox.

There were lots of messages. None from Paul-Henri himself, though Suzanne had sent him some torrid stuff, judging by their titles. He scrolled past them without interest and set about the serious business of finding out what he ought to do next for Cleo.

It took him a couple of hours, a trawl through some mind-boggling papers in the international journal, *Neurology,* and a jolly exchange about international fencing rankings before he was talking online to a helpful neurologist in Brisbane.

'Transient global amnesia, interesting,' wrote this genius with relish. 'Post-traumatic not as interesting as spontaneous.'

'Sorry about that,' muttered Rafael.

'But your friend displays some of the indicators of non-traumatic. If you are certain there is no skull fracture or major injury to the head, most probably the amnesia was caused by a temporary vascular insufficiency affecting the brain tissue. Effects can be dramatic but are usually very short-lived. In my experience, there are no signs of permanent brain damage after remission.'

'Thanks for the reassurance,' wrote Rafael. 'What's the prognosis?'

The professor had to be sitting at his machine. The reply came back at once.

'Depends what caused it in the first place. Often episodes are the result of physical exertion or mental stress. If it's the latter, there may be some behavioural element involved.'

Rafael stared at the screen. Behavioural? What on earth did that mean?

'Explain!' he typed back.

'Freud would have said some unacceptable memory was being repressed. We all hate Freud these days but there does seem to be a core of truth there. The brain is good at defending itself. If there was something she couldn't bear – or couldn't deal with – the brain may have decided to use the opportunity of a bop on the head to take time out.'

Rafael stared at the screen. 'I don't believe this guy,' he muttered. 'What sort of scientist says things like "the brain decided to take time out"?'

And then he thought – a guy who doesn't need to falsify his research findings. Paul-Henri's papers were couched in impeccable professional terminology. It didn't make them true.

Humbled, he wrote back, 'So does that mean that the stuff she couldn't bear has gone forever?'

'Unlikely,' came the reply, accompanied by a lot of stuff about variable ability to lay down new memory after an injury which David had gone through with him that first day at the hospital. 'If she can remember what she had for breakfast this morning, she's probably OK.'

She could remember what she had for breakfast, thought Rafael. And she remembered everything he had said to her since she'd woken up on David's trolley.

*'I haven't forgotten what you told me about how I – looked – when you first found me.'*

*'Looked?'*

*'Designer rags was how you put it. You obviously thought I'd discarded the underwear with you in mind.'*

He winced. 'She's laying down new memory, no sweat,' he typed.

Back came the reply. 'The more normal she seems, the more normal she probably is. Don't worry about her.' The professor ended on a practical note. 'Basically, when she wants to remember, she will.'

'Great,' muttered Rafael. He wrote 'What will make her want to remember?'

'She's *your* friend. You tell me.'

There was no answer to that. Rafael thanked him and signed off.

Restlessly, he went back to Cleo's room. But Maria was sitting sentinel by the bed.

'She is sleeping,' she told him curtly.

He looked down at the quiet figure. Her sleep looked natural, as far as he could tell. It was long time since he had taken a pulse, but he raised her flaccid hand, feeling for the beat. Even in sleep, her fingers curled in response. He felt his flesh jump in reply and hurriedly returned her arm to her side.

Maria gave him a long look.

'She has bruises all over her leg,' she announced. She folded her arms across her bosom, awaiting an explanation.

Rafael gave her an equally long look back. 'She fell down the spiral staircase at the tower.'

She stayed suspicious.

Fine, he thought. She wants to know, I'll tell her. Nosy old bat.

He said deliberately, 'We both did. Together. We weren't watching our feet at the time. We were too busy trying to haul each other's clothes off.'

There was a complicated silence. But Maria would have died rather than let him see he had shocked her and he knew it. As far as Maria was concerned, he was seven-years-old and she knew more than he did about everything.

She sniffed. But all she said was, 'Then you'll have bruises too. You'd better put arnica on them. There's some in your

Aunt Violetta's bathroom.'

Rafael laughed aloud at that. 'Maria, you're a star.'

She shrugged.

No doubt so she could tell his aunts the moment they called, he thought wryly. Then stopped – tell them what? He looked down at the sleeping woman.

He said slowly, not to Maria, 'I'm in very deep here, aren't I?'

Cleo woke slowly. Brilliant, blinding sun bathed the room in a spotlight. For the first time for days – maybe months – she felt peaceful.

*I know what I've got to do.*

She got up, as if she was still in a dream, and went to the old chest of drawers which held so few clothes. She opened the thin top drawer and found what she was looking for.

Yes, it was there. As she had known it would be. A flower, like an exotic face, dry but not yet papery. Its darkened petals were like suede to the touch. She touched a gentle fingertip to an outer petal.

She remembered him giving it to her. It had been attached to a black velvet band. She had worn it on her wrist. When they were in bed – she gave a slow voluptuous shiver – it was the only thing she had worn.

She was a bit hazy on the intervening period. But, some-time in between then and now, she must have married him. She *felt* married to him. Heck, she had felt married to him that first night, though she had tried to pretend that she didn't by bolting the next morning.

No wonder Rafael had been so suspicious, so angry, ever since she woke up in the little jungle hospital and did not know him. He must have felt utterly betrayed. How could she have forgotten?

She bathed and dressed quickly and ran down the staircase.

Maria came out from the kitchen wing, wiping her hands on tea cloth.

'Rafael?' Cleo said eagerly.

The woman hesitated. Then waved a hand at the salon.

Cleo ran through.

He was sitting on the veranda, frowning over a sheet of paper. He must have been out riding. He was wearing breeches, though cleaner than the ones she was used to seeing on him, and an open-necked shirt. His riding boots stood on the bottom step. There was a tall coffee pot on a table covered with a spotless embroidered cloth and a tiny cup of the fearsome brew untouched in front of him.

She ran through the salon to him, her hands out.

Hearing her steps, he looked up and sent her one incredulous look. Then flung his arms wide to receive her.

Their mouths met in a long, heart-stopping kiss.

'I'm sorry,' said Cleo, breathless, but able to speak again. 'I woke up this morning and I remembered, and I realised I should have known I was your wife all along. I don't know what happened. I mean, I still can't remember the accident, whatever it was. But I know who I am. I remember how we met…'

Her hands were busily pulling his shirt out of his waistband while she dabbed little kisses along his unshaven jaw between her tumbling words.

'I remember I love you. You're the other half of me,' she said, gasping as she struggled with the tailored jodhpurs. 'You're my knight in shining armour. I knew you even before I met you. I've waited for you all my life.'

He stilled her questing fingers with a groan.

'Slow down. Slow down. What exactly do you remember?'

She thrust a hand into the pocket of her skirt and brought out the orchid. It was brown and battered but it was still recognisable.

'See?' she said gleefully. 'I went looking for it this morning. I knew exactly where I'd put it. And it was there. David was right. My memory came back when I was ready for it.'

Rafael took the flower between his thumb and forefinger and turned it round blankly. He looked stunned.

'It's the orchid you gave me,' said Cleo, disappointed.

'I know what it is. Why did you keep it?'

She stared. 'Because I love you, of course.'

His jaw was rigid.

'When did that happen?'

'Well, I'm not sure exactly. I haven't got quite *all* my memory back yet…'

'You haven't got any of it yet,' he said, with a brutality that shocked her into silence.

'But, the orchid, I knew where…'

Rafael cut across her. 'But you don't know why.' He put the flower down on the table and set her away from him. Then he said with great deliberation, 'You are not my wife. You have never been my wife.'

He watched the bright happiness drain away.

For a moment, Cleo stared at him as if he had spoken in a foreign language. She made a move towards the little brown blossom on the tablecloth.

'But…'

She stopped. He saw her eyelashes flutter, as she tried to assimilate it. He had never seen her look so lost, not even when she woke up in the hospital and didn't know her own name. He wanted to take her in his arms so badly, it was like starving.

But he knew that anger was coming. He could not expose her to danger. He could not expose her to anything more than he already had.

She looked up at him. No disguise now. No pretence not to care. *Tell me something real.* Well, he had got what he wanted in that naked look of hers. And he could not afford to respond. It made him feel like a traitor.

She swallowed. 'But I was so sure. I mean – yesterday. We felt – it felt – so right?' She moistened her lips. He could see what it cost but she met his eyes bravely. 'Didn't it?'

He could not lie. 'Yes.' His lips barely moved.

But she gave a little sigh of relief and moved closer again. 'Well then…'

He said brutally, because he wanted her so much, 'We spent one night together.'

Cleo stopped as if he had pointed a gun at her. 'What?'

'One night. Weeks ago. In LA. You didn't tell me the truth then. I didn't tell you the truth this week. That's all there is to it.'

She went so pale, he thought she was going to faint.

'I – don't believe you.'

But she did. He could see it in her face. Her eyes looked blind.

Before he could help himself, he said roughly, 'Cleo, my darling, don't look like that.'

In spite of all his noble resolutions, he took a hasty step towards her. But she held out a hand to ward him off.

'I see.'

He watched her struggle to assimilate it. Saw her remember…

'Of course, your wife would have to – what was it you said? Read books. Listen to music. Speak languages. And I don't, do I?'

'That's not…'

Her lips stretched in a travesty of a smile. 'How embarrassing,' she said, with a brave attempt at mockery. 'I should probably apologise.'

He set his teeth. '*Don't*. I…'

'It would have been so much easier if you'd told me.' Her voice was very level. 'Am I allowed to ask why?'

'I wasn't sure of you.'

She gave a laugh that broke. 'Can't imagine why,' she said with vicious self-mockery.

'I didn't mean that.' He was getting deeper and deeper in the mire, while he kept one eye on the clear sky for the plane that he had known would arrive from the moment he had sent that e-mail last night. 'I meant, I was suspicious of you. I'm involved in something…you don't know about it but…'

And then he saw the plane, lining up for its final approach.

Cleo saw his eyes widen. She turned, following his eyes. And saw the little Cessna before the gable of the house hid it from sight. And, of course, she leaped to the obvious, the cruel conclusion. She flinched as if he had flung boiling water at her.

'I see.' She swallowed. 'You're expecting guests.'

'Yes,' Rafael said grimly. 'But it's not what you think…'

But Cleo was not listening. 'I think I'd better go at once,' she said, cool and courteous, and terribly pale. 'You've been very kind. But it's time I took my funny memory back home and started sorting myself out. Perhaps I could go back on that plane there. I'm sure I could pack quickly…'

She fled before he could move or speak.

Maria stood in the hallway, looking worried. Cleo gave her a glassy smile as she pelted up the stairs.

All she could think was, *I must get away. I must get away now.*

She flung everything into a bag very fast. There was not much. She found her passport easily too. For some reason, she had put it in her make-up bag in the bathroom. There was even an open, return ticket to Los Angeles. She was packed long before she heard the jeep coming up from the landing strip. Only when she heard voices, did she come downstairs.

The woman in the hallway was spectacular. Tall and amazingly well-dressed, with perfect legs and that glacial composure that freezes other women in their tracks. She looked Cleo up and down with indefinable mockery.

'I didn't know you had friends staying, darling,' she drawled.

Cleo saw that Rafael was standing behind her. A muscle was working in his cheek. But he said without expression, 'Miss Darren was with the film company. She's leaving today. I'm sure you know all about the movie, Suzanne.'

'So thrilling,' said the newcomer, bored. She put a hand on Rafael's arm. He did not shake it off. But that was not what told Cleo that Suzanne-whoever-she-was had done exactly that many times before. There was something about the way they stood together . . .

Maybe this was the woman who *was* going to be Senhora Rafael Dourado, Cleo thought painfully. Of course, he was the *patrão*. This expensive lady would be much more able to fulfil the role of his wife than a waitress from a downtown diner.

She didn't look at him again. She didn't shake hands either. She didn't think she could bear it. Instead, she gave him a quick, blind nod.

'Thank you for the room,' she said formally. 'You've been very kind. Now, can I go back to wherever that plane is going?'

Even then, she thought Rafael would try to stop her. But he did not. In fact, she sensed that he could not wait to get her out of the house.

'I'll come out with you to the jeep.' He took her bag, one-handed, and threw it easily into the back of the car. Under his breath he said, 'You don't understand and I can't explain. But I will…'

And the lovely Suzanne came out into the sun, her high heels clipping on the old paving stones. Her eyes narrowed with suspicion. She hardly bothered to disguise it.

'Oh, for God's sake, let the girl go, Rafe.'

And he did. He *did*.

He stepped back. Suzanne linked an arm through his possessively and walked him towards the house without a backward look.

Her voice came back to Cleo, who had been left disregarded to climb into the jeep.

'Now darling, you're just going to have to stop being so puritanical about things. We just need to meet halfway. But we can do that. We always have in the past.' Her voice was heavy with sexy innuendo. 'Oooh, you and I have got so much to talk about.'

He listened, head bent courteously, as if he were agreeing with her. He could not have shown more clearly that Cleo was of no further interest.

And she heard, like a blow to the heart, his reply.

'More than just a talk, I think.'

How could anything hurt this much and not show?

But she would survive. She felt numb, but she had to get on with the business of surviving.

So she nodded to the driver and set off for the airstrip. And Manaus. And a life without Rafael.

## chapter thirteen

Christmas in London. It sounded so exciting!

Cleo tried hard to feel excited. She was going home, after all. She was going to see her father again, for the first time in ten years. Going back to the suburb where she was born. Where she could remember, vaguely, being a happy seven-year-old. Home!

Except that nowhere felt like home without Rafael. It had taken her five months, but she had already proved that, over and over again. Her memory had come back without difficulty. And every single thing that slipped back into place told the same story – she loved him. She had lost him.

'I've always wanted to go to London,' sighed Mikey who didn't even own a passport.

George frowned at him. 'Cleo's not going on vacation. This is work.'

'We should all have such work! A premiere, no less.'

'I know. It feels weird,' agreed Cleo.

'Cloud Orchid' had been what they called a sleeper. Opening in obscure cinemas throughout the US, with a minimal advertising budget, its popularity had grown by word-of-mouth, until the trade press were calling it a movie phenomenon. So the producers had decided that the European opening should have more of a fanfare. Anyway, by then they could afford it.

Cleo was travelling to London first class, along with Michelle, Ed, Roger and the director. She was going to be staying at a new and fabulously stylish hotel in the centre of town. She had taken advice from fashion lecturer Naomi on her wardrobe and urban philosopher George on self-presentation. Mikey and Jill had written her a brief but telling paragraph on the plight of ex-child stars. It was, they all assured her, going to be the performance of her life.

They could not understand why she was not excited. Especially as her major problem, her mother, had unexpectedly faded away. Well, she did not mention her anymore and Margaret had stopped turning up at the diner, so they supposed she had.

What they did not know, because Cleo had not told them, was that she had taken charge of her life at last.

When she had returned to LA, after the worst journey of her life, she had known that there was one dark area of her life, at least, that she could do something about. She could not heal her bleeding heart, but she did not have to be on the edge of panic every time the phone rang.

She had gone straight to Margaret's condo.

'Mother, you have to be clear about some things.'

Margaret had not wanted to listen, of course. But somehow, something about the new steady-eyed Cleo stopped her fantasy forward planning as nothing else had ever done.'

'I'm leaving LA,' Cleo said clearly.

'Darling, don't be silly. Your career…'

'I need to think about my *life*, mother.'

'But…'

'You,' said Cleo levelly, 'put me into television because that's what you wanted to do yourself. I had a bit of talent and I enjoyed showing off, as kids do. I stopped enjoyed it long before you did.'

Margaret looked genuinely shocked.

Cleo saw it with grim humour. 'Heresy, isn't it?'

Margaret rallied. 'You were so successful. Nobody could have been that good if they hadn't enjoyed it.' But, for the first time in her life, she didn't sound certain any more.

Cleo did not bother to answer.

'I wanted you to know what I'm going to do. Then you can make up your own mind about your future. I'll do whatever I have to on "Cloud Orchid", of course. I'm going to finish this module of my law course, and then I'm going to travel.'

*'Travel!'* If she had said she was going to Mars, Margaret could not have been more astonished. Or affronted.

'I'm twenty-three. I've been to London, LA, and the Amazon Jungle. Time I saw some more of the world. I'm going to travel and learn other languages and read books and listen to music. I should have done it years ago. Now I'm going to before it's too late.'

Margaret began to look scared. 'But what am I going to…?'

'That's why I'm here,' said Cleo gently.

Looking at her, Margaret saw that the gentleness was deceptive. She was used to Cleo fighting and funny, all smart remarks and fire. She knew how to handle that. This gentleness was all steel and she did not know where to begin.

'I don't know if you need professional help or not,' Cleo said with deadly calm. 'I do know you need to get out of Hollywood. Everything you touch here feeds the fantasy.'

'Leave Hollywood?' Margaret was aghast.

Cleo shrugged. 'Up to you. Your life. But if you want me to help, here's my suggestion. You have family in England. Even if you don't want to go back to Dad, there's Grandad and Aunt Elaine and Uncle Chris.'

'Your father isn't interested in me,' said Margaret with sudden bitterness. 'All he has ever cared about is his beloved cricket. Whenever England were losing, he'd just stop noticing me. And England lose so much!'

Cleo shrugged. 'Whatever. Settle your debts and I'm willing to pay your fare back to the UK. And six months' rent on somewhere while you get your head back together, if you don't want to stay with any of the family.'

Margaret brightened. 'In that case…'

'And that's all I'll pay for,' Cleo said, as if she had not spoken. 'If you want to do anything else, you fund it yourself. Let me know.' She gave a brief, wry smile. 'I'm telling you something real here, mother. Goodbye.'

Cleo's self-education programme began immediately. She bought a copy of 'Cloud Orchid' in Spanish and found a neighbour in her block who would give her Spanish lessons in return for English ones. She went back to waitressing at the diner, but reduced her hours. She completed the next two modules of her law course ahead of time and negotiated a sabbatical on the next stage. She did some lip-syncing for the movie in post-production, visited Yellowstone and Napa for the first time, and began to read about Europe.

It all took longer than she expected. It would have been easy, in those long, crowded months, for Rafael to have found her. If he had wanted to. He clearly didn't. So now she was off on her adventures, at last, starting with London.

She stayed at the 'Ritz' for the first few days. It was useful, anyway, as Anitra had organised some major PR. Journalists trooped through her room at hourly intervals to talk about 'Cloud Orchid'.

'How frightful,' said her father, coming to visit and finding himself banished to take tea in the sumptuous lobby.

Cleo laughed. 'I'm lucky. I'm only a supporting player. Michelle is doing them at fifteen minutes a pop.'

He put an arm round her and gave her a quick, awkward hug. 'I'm proud of you.' He was not talking about the movie, and they both knew it. 'Look, I'm taking Margaret out of London for Christmas. Well…' he met her eyes ruefully, 'I'm taking her away until all the razzmatazz of the premiere has died down. We don't want her getting over-excited again, do we?'

For Margaret had, unexpectedly, gone back to Cleo's father and was making genuine efforts to re-adjust to reality.

'No,' agreed Cleo. She did not say, *So that means I go to the premiere on my own*. She had half-expected it.

Anyway, without Rafael, she would always feel alone.

'I'm really sorry not to be there, chick. But – I wondered – do you want to get out of all this?'

Cleo looked round the luxurious lobby, the carpet deep as

fur, the flora rococo décor, and the mirrors. The *people*.

'Yes,' she said.

'Well, what about borrowing my house while we're away? You'd have to take the dog for walks but you can handle that.' He hesitated. 'I kept away because I thought you and your mother didn't want me. It would be nice to feel that my daughter was in my house.'

Cleo's eyes filled with tears. It astonished her. Since that day in Ruprechago when Rafael walked away from her, she had not cried.

'Oh *yes*,' she said.

The day of the premiere was cold and rainy. London in December was dark by four o' clock in the afternoon. Cleo took the dog for a jog round the Battersea Park and enjoyed the feel of rain on her face and the smell of leaves under foot. She even enjoyed the muddy interval in which she hosed down the mongrel and the mongrel jumped all over her.

By the time she had to get ready for the premiere, she was as close to happy as she thought she was likely to get. Well, until she had got over Rafael Dourado. And she would. She *would*.

She was wearing black velvet tonight. It looked stunning with her Renaissance hair. She was styling it herself, as she had done that day in the back of the limo. Wash it in the best shampoo you can afford, then wind small strands round tissue paper and let it dry naturally. Then fluff out and add stardust to taste, she thought, amused.

'Full circle,' she said, turning down the offer of a top London stylist with a private smile.

'Oh well. We'll send a car, for you,' said Brian Ross's assistant, trying to be helpful. Cleo had received some surprisingly good reviews. 'Would you like an escort, now that your father can't come?'

Cleo's smile died. She shook her head. 'I don't think so.' *Not after last time.*

So the evening of the premiere found Cleo padding barefoot around her father's kitchen. She had pulled on the wrap from behind the bathroom door over her first-time-on black silk underwear. She would keep her hair twisted up in its dozens of tissue paper knots until the very last moment. She made herself a cup of tea and some hot buttered toast and listened to the news on the radio.

It was nothing very interesting – a stock market shimmy, a peace negotiation restarting, a scientific research scandal exposed, the England cricket team beaten somewhere tropical. No change there then!

'Welcome home,' said Cleo, grinning through toast crumbs.

The mutt raised his head. She threw him a crust. He caught it but was too exhausted after his walk to get out of his basket. The doorbell rang. The dog pointedly put his nose under his paws.

'Fine watchdog you are,' Cleo told him. She went to answer it.

And the world split apart into rainbows. Birds sang. Sun shone.

'Hello,' said Rafael.

He did not wait to be invited in. He closed the door behind him. Cleo backed up, her eyes widening and widening. She opened her mouth and shut it again, helpless. Her father's dark Victorian hallway seemed to have turned into paradise and she was just not ready for it.

'Aren't you talking to me?' said Rafael. 'I don't blame you. I can explain but you have to give me a chance to get my breath back.'

He was wearing a tuxedo again. He looked wonderful, so vibrant and full of energy. She wanted to touch him…

*Why* was he wearing a tuxedo?

'I couldn't get in touch before. It could have put you in danger. Until the news broke tonight, I was never certain how Toussaint would try and get to me next.'

She *had* to touch him.

She said in a voice she didn't recognise, 'Take your jacket off.'

'What?' he was startled. 'No, it's all right. The rain has nearly stopped. I didn't get wet. I want to *explain*…'

'Take it *off*.'

Rafael stopped dead then. He said in an odd, uncertain, disbelieving voice, 'Cleo?'

Whatever he saw in her face gave him his answer. Not taking his eyes from hers, he shrugged off the jacket and did not even look to see where it fell.

Her lips parted. If she had wanted to keep her feelings hidden, there could have been no more of a devastating betrayal. But Cleo was way beyond secrets and she knew it.

'Tell me something real,' she said harshly.

'I need you.'

The shirt followed the jacket. Her heart was beating so loud it seemed to shake the universe.

'And?'

'I need you so much, I'm not even going to ask who he is.'

Her eyes flickered, confused. 'He? Who?'

'The man who's robe you are taking off *now*.'

'I…'

But he took it off for her. And put his arms round her, so that his fingers slid under all the pretty new underwear. Suddenly Cleo saw the point of silk. Her skin felt as if he was turning it into sunshine. She placed her palms against his chest and his body heat struck through them, entering her, making her come alive. She began to fumble for unfamiliar fastenings, panting.

He kissed her open mouth and her bones liquefied.

He walked her backwards to the stairs. She was hopeless, could not find the trouser mechanism at all. He flicked it open and let her unzip him, while he moulded her, cupped her shoulder blades in powerful, sure hands, tipped her back, his head bending to her breast, her hips, every inch of her that was already his and knew it. She arched to him, eager for repossession…

They hit the stairs together. Cleo thought, *This is going to be geometrically impossible.*

And then she stopped thinking.

And it wasn't.


Later, they were lying at the foot of the stairs in a dusty, satisfied tangle of limbs at the time. Rafael said lazily, 'Wanna go to a movie?'

'Mmm?'

'There's this thing on at the cinema…'

That's when Cleo came back to earth with a bang. 'Jeez. The premiere! I'll be late.'

He kissed her lovingly. 'Not unless you insist.'

'What?'

'I'm on Rent a Hunk duty again,' said Rafael, odiously pleased with himself. 'By my reckoning, we've got thirty minutes.' He ran a hand possessively across her body, making her catch her breath. 'Unless there's something else you'd rather do.'

She scrambled to her feet. 'Lots of things, including walk the dog and scalp you. But they'll have to wait.'

She galloped upstairs.

Rafael followed at a more leisurely pace. He brought his clothes and her robe with him.

Cleo did a quick pirouette under the shower and began to scramble into her clothes. He reclined on the bed, magnificently naked, and watched her with appreciation.

'Aren't you going to dress?' Cleo was finding herself slightly embarrassed. Even – crazily – shy. She looked up and met his eyes in the mirror.

His eyes were warm, as she had never seen them. She held her breath.

He said softly, 'This is the first time. I want to remember it.'

'The first?' She frowned. 'I should warn you, I've got my

memory back. I know we've had volcanic sex in two continents. Well, sub-continents.'

'Make that three,' he said amused. 'And I meant that this was the first time I've seen you get dressed. Undress, sure. But dressing is different, don't you agree?'

'What?'

'I like lying here watching you get dressed to go out. It makes me feel like we're married.'

'Oh.'

'You were so sure you were my wife,' he said quietly.

She blushed, remembering.

'You were right.'

Cleo looked away. 'I told you,' she said with an effort at mockery, 'The memory is all back and functioning. No wife. Clocked it.'

'There was never anything wrong with your perception,' he said dryly. 'Your timing was a little off, that's all. We should be married. If you give me the chance, we will be.'

She turned away from the mirror.

'And the woman in the business suit?' She flinched remembering. 'She said you had to talk. And you said "more than talk".'

He got off the bed and came and put his arms round her. 'More than talk was right. They were trying to kill me.'

She looked at him doubtfully. 'But you were lovers.'

Rafael raised his eyebrows. 'Nothing wrong with your perception at all. Yes, for once, I admit it. I was stupid and she was clever.'

'I saw what she was,' said Cleo dryly. 'Sex incarnate.'

His arms tightened. 'No. Sex incarnate is a woman with her hair in rags who can't wait to get my clothes off. Suzanne was well-packaged – but definitely synthetic. I wouldn't fall for that now.'

Cleo held on to him. 'W-wouldn't you?'

'No. Not even if you turn me down,' he said gravely. 'And I wouldn't blame you if you did. Are you?'

'Going to turn you down?' Suddenly, gloriously, all her doubts and the last months of misery flickered out like a spent match. 'Not if you take me to a movie. And tell me something real.'

His eyes began to dance. 'Just try and stop me.'

*epilogue*

If you compared the pictures of Patti Darren at the Diamond Awards with the footage of her arrival at the premier of 'Cloud Orchid', you would hardly think she was the same woman.

Oh, the gleaming urban curls were the same. And the wide aquamarine eyes. She was even with the same gorgeous man. But in her long, black velvet dress she had somehow grown. The photographers, lined up on their boxes and stepladders for the stars' arrival, all noticed it.

Rafael agreed. 'You look like a queen,' he murmured in her ear, as they progressed along the clear way from car to glittering entrance.

'I feel like a queen,' Cleo said out of the corner of her mouth as she waved to a TV camera. She glanced up at him naughtily. 'Thanks to you.'

His arm tightened. 'Behave.'

She pulled a face. 'Bor-ing.'

'Oh you think I'm boring, do you?' he growled, mock indignant.

One of the crowd of reporters for the entertainment programmes called out, 'How are you doin', Patti?'

'I'm good,' she said.

'She's brilliant,' corrected Rafael. He glanced sideways at her and she realised, with a little kick of excitement that he was taking up her challenge. 'She was taught to kiss by experts.'

Cleo choked and nearly fell off her designer stilettos. The cameras clicked furiously.

'Traitor!' she muttered.

'Never issue a challenge if you're not prepared to follow

through,' he advised cheerfully. He put a possessive arm all the way round her waist and brought her to a halt to face the crowd.

'I have an announcement. Well…two. The lady is called Cleopatra. And the lady is mine.'

There was almost a shout of glee.

'And the gentleman,' said Cleo vengefully, 'is the genius who uncovered the cancer research fraud you all heard about on the news this evening.'

A clutch of entertainment correspondents pressed forward. This was the stuff that got them slots on the main news.

Rafael laughed down at her. 'Challenge returned in full,' he conceded.

She wriggled against him. 'You'd better believe it. What about passion indeed?'

He touched her cheek. Fifty photographers clicked in ecstasy.

'I'll tell you something real,' he said, for her alone, though anyone who wanted to could hear his words. 'I love you with my whole heart and I'll never let you go.'

Cleo looked at him. He brushed her hair back off her neck gently. It was the tenderest caress. It was the height of dreams she had never known she had.

She leaned against him, in perfect trust, and smiled up at him.

'Then you'd better ask me to marry you.'

Their eyes met. Total love. Total laughter. Rafael kissed her.

'I am not asking,' he said magnificently, 'I'm telling you. You *are* mine. Live with it!'

Why not start a new romance today with Heartline Books. We will send you an exciting Heartline romance ABSOLUTELY FREE. You can then discover the benefits of our home delivery service: Heartline Books Direct.

Each month, before they reach the shops, you will receive four brand new titles, delivered directly to your door.

All you need to do, is to fill in your details opposite – and return them to us at the address below.

**Please send me my free book:**

Name (IN BLOCK CAPITALS)

_____

Address (IN BLOCK CAPITALS)

_____

_____

_____

_____ Postcode _____

**Address:**
HEARTLINE BOOKS
PO Box 400
Swindon  SN2 6EJ

We may use this information to send you offers from ourselves or
selected companies, which may be of interest to you.

If you do not wish to receive further offers
from Heartline Books, please tick this box ☐

If you do not wish to receive further offers
from other companies, please tick this box ☐

Once you receive your free book, unless we hear from you otherwise,
within fourteen days, we will be sending you four exciting new romantic
novels at a price of £3.99 each, plus £1 p&p. Thereafter, each time you
buy our books, we will send you a further pack of four titles.

You can cancel at any time! You have no obligation to ever buy a
single book.

# Heartline Books –
# romance at its best!

What do you think of this month's selection?

As we are determined to continue to offer you books which are up to the high standard we know you expect from Heartline, we need you to tell us about *your* reading likes and dislikes. So can we please ask you to spare a few moments to fill in the questionnaire on the following pages and send it back to us? And don't be shy – if you wish to send in a form for each title you have read this month, we'll be delighted to hear from you!

# Questionnaire

Please tick the boxes to indicate your answers:

1 Did you enjoy reading this Heartline book?

   Title of book: _____

   A lot ☐
   A little ☐
   Not at all ☐

2 What did you particularly like about this book?

   Believable characters ☐
   Easy to read ☐
   Enjoyable locations ☐
   Interesting story ☐
   Good value for money ☐
   Favourite author ☐
   Modern setting ☐

3 If you didn't like this book, can you please tell us why?

   _____

   _____

**4** Would you buy more Heartline Books each month if they were available?

Yes ☐
No – four is enough ☐

**5** What other kinds of books do you enjoy reading?

Historical fiction ☐
Puzzle books ☐
Crime/Detective fiction ☐
Non-fiction ☐
Cookery books ☐

Other _____

_____

**6** Which magazines and/or newspapers do you read regularly?

a) _____

b) _____

c) _____

d) _____

And now a bit about you:

Name _____

Address _____

_____

_____ Postcode _____


Thank you so much for completing this questionnaire.
Now just tear it out and send it in an envelope to:

HEARTLINE BOOKS
PO Box 400
Swindon  SN2 6EJ

(and if you don't want to spoil this book, please feel free
to write to us at the above address with your comments
and opinions.)

Code: IHTBY

**Have you missed any of the following books:**

The Windrush Affairs *by Maxine Barry*
Soul Whispers *by Julia Wild*
Beguiled *by Kay Gregory*
Red Hot Lover *by Lucy Merritt*
Stay Very Close *by Angela Drake*
Jack of Hearts *by Emma Carter*
Destiny's Echo *by Julie Garrett*
The Truth Game *by Margaret Callaghan*
His Brother's Keeper *by Kathryn Bellamy*
Never Say Goodbye *by Clare Tyler*
Fire Storm *by Patricia Wilson*
Altered Images *by Maxine Barry*
Second Time Around *by June Ann Monks*
Running for Cover *by Harriet Wilson*
Yesterday's Man *by Natalie Fox*
Moth to the Flame *by Maxine Barry*
Dark Obsession *by Lisa Andrews*
Once Bitten…Twice Shy *by Sue Dukes*
Shadows of the Past *by Elizabeth Forsyth*
Perfect Partners *by Emma Carter*
Melting the Iceman *by Maxine Barry*
Marrying A Stranger *by Sophie Jaye*
Secrets *by Julia Wild*
Special Delivery *by June Ann Monks*
Bittersweet Memories *by Carole Somerville*
Hidden Dreams *by Jean Drew*
The Peacock House *by Clare Tyler*
Crescendo *by Patricia Wilson*
The Wrong Bride *by Susanna Carr*
Forbidden *by Megan Paul*
Playing with Fire *by Kathryn Bellamy*
Collision Course *by Joyce Halliday*

**Complete your collection by ringing the Heartline
Hotline on 0845 6000504, visiting our website
www.heartlinebooks.com or writing to us at
Heartline Books, PO Box 400, Swindon SN2 6EJ**